MURDER COMES TO CALL

Roger Keevil

MURDER COMES TO CALL

Three Inspector Constable murder mystery stories

by

Roger Keevil

mail@rogerkeevil.co.uk

www.rogerkeevil.co.uk

Printed by CreateSpace, and Amazon.com company

Available on Kindle and other devices

In memory of John Robbins

Friend, detective, and very discerning book reviewer!

MURDER COMES TO CALL

Three Inspector Constable murder mystery stories

*   *   *   *   *

DEATH BY CHOCOLATE

"Chocolate, guv?"

"First thing in the morning? Oh well. Why not?" Detective Inspector Andy Constable's hand reached out and hovered over the proffered box. "Is that a coconut fudge? That'll do me. Thank you."

"No problem." Detective Sergeant Dave Copper selected a sweet of his own and began to munch abstractedly as he pored over the papers littering the desk in front of him.

Constable shot a glance of suspicion in the direction of his colleague. "What's all this then, sergeant? You're not usually so generous in handing out the sweeties. This wouldn't be the start of some elaborate scheme to butter up the boss, would it?"

Copper's face was a picture of innocence. "Honestly, no, guv. I ... er ... I just happened to have these, and I thought you might fancy one. No agenda, I promise."

Constable settled back in his chair. "Copper, for a detective, you make a rotten liar. I smell a story. Come on, out with it. Where did these come from?"

Copper sighed. "Actually, guv, they're Sam's."

"Sam who? Don't tell me you've been getting unsolicited gifts from the latest intake of rookie recruits? Or were you forced to confiscate them because you caught someone running in the corridors?"

"Guv ..."

"Anyway, I can't think of anyone round the station called Sam. So come on, who is he?"

"She, guv. Sam, short for Samantha."

"Ah." Light dawned. "The girlfriend." A nod. "So what's she doing getting you chocolates? Isn't that supposed to be the other way around?"

"It was, sir. You see, it was her birthday last week ..."

"You didn't mention."

"Well, no, guv. What with all the aftermath of that woman getting killed at the restaurant and all the late overtime, I kind of got distracted. I mean, I was going to take her out for a meal and everything ..."

"Not to the 'Palais de Glace', I hope," interpolated Constable wryly.

"But, well, it sort of slipped my mind until two days afterwards."

"Until the lady gently reminded you," deduced Constable. "I have a feeling I know what's coming."

"You probably do, guv. Sam wasn't best pleased, so I rushed out and grabbed a box of chocolates as a sort of peace offering ..."

"Don't tell me," said Constable with a sigh of despair. "From the local petrol station."

"It was the nearest place open," pointed out Copper defensively. "So I got back, tried to make it up to her ..."

"And I'm guessing, probably got the chocolates thrown at you for your pains."

Copper gave a rueful chuckle. "Are you sure you haven't met Sam, guv? Anyway, she missed. Just."

"Leaving you with a box of chocs, a girlfriend who I suspect has now become an ex-girlfriend, and a diary which is now considerably emptier of social engagements. Am I right?"

"Ten out of ten, guv. Which is why I've come in early today. So if there's any more overtime going spare, feel free to ask."

"You will be doing plenty of overtime, spare or not, if you don't get those reports sorted out by the deadline," retorted Constable. "So, having given us the latest update on your perpetually convoluted love-life, may I suggest that you turn your attention from scoffing sweets to writing up your notes about the late Miss Stone, or whatever it is you're doing."

"Righty-ho, guv." With his customary cheerful grin, the sergeant bent his head back over the paperwork on his desk.

Andy Constable continued to gaze at the shock of light brown hair before him with a faint indulgent smile. Sometimes, he mused, I wonder what possessed David Copper to become a policeman. The younger man had joined the force, seemingly on some sudden and unaccountable whim, from what he had described as a dead-end job working in a sports store, and after a surprisingly short time in uniform, had moved to the intelligence section. A combination of hard work and luck had given him the opportunity for promotion to sergeant and a further transfer to C.I.D., where a fortuitous re-arrangement of staff had placed him in the position of assistant to Detective Inspector Constable. Luckily for both of us, thought Constable. I doubt if anyone else could put up with him. Or me, he admitted to himself in a moment of self-recognition. Dave Copper, now in his late twenties, not exactly chubby but well-covered, had an irreverent view of police work, and always seemed ready to recognise the humorous side of even the most gruesome situation, traits which did not endear him to the majority of the more strait-laced senior officers on the force. But his capacity for dogged routine, combined with occasional flashes of startling intuition, had turned him into the ideal colleague for Constable, a detective who himself was not always beloved of the authorities on the higher floors.

The inspector was the first to confess that he found some of the demands of the job and the personalities he worked under both irksome and ludicrous at various times, and he was not always able to conceal the fact. In his forties, lean, around six feet tall and with slightly greying dark hair, he was in noticeably better shape than many of his plumper and balder contemporaries, a fact which he tried his hardest not to make him feel a degree of self-satisfaction. Some of his colleagues were a touch wary of him – his talent for knowing the most surprising facts on an almost unlimited range of subjects meant that he had long ago been barred from the occasional police station quiz nights, and he often had a way of looking at a case which led him straight to correct conclusions with no discernible intervening process, much to the bafflement of his fellow officers. His dry sense of humour was not always appreciated by those above him, but the fact that he was undeniably the best detective on the force at producing results encouraged them to overlook both that, and the fact that a rigorous pursuit of procedures was often not his first consideration. And if Constable was content to work with Copper, barring the occasional mild slap-down when the sergeant overstepped the mark, at least it kept the pair of them out of everybody else's hair. With a quiet sigh, the inspector turned his attention once more to the sheaf of papers awaiting his attention.

It was only a short while later, an interval whose silence was punctuated by only the occasional tut from Constable at some of the more bureaucratic demands of his job, and the riffle of turning pages as Copper leafed back and forth through his notebook and the click of keys as he typed up a report, that the phone on the desk rang. Dave Copper's hand shot out.

"Yup? ... Really? Right, hold on a sec while I make a note ... Yes, I know, in Rownville ... Is he, indeed? Well, that's going to cause a few ripples, isn't it? ... So are we sure this is one for us? How do we know he didn't just flake out? ... *Chocolate*?!?"

"No thanks," returned Andy Constable absently, his attention still concentrated on the form before him. "One's enough for me."

"Right, we'll be over. And how about ...? ... He's on his way? Well done. Okay, I'll tell the guv and we'll be with you as soon as we can." Copper replaced the receiver with a slightly bemused expression on his face.

Constable lifted his head and gave his junior colleague a look of enquiry. "So what was all that about?"

"They have a body for us, sir. At Wally Winker's Chocolate Factory in Rownville."

"And the circumstances require our immediate attention, I take it? Well, halleluia!" said the inspector. "Now I can dump this mindless bumf and do the work the public pay me for." He closed the file in front of him and consigned it to a desk drawer which he slammed shut with some satisfaction. "So, what's it all about?"

"Well, guv, you ain't gonna believe this, but ..."

"If this is going to be a long story," interrupted Constable, "you can tell me in the car." He stood. "Let's get out of here."

*

Wally Winker's Chocolate Factory was a rare survival. In the world of international conglomerates, it had somehow escaped being gobbled up in the almost irresistible process of consolidation and rationalisation which had seen so many of its peers in the confectionery business consumed by gigantic companies whose interests ranged from detergents to computers. The firm was founded in the 1900s by the first Walter Winker, great-grandfather and namesake of the current president, who had believed that the innocent pleasures of chocolate provided the perfect antidote to the evils of the Demon Drink. After his death at the relatively young age of fifty-seven and the relatively advanced weight of twenty-five stone, the company had passed to his son, and subsequently down the dynasty to his great-grandson. It continued to trade on the continuing affection for its traditional old-fashioned products like the Pup-e-Dog Bar with its rascally mascot, Boxer Trix, while combining these with a constant search for innovation and a flair for finding new niches in the market for quality designer chocolates for special occasions. The firm's offices were still located in its original striking but modestly-sized red-brick factory, a tribute to Edwardian industrial design with its ornate terracotta detailing and its palatial use of mosaic and stained glass in the cathedral-like entrance, while across the road, a more anonymous building of steel and concrete housed the main but still moderately-scaled manufacturing facility.

Approaching the factory along Meltinga Way, the detectives were aware of small knots of people, several of them white-coated and -booted, standing in disconsolate groups on the pavement, some huddled in conversation. As Copper turned the car off the road into what had to be regarded as a carriage-drive leading to the factory doors, the way was barred by a red-and-white striped pole across the entrance. A man in his forties, his peaked cap declaring his status and function, emerged from a small gate-house and held up an officious hand. Copper wound down his window.

"You can't come in," declared the employee in a characteristic accent which Copper deduced had never strayed further than ten miles from the West Midlands in its life. "We've got a ..." He searched briefly for an appropriately portentous epithet. "... a situation inside." He nodded slowly to give his words extra emphasis. "Nobody's allowed in except accredited staff."

"How about the police?" enquired Copper mildly.

"Well, obviously," sneered the man.

"Isn't that handy?" replied Copper. He produced his warrant card. "Because that's exactly who we are. I'm Detective Sergeant Copper, this is Detective Inspector Constable, and your situation is what we're here about. So if you wouldn't mind lifting your little pole out of our way, Mr ...?"

"Barry Herman," replied the man, wriggling with embarrassment. "Sorry and all that, gents, but I wasn't to know, was I? I'm just doing my job. Only it's been a bit of a morning, and I'm not properly supposed to be here at all, what with being on

11

night duty really, but you see, what happened was ..."

Copper swiftly forestalled further ramblings. "If you wouldn't mind, Mr. Herman. If we can just get on. Perhaps you can tell us later. But in the meantime, maybe you can carry on keeping unwanted callers out ... Oh, except for SOCO, of course."

"SOC-who?" The guard was baffled.

"Scene Of Crime Officers," explained Copper patiently. "Big white van – people in overalls."

"Of course, gents. Sorry again. Won't be a second." Barry Herman disappeared into his little hut and, a moment later, the barrier began to rise. Copper parked the car in the small car park at the front of the factory, in the one remaining space marked 'Visitor', between a vividly-liveried police patrol car and the huge and ostentatious Rolls Royce which lolled in the bay marked 'M.D.'. The detectives were met at the factory door by a uniformed officer, evidently the driver of the police car, whom Constable recognised.

"Morning, Collins."

"Morning, sir."

"How's that cousin of yours over at Dammett Worthy? Got over all the excitement yet?"

"Pretty much, sir."

"And now you've got some excitement of your own here? So what's the story?"

"I haven't actually been inside, sir, other than a couple of minutes when we first got here. And once we'd seen the score, Jenkins stayed inside, and I came out to put the word through to Control, and to stop anyone else going in or out. Oh, except the doctor, sir. He just got here a couple of minutes ago, so I had to vouch for him to our jobsworth on the gate, and he's just gone on through."

"Well done, Collins. So, if you can stay here wielding your fiery sword against all-comers, we'll check out what's going on inside." The inspector pushed open the door and, followed closely by Copper, entered the building. On the far side of the lofty foyer, whose walls were adorned by life-size portraits of the four generations of Winker patriarchs, a second uniformed officer was emerging through a set of double doors.

"It's through here, sir, on the factory floor," he greeted the detectives.

"What's the state of play, then, Jenkins?" Constable's enquiry was brisk and business-like. "Fill us in on the facts so far."

"We got a call just after eight-thirty, sir. That's when people start to arrive in the offices on this side of the road, sir. And that's when they found the body."

"And who found it?"

"Lady by the name of Mrs. Hart, sir. I gather she's some sort of cleaner-cum-tea-lady. She was first in, came through into the factory, found the body, and rushed out to tell the security guy. He phoned us – that's pretty much it so far."

"What, nobody else about?"

"Oh yes, sir. Most of the senior management had turned up here by the time Collins and I arrived, so we decided to keep them here, upstairs in their offices. I hope that's okay, sir, but I thought you'd want to speak to them. I made a list of who's who, sir." The P.C. delved into a pocket, fished out a notebook, and tore out a page which he proffered to the inspector.

"Very good thinking, Jenkins. And the Doc's here, I gather. Right, we'd better take a look. Lead the way." Andy Constable paused. "By the way, Jenkins, I don't normally like to make comments on the junior ranks' personal appearance, but don't you think you could do with smartening yourself up a bit?" He gestured to the smears of what looked like mud adhering to the officer's uniform in generous quantities.

"Sorry, sir, but there's a reason for that. You'll see why." Jenkins held the door for the detectives, who passed through.

After the splendour of the foyer with its marble columns, crystal chandelier and mahogany staircase, the factory floor was a total contrast, with everywhere the gleam of stainless steel set against the brutal strength of white-painted concrete, all under the harsh glare of powerful fluorescent lighting. The odour of chocolate was overpowering.

"Reminds me of a brewery I visited in Belgium," commented Dave Copper in an undertone to his superior. "Wonder if they're giving away free samples here as well."

Rounding a tall tank with a forest of copper piping disappearing aloft, the three officers were greeted by a bizarre sight. Sprawled on the floor alongside an open tank with a raised walkway around it, lying on his back, was the body of what appeared to be a middle-aged man, clad from the feet upwards in

13

white – boots, over-trousers, lab-coat. The clothing on the top half of the body, and the hat which lay alongside on the floor, must presumably have initially been white, but they were now overlaid with a thick layer of rapidly-congealing brown goo, as was the face. Alongside, examining the body, knelt the police doctor.

"Andy!" he cried cheerily, rising to his feet. "I wondered how long it would take you to get here. I must say, your boys do have the jolliest ways of keeping me occupied. I've not had one like this before."

"Good morning, Doc," returned Andy Constable. "I'm glad you're happy, although I'm sure we can't say the same for the gentleman here. I take it he is dead?"

"Oh yes, no doubt of that. Of course, I had to make sure, so between us, Jenkins and I managed to haul him out of the vat."

"So this isn't how he was found?"

"Oh no. When I got here he was up on the walkway, bent over the edge of the tank with his head down in the merrily-bubbling molten chocolate. Most bizarre - never seen anything like it. So just to be on the safe side, I took a couple of quick photos, because I knew you and SOCO would give me a hard time otherwise - thank the lord for smart-phones! - and then we somehow managed between us to get him down on to the floor, just to be certain that life was extinct. Had a devil of a job, but well done Jenkins for doing most of the heavy work."

"That's how come I got messed up, sir," explained Jenkins anxiously. "I mean, I didn't mean to ..."

"Perfectly understandable, constable, so stop worrying," replied the inspector. "We'll take things from here. Tell Collins to keep station at the door – his family seems to be developing quite a talent for that – so that he can point SOCO and the body-wagon in the right direction when they arrive. Why don't you go and tell the chap on the gate that, apart from them, nobody else goes in or out, and we'll come and have a chat with him later, and then you can go off and get yourself cleaned up. Oh yes, and before you go, pop up to the offices and tell everyone to sit tight, and we'll get up to them shortly."

"Will do, sir. Thank you, sir." The P.C. headed for the foyer.

"So, Doc," said Andy Constable, turning his attention back to his medical colleague. "Do we know who our dead man is?"

"Oh yes. It is in fact the eponymous Wally Winker himself, although I can't say I'm surprised that you don't recognise him in his present state. But as it happens, I was at a do the other week where he got some sort of award for civic virtues or some similar nonsense, and I knew him from that."

"Time of death? Any ideas?"

"Not a clue," responded the doctor cheerily. "With a bubbling cauldron of molten chocolate in the mix, any temperature calculations are going to be knocked for six. You might as well wet your finger and stick it in the air."

"And as for how he was found. Couldn't he simply have overbalanced and tipped in?"

"Hmmm." The doctor sounded dubious. "Looking at the height of the guard-rail, I'd be inclined to say no. If you want a strictly non-medical hunch, I'd say he was pushed and held."

"And cause of death? Do I need to ask?"

"Probably not," replied the doctor, "although it doesn't do to be too hasty about these things. Can't give you a definitive cause at the moment, although from what I can see so far, there don't seem to be any wounds or any sort of cranial trauma."

"So not bashed on the head, then?" interjected Dave Copper.

"The obvious explanation," continued the doctor, "considering the position in which he was found, is that he drowned. Tell you more when I've got him on my slab. Of course, in normal drowning cases, you'd probably find that the victim's lungs are waterlogged, but clearly in this case, Mr. Winker is more likely to be ..."

"Chocolate-logged?" suggested Copper helpfully.

"On which note," said Constable with a stern sideways look at his junior colleague, as a team of overall-clad officers pushed through the foyer doors and headed for the group around the body, "we will leave you with the SOCO boys and girls, and see what we can find elsewhere."

"Here, guv – my gran's always telling me I'll come to a sticky end," murmured Copper in an aside to his superior. "Do you suppose this is what she had in mind?"

The inspector elected to ignore him. "Come along, Copper," he said severely. "Let's see if we can't find a more productive outlet for your warped sense of humour."

15

As they climbed the stairs, Constable and Copper became aware of the sound of trundling wheels and rattling crockery, and on reaching the landing they were greeted by a dumpy grey-haired woman clad in an old-fashioned wrap-around apron, pushing a trolley laden with cups and saucers.

"Morning, dears," she said, evincing no great surprise at the detectives' presence. "I expect you're the police, aren't you? I thought you'd be along soon. And you're just in time for a cup of tea." She gestured to her trolley. "I've just made one for the others, because they've all had a bit of a shock, haven't they, and you know what they say, nothing like a nice strong cup of sweet tea when you've had a shock. I'll go and get a couple of extra cups for you two gents in a moment, once I've delivered this lot, but you'll have to make do with the ordinary china, dears, because this is the special tea set for the board, because I thought everybody needed a little bit of pampering, what with everything."

Constable managed to interrupt the flow with some difficulty. "Would you be Mrs. Hart, by any chance?"

"That's right, dear, Val Hart. Cleaner, tea lady, chief cook and bottle-washer – you ask, and I'm probably it."

"And from what I gather, you were the one who found Mr. Winker's body this morning."

"I did. I went through to the factory to get my mop and bucket to do the foyer, and there he was. Of course, I didn't know it was him at the time, because all I could see was a pair of legs sticking up over the edge of that tank thing. It could have been anybody. But then that nice young policeman came up just now and told us who it was, which of course took the wind out of everyone's sails, so that's when I decided to go and make the tea. Which," she added meaningfully, "I had better get on with pouring out, otherwise it'll all be stone cold, which will be no good to anybody. You'd better follow me, dears. Everyone's through here in the boardroom. If you can just get that door for me, young man." Copper opened the indicated heavyweight panelled mahogany door, and Val pushed her trolley through into the room, where half-a-dozen faces turned to look with varying degrees of surprise and apprehension.

"Here's your teas, dears," announced Val cheerfully, "and

16

these gentlemen are policemen, so that's nice, because I'm sure they'll be able to sort everything out. Right, then, dear, it's over to you, I think." She turned to the inspector with an expectant beam.

Constable, slightly taken aback at the style of introduction, pulled himself together rapidly and strove to inject a more formal tone into the situation, as Val busied herself with teapot and cups. "Good morning, ladies and gentlemen. I'm Detective Inspector Constable and this is my colleague Detective Sergeant Copper, and, as Mrs. Hart says, we are here to investigate the death of the gentleman who has been provisionally identified as Mr. Walter Winker. In fact, it might be helpful to us if one of you were able to provide a positive identification while the body is still on the premises. Would one of you be prepared to assist us with this?"

A heavily-built man, apparently in his fifties, rose from his seat at the head of the table. "I'll do it if you like."

"Thank you, sir. And you are ...?"

"Ivor Sweetman. I'm the company's Quality Director."

"Would that mean that you're the senior person here?"

Ivor looked around his companions. "Well, yes, I suppose so."

"Then you will do very nicely, sir, since you are so kind. Copper, would you take the gentleman downstairs for the necessary. Quick as you like, and then back up here, please."

"Right, sir. If you'd come with me, Mr. Sweetman ..." The two left the room.

Constable turned his attention to the remainder of those seated around the table. "I am going to need to speak to each of you to try to get an impression of the circumstances leading up to Mr. Winker's unfortunate death. I wonder, is there somewhere suitable I can use."

"There's always Mr. Winker's office," piped up Val. "It's a bit more comfortable than the other offices, and he won't be needing it, will he?"

"Certainly, if nobody has any objections." Constable's look of enquiry was met with a variety of murmurs, shrugs, and shakes of the head. "So if you would be good enough to wait here, and I'll ask my colleague to come and fetch you as soon as possible."

"You come along with me, dear," said Val. "I'll show you

where it is." She led the way as Constable, quietly amused at the elderly woman's taking charge, followed her meekly along the corridor, past various partitioned-off sections and open-plan areas, to a door identical to that of the boardroom at the other end. "Here you are, inspector." The room was comfortably furnished with a large desk in dark wood, with matching leather-upholstered chairs. Bookshelves laden with a variety of books, folders and box-files stood against one wall, while other walls bore framed enlarged photographs of many of the company's iconic products. Opposite the window overlooking the front car park, a further window looked down over the factory floor, with a door adjacent which opened on to a staircase which led downwards. "Make yourself at home, and I'll go and get a couple of cups of tea for you and that sergeant of yours. Just let me tidy up a bit." She made to move the newspaper lying open on the desk.

Constable forestalled her. "Best leave everything as it is until we know what's what, Mrs. Hart."

"Oh, alright, dear. You know best. And I suppose you'll need to talk to me as well, what with me finding the body and everything."

"We shall, Mrs. Hart."

"I should think you would, dear. There's not much about this place I don't know."

"Have you been here long?"

"Oh, donkey's years, dear, so if there's anything you want to know, you just ask me. I know all their little secrets. For instance, ..."

Val appeared prepared to launch into a lengthy speech, but she was forestalled by the re-appearance at the head of the stairs of Dave Copper and Ivor Sweetman.

"Through here, sergeant," called Constable. "And Mr. Sweetman, if you wouldn't mind joining us, perhaps we could make a start with you."

"Oh. Right." Val seemed miffed at the interruption. "I'll just go and get those teas, then, shall I?" she harrumphed.

"If you wouldn't mind, Mrs. Hart." Constable sought to soothe the ruffled feathers. "And we'll have our little chat when I've got a few more facts. I'm sure that what you have to tell us will be much more useful then. Don't you think?"

18

"All right, then, dear," responded Val, mollified. "I'll be back with your tea in a minute."

*

"Please take a seat, Mr. Sweetman," said Constable, seating himself in one of the pair of leather tub chairs in front of the large desk and indicating the other. Dave Copper discreetly took a smaller chair to one side, just out of Ivor Sweetman's eye-line, produced a notebook from his pocket, and prepared to make notes. "First, may I take it that the gentleman downstairs is in fact Mr. Winker."

"Yes, it's Wally all right. Though how he … well, that's your job, isn't it, finding out what happened. So, how can I help?"

"Firstly, sir, perhaps you can tell us if there's anyone we should be notifying. I mean, is there a Mrs. Winker?"

"No, Wally was a widower. No children." Ivor broke off as something seemed to strike him. "That's a thought."

"Sir?"

"I wonder who'll take over the company now. I mean, there's no obvious successor in the family, so …" Ivor tailed off.

"Now, Mr. Sweetman," resumed Constable. "It's Mr. Ivor Sweetman, I think you said?" A nod in confirmation. "And if I remember aright, you say that you're one of the company's directors. Which I imagine would make you one of the most senior members of staff. Perhaps the most senior, after Mr. Winker?"

"That is correct, inspector. Quality Director for the Winker Chocolate Company, if you want it in full, as stated under my signature on letters." There was an air of pompous satisfaction in his words.

"Which means what, exactly, sir?"

"To put it in layman's terms, inspector, Chief Taster. In other words, if anyone has an idea for a new product, they have to get it past me first. So all the research and development happens on this side of the road – we have a small team working under me - and when we go into production, it all transfers over to the other side."

"At present, Mr. Sweetman, I'm rather more concerned with events on this side of the road, and one of the first things I'd like to establish is who last saw Mr. Winker alive and when."

"I saw him last night, if that's any help to you. Well,

19

yesterday evening, anyway."

"Can you be more specific, Mr. Sweetman? What sort of time are we talking about?" Constable flicked a brief sideways glance at Copper to verify that the sergeant was recording the information. Copper's pencil stood poised.

"Normally I would go home at around six, inspector, although having said that, I do quite often stay late at the office, but my wife has grown used to that. And frequently I stop for a meal on the way home, to save putting her to any trouble. But I was working late last night, because Mr. Winker had had the idea of introducing a range of garlic- and prune-flavoured chocolates for people to give to unwanted trick-or-treaters, so I was looking into ways of making the sweets revolting enough." Ivor gave a self-satisfied chuckle. "Of course, that's something of a challenge in our business, and I thought my research bods probably wouldn't have the first idea of where to start, so I was doing a little background research. I don't like to take my work home. Wally was still in his office, and he and I exchanged a few words at one point, and I left at around quarter past seven, I suppose."

"Leaving Mr. Winker alive and well at that stage?"

"Of course, inspector."

"Then thank you for that, sir. I think that will do for the moment."

"So does that mean I can go back to my office? As you'll appreciate, I'm sure, as senior executive I shall have a great deal to do today to sort out all the ramifications of this business."

"Of course, Mr. Sweetman. We'll come and find you if we discover that we need to speak to you further."

Ivor made to get up, but then stopped. "Inspector, just a moment. These questions – are you implying that Wally's death isn't some sort of horrible accident? But who on earth would ...?" He broke off, seemingly bewildered.

"Who indeed, Mr. Sweetman? My thought exactly. Which means that, if you don't mind, I should be talking to your other colleagues."

"Oh. Well." Ivor seemed at a loss for a moment. "You'd better start with Bernard Rabbetts, in that case," he advised. "He's the other senior director, and he'll only take the huff if you keep him waiting too long."

"Thank you for the suggestion, sir. Copper, if you'd get

20

the door for Mr. Sweetman, and then pop along and ask Mr. Rabbetts if he'd join us."

"Will do, sir."

*

Bernard Rabbetts was a shortish plump middle-aged man with a round eager face. As he took his seat opposite the inspector, his handshake was slightly warm and damp.

"I must say, this is all something of a shocker, inspector. Goodness knows how this is going to affect the company, but I suppose we shall all have to just carry on as best we can and see how things work out."

"And what exactly will your part be in this, Mr. Rabbetts?"

"Please, call me Bernie – everyone does. Wally runs a very informal ship."

"I think, if you don't mind, Mr. Rabbetts, we'll stick to the formalities," replied Constable. "I find it's easier to elicit the facts that way. Now, I understand from Mr. Sweetman that you too are a director of the company."

"That's right, inspector. I've been here for years, man and boy – I shudder to think how many, really!" He gave an open beaming guileless smile. "I started off on the factory floor, and I've worked my way up to the Board – my actual title is Director of Seasonal Products."

"And what does this entail?"

"Oh inspector, I'm sure you can work that out for yourself. Anything that's over and above the normal range of items which are available all year round. Christmas of course, and Easter. It's a constant process to find new ways of extending the range. For instance, we had machines which were used for making Easter eggs which were sitting idle the rest of the year. But then I had the idea for a mould which would use the same machine to make chocolate hearts, so now we can take advantage of the St. Valentine's Day market as well. It's the same with Easter rabbits – a little tweak on the mould and the packaging, and you have chocolate reindeer for Christmas."

"Very resourceful, sir."

Bernie glowed with enthusiasm. "And now I'm working on a really exciting project I've thought of – Easter chicks made out of yellow chocolate! Which meant I had to stay on a little last night, because there's a Board meeting coming up, and I wanted to go through a new European Union directive on food colouring for my report."

"Ah, so you were here after normal office hours as well, sir. And did you see or speak to Mr. Winker during that time?"

"Oh yes, inspector. I'm in and out of his office all the time. He likes to be kept abreast of everything that's going on, so that nothing comes as a surprise to him when it reaches the Board."

"And can you tell us, just for Sergeant Copper's notes, what time you left the premises yesterday?"

"Goodness, I'm not sure I can, inspector. Sometime in the region of seven, I suppose, but I expect that's a bit too vague for you." Bernie smiled helplessly. "I'm sorry, but I'm not very good with times."

"No matter, Mr. Rabbetts," said Constable affably. "Perhaps one of the others will be able to confirm your movements."

Bernie stopped smiling. "Inspector ..." he faltered. "Does this mean that you think that one of us may have had something to do with Wally's death?"

"I can't rule out any possibilities at this stage, sir," was Constable's un-reassuring reply. "I'm just attempting to get an idea of the general shape of things. Which means, if there's nothing else that occurs to you that I may have missed, sergeant ...?" He cast an enquiring look in Copper's direction.

"Not a thing, sir."

"Then we'll let you get on, and perhaps have a word with whoever is next on our list. Which would be ...?"

Copper consulted the list which Jenkins had provided. "That would be a Miss Marr, sir."

Bernie stood. "Trixie? Would you like me to send her down to see you? That's if you're sure you've finished with me?"

"Certainly for the time being, sir," said Constable. "So yes, if you would ask Miss Marr to join us, that would be very kind."

As Bernie opened the door, he was met with the sight of Val attempting to juggle two cups and saucers in an effort to leave a free hand to knock. She sidled past him as he left.

"Here you are, dears," she said, depositing the cups on the desk. "I've put two sugars in each." Constable smiled in thanks, while giving an inward shudder. "And if you open that bottom drawer, you'll find a tin with Mr. Winker's special chocolate biscuits in it. I'm sure he wouldn't mind, and you need to keep your strength up." She glanced at Dave Copper. "And I've never met a young lad yet who could resist a choccie biccie. So you help yourself, dear." Copper gave an embarrassed half-grin. "Oh look, here's Trixie." A trim dark-haired woman who looked to be in her late thirties was hovering uncertainly in the doorway. "Well, I'll leave you to get on – I'm sure you've got lots of important questions to ask." She gave a meaningful look. "And don't you forget me, will you, because I ..."

"Yes, thank you, Mrs Hart," said Constable, interrupting the flow of prattle and gently ushering the garrulous cleaner to the door while indicating to the newcomer that she should take a seat. He closed the door with an almost inaudible sigh of relief. "Sergeant, would you like to ask Miss Marr a few questions?"

"Righty-ho, sir." Copper moved to the chair behind the desk as Constable picked up his teacup, took a sip and, wincing at the unwelcome sweetness, hastily deposited it again on the windowsill.

"So, Miss Marr," began Copper. "It is *Miss* Marr, isn't it?"

"Yes ... that's right." Trixie Marr seemed faintly ill-at-ease.

"And you're what ... another of the directors?"

"Actually, no. I'm the Production Manager for Bars. I'm in charge of the production line for all the mass-market products."

"Now we were under the impression, Miss Marr, that the production all took place in the main plant across the road."

"It does, sergeant, but I have my office over here, because everything has to go through various stages before it's finally handed over to me, so it's convenient to be closer to the development people." A pause. "Sergeant ... Bernie said that you're looking at the possibility that one of us might have had something to do with Mr. Winker's death. Surely that can't be true."

"I'm afraid it is, Miss Marr. We're going to be looking into the movements of everyone who was on the premises after the last time Mr. Winker was seen alive, after normal going-home time yesterday."

"Oh." Trixie grimaced. "Then that's why you want to talk to me? Because I stayed on late last night?"

"Not another one!" groaned Copper, half to himself. "No, I

wasn't aware that you were on the premises yesterday evening, miss. Perhaps you'd like to give me the details."

"I decided to work on a little because I had to do some work on a report Mr. Winker had asked me to write for the Board meeting which is coming up soon. You see, we'd had a few problems with the machines on the last new product – that was the 'Tiger' bar – and because of that, the launch didn't go quite as we planned."

"The 'Tiger' bar? That's one of yours? I love those – they're great. But they're not easy to find – our local shop's never got them."

Trixie gave a faint rueful smile. "That was the problem, sergeant – we failed to de-bug the production fully, and as a result, I'm afraid the launch was a bit of a flop. That's why Mr. Winker had insisted on a report for the next Board, to make sure nothing went wrong with the next new product, which is even more intricate."

"Oh?"

"Yes, it's the 'Box-o-Chox' Bar. One cream bar with different fillings in each of the six compartments."

"Sounds complicated. Plenty of scope for mistakes, I bet."

"Yes. And Mr. Winker didn't like mistakes."

"And did your path and Mr. Winker's cross yesterday evening?"

"Only briefly, sergeant. We just had a short conversation about a little production problem, but that was all sorted out downstairs."

"And you know of no reason why anyone would wish to do Mr. Winker harm?"

"No." There was a clear note of reserve in Trixie's voice.

"Including yourself."

"No!" Trixie was unexpectedly emphatic, but then her voice fell. "Quite the opposite. In fact, he … I don't know how …" Her voice broke, and she pulled a handkerchief from her sleeve to wipe a sudden tear.

Andy Constable intervened. "I think we'll leave it there for a moment, Miss Marr. I understand all this must be very upsetting for anyone who knew Mr. Winker well. But if you wouldn't mind remaining on the premises, and perhaps we can speak again later."

"I'm sorry, inspector. It's just that ..." Trixie made a concentrated effort to master herself. "Is it all right if I go to my office?" she asked in firmer tones. "I should get on with that report. Someone will want it."

"Of course." Constable held the door open for her. "Oh, would you just ask the next of your colleagues if we could have a word? Sergeant, that would be ...?"

Copper consulted his list. "Mr. Laurie, sir, according to this."

"You want Carson? I'll send him along." Self-control fully restored, Trixie closed the door behind her.

Dave Copper exchanged glances with his superior. "Well, guv, that's the first hint that we've had of something a bit iffy. The lady's obviously upset about something, over and above the obvious of her boss being found taking an unscheduled swim in the company product. Do you reckon this is one of those little secrets Mrs. Hart was going on about?"

"Could well be, sergeant, but we'll put that on the back burner for the moment until we've had our talk with our little group of ..."

"Suspects, guv?"

"Hmmm. Very possibly. I'll tell you one thing – I'm going to be highly astonished if everyone doesn't turn out to have been working late last night. I swear the fates do it just to annoy me."

Andy Constable's musings were cut short by a robust rap at the office door. Before there was time to respond, it was pushed open forcefully, and the next visitor strode confidently into the room. Fortyish, with an athletic build and thick brown hair swept back, Carson Laurie advanced with a friendly smile and a hand outstretched in greeting.

"Inspector Constable. Good morning. I'm Carson Laurie. I understand you have some questions for me."

Constable was slightly taken aback by the vigour of the approach, and took the other's hand after only a moment's hesitation. "Indeed yes, Mr. Laurie. Do please take a seat." He allowed himself a small smile as Carson took the chair in front of the desk. "I'm guessing, sir, from the accent, that you're not originally from round here."

"Detroit, Michigan, inspector, although I've been living over here for a while."

"Really, sir? And what brought you so far from home?"

"Well, I used to be with the Satsuma Motor Corporation over there – I was on their design team for a while."

"Sounds exciting, sir, working for a big car company in the States," broke in Dave Copper.

"I guess, pretty much." Carson seemed happy to bask in the sergeant's admiration. "And I spent time at Corporate Headquarters in Washington too. Sometimes you had to be close to where some of the big decisions on laws and regulations got taken. Lot of money tied up in these things. But then, you know how it is – things not so good in the automotive industry in the States, so I figured it was time for a change of scenery and a change of direction, so to cut a long story short, I'm now the Winker Company's Transport Manager."

"So not a total abandonment of the old field of activity, then?"

Carson smiled. "No, I guess not. Now anything with wheels on it is my responsibility, and I've just been starting work on this great new project Wally had thought of. Because I've got this design background, and to boost this big new product we're launching, Wally had the idea of turning all the company vehicles into 'Box-o-Chox' bars – everything from the reps' cars up to the forty-ton trucks. Believe me, that's some big decals!"

"And would that have been one of the reasons you were here after normal office hours yesterday?" asked Constable innocently.

"Yeah, that's right," nodded Carson, and then paused. "Hey, how did you know?"

"Lucky guess, sir," responded Constable mildly. "So you did stay on late yesterday?"

"As it happens, inspector, yes, I did. This plan of Wally's, it's a fabulous idea, but there are plenty of things that aren't easy to achieve. That's why I was here - Wally and I were talking about some of the factors involved, and I had some drawings I wanted him to see, but it wasn't easy to get in to see him, because so many of the others were around as well. But I have to tell you, inspector, in case you're wondering, Wally was alive and well when I came out of his office, and you can ask anyone you like about that."

"And I imagine we probably will, sir," replied Constable

comfortably. "But just before you go, can you think of any reason why anyone would wish to do Mr. Winker harm?"

Carson shook his head. "Not at all, inspector. Wally was a very good boss. You know, good to people. Surprisingly so, sometimes." He seemed lost in his thoughts for a moment. "Beats me."

"Then we'll let you get on for now, sir." Carson stood. "And we'd like a chat with whoever is left in the boardroom – sergeant, that would be ...?"

"Miss Kane or Miss Lockett, sir."

"Let's have them alphabetically. If you could ask Miss Kane to join us."

"Sure." A nod. "Inspector - sergeant." With a fresh shake of the hand with each, Carson strode from the room.

"A forty-ton chocolate bar?" remarked Copper incredulously. "That's a bit of overkill, isn't it? Sorry, no pun intended."

"Times is hard," observed Constable. "I dare say there's a lot of competition in this business, what with getting squeezed between the big boys and the supermarket own brands, so if they're launching a new product, they probably need to go overboard with everything they've got."

"Do you suppose this business is something to do with these new products, guv?" asked Copper. "That's the fourth in a row who's had some job on involving something that was being brought into the range. Do you reckon somebody was having trouble getting a pet idea past the big boss, and they somehow snapped when whatever-it-was didn't happen?"

"It's not out of the question," mused Constable, "but there's nothing that points me in that direction at the moment. Let's see what the others have to say."

At that moment, as if on cue, a woman appeared in the office doorway. She looked to be in her late twenties, with a trim figure clad in an almost severe dark blue suit. Pale blonde hair tied straight back off the face, and touches of make-up subtly applied, gave her a restrained glamour.

"You wanted to speak to me, I think, gentlemen." She advanced into the room. "I gather you have some questions. Shall I sit here?" With calm self-possession, she seated herself in front of the desk and looked up at Constable expectantly.

"Indeed, yes, Miss ... er ... Kane, isn't it?" The inspector was thrown slightly off-balance at the newcomer's assumption of control.

"That's correct, inspector. Candice Kane, if your sergeant wishes to make a note of the full name. My friends call me Candy." She favoured Dave Copper, seated to one side, with a smile. He flashed a look at his superior, raised one eyebrow, and obediently started to write in his notebook.

"And your position with the company, Miss Kane?" continued Constable.

"Officially, Managing Director's Secretary, inspector."

'And unofficially?' wondered Constable, but kept the thought to himself. "I see. So, does that mean you're the Company Secretary?"

Candy shook her head. "Oh no, that's quite different. I'm the managing director's confidential personal assistant – was, I suppose I should say. Everything Mr. Winker did tended to go through me – letters, calls, emails, all that sort of thing."

"That sounds a highly responsible position, Miss Kane. And I imagine, from what little I know about business, that whenever the boss needs you, you have to be there."

"That's usually the way it is." Candy gave a small smile.

"Which would mean that, like the others, you would have been staying late at the office yesterday, as long as Mr. Winker needed you."

"Yes. Mr. Winker very often stayed on, but usually he would let me know when he didn't want me any more. It wasn't as if I had to work late every night."

"And yesterday? Perhaps you are best placed to give us an idea of Mr. Winker's movements up to the last time he was seen. Although I assume you didn't work in this office with him?"

"No, inspector. I have my own office, through that door there." Candy pointed to a door adjacent to the entrance to the corridor. She paused a moment in reflection. "So, I took Mr. Winker his evening paper as usual yesterday teatime ..."

"That would be this one?" said Constable, gesturing to the copy of the Rownville Evening Mail still lying open on the desk before him.

"Yes. Mr. Winker always liked to keep up with the local news – it meant that whenever he went on one of his regular walks round the factory across the road, he always had something local to chat to the employees about. He liked to keep in touch."

"So, coming back to yesterday teatime, by which I assume you mean around five or six?"

"That's right – probably closer to six, actually. I remember it was just before Mr. Laurie went in to see him. So then I had some correspondence to see to, so I finished off Mr. Winker's letters and took them down to the post-room. Then I went and had a word with Ivor – that's Mr. Sweetman – he was looking into something for Mr. Winker, I believe. I wondered if there was anything I could do to help him with it. And when I went back to my desk, Mr. Winker wasn't in his office any more."

"Do you know where he'd gone?"

"No, not really, inspector. He might have been in one of the other offices, or sometimes he went down to the factory floor for some reason. But it was a sort of unspoken thing, that if he wasn't in his office after six, he wouldn't be needing me any more. So then Mr. Sweetman very kindly gave me a lift home."

"And you didn't see Mr. Winker again after you left your office with the post?"

"No, inspector, I'm afraid not. I think that's about all I can tell you."

"Well, we'll leave it at that for the moment, Miss Kane," said Constable. "I expect you probably have a great deal to get on with, under the circumstances."

Candy's lip trembled slightly. The efficient façade seemed in danger of crumbling, but she then took a deep breath and stood. "I'd better start making some phone calls. I don't really know where to begin. Will it be all right if I use my office? I mean, I won't disturb you?"

"No, Miss Kane," Constable reassured her. "We shall be off and around shortly anyway." And as Candy disappeared through into her own room, a brisk knock came at the door to the corridor.

"I bet that'll be Miss Lockett," speculated Copper. "She's the last on my list. She sounds a bit eager, doesn't she?"

"In which case," returned Constable, "we'd best not keep her waiting. Let her in."

Copper opened the door to reveal, not the expected

individual, but the young officer who had first greeted them on their arrival at the factory.

"Sorry to butt in, sergeant ..."

"Yes, Collins, what is it?" asked Constable.

"We've got a little bit of a kerfuffle at the gate, sir. There's a chap just arrived who says he's working here and he needs to come in, but the guy on the gate is refusing to let him through and says he's only obeying orders, but the new chap is quite insistent, and the temperature is rising a bit, so I thought I'd better check with you."

"Sounds as if Barry Herman's doing the traditional 'more than my job's worth' routine, guv," remarked Copper. "Want me to go down and sort it out?"

"I've got a better idea," said Constable, getting to his feet. "We'll both go. We'll pop along and have a word with Miss Lockett, who I assume is probably getting rather fed up with cooling her heels in the boardroom, and then we'll come down and find out what this is all about. I want to speak to the gate-keeper anyway, so we can kill two birds with one stone." He paused to reflect on his choice of words. "So to speak. Copper, you must be a bad influence – I'm getting as bad as you. Collins, you'd better go down and try to keep the warring parties from coming to blows, and tell them we'll be with them in a few minutes."

"Sir." The P.C. nodded and disappeared swiftly towards the stairs.

*

As Constable opened the door to the boardroom, he immediately launched into an apology to the woman seated alone at the table. "Miss Lockett, I am so sorry to have kept you waiting so long, but I'm afraid these investigations take time, as I'm sure you must know."

"Better than you probably realise, inspector," came the reply.

"Oh?"

The woman rose and came towards Constable, hand outstretched in greeting. She appeared to be in her forties, tall and sturdy with neat short brown hair, a matching dark top and trousers, and a confident professional air. "Heidi Lockett. We're colleagues, or rather, former colleagues. I used to be on the force. Oh, not this one," she explained in response to Constable's

30

quizzical look. "That was when I lived in London."

"And now?"

"Now I am Head of Security for the Winker Chocolate Company."

"Something of a change, Miss Lockett," commented Constable.

"Not so much," said Heidi. "I was in the same boat as quite a lot of the chaps a while back – cuts in resources, and so on. I'm sure you must have the same problems. But I was lucky enough to be able to walk into a job with a private security company, and then a little while after that, the position arose at Winker's. So here I am."

"And I'm very glad you are," said Constable. "Another professional pair of eyes won't do any harm at all in looking at this case. Maybe you can fill us in on some more details about yesterday."

"In fact, inspector, I wasn't supposed to be here at all yesterday, because I was taking a day off."

"But the way you say that makes me believe that you in fact were around."

"Oh, not during the day, but then, I don't suppose that makes much of a difference, because what happened to Wally took place later, from what I gather. No, I arrived later, because we're just testing a new security system, with sensors and concealed cameras and so on." She smiled. "It may sound all very cloak-and-dagger, but there is a lot of industrial espionage in the confectionery business, with manufacturers wanting to steal a march on their rivals over new products and so on. Anyway, we've been using this freelance company to devise the system, and Wally Winker called me and asked me to come in after hours and be an intruder, just to test how it was working. I got in at about six, I suppose, but at that time, pretty much everyone on this side of the plant was around, so it was all a bit pointless."

"And presumably you saw Mr. Winker during the course of your visit."

"Oh yes. We spoke in his office, because I wanted to point out to him that I wouldn't actually be able to do what he had in mind, and then I had a few words with the I.T. guy, but after that I just mooched about, really, until I finally decided that there was absolutely no point in my hanging around any longer, so I went home."

"And have you any ideas about other people's movements?" enquired Constable.

"Not really," said Heidi. "Of course, I was rather hoping that there wouldn't be anyone about at all. But there may be something on the CCTV, that's if it was up and running by then. You'll have to ask Mike, except that I haven't seen him today."

"Mike?"

"Mike Rowe, the freelance I.T. chap we're using."

"CCTV could certainly be helpful, if there is any, guv," pointed out Copper. "Might save us a lot of chasing about."

"Can we get hold of this Mr. Rowe?" asked Constable.

"I'll see if I can reach him," said Heidi, producing a phone from her jacket pocket. "Being freelance, he's a bit here and there, and you never know when you've got him, but I'll see what I can do. That's if there's nothing else?"

"Only to wonder if you might be aware," said Constable, "given your position with the company, of anyone who might have an interest in doing Mr. Winker harm."

Heidi laughed quietly. "Over and above the usual office politics, I can't really imagine it, inspector. I think if you ask anyone, you'll find that they all say that Mr. Winker was a very good employer." She smiled. "If that's it, I'll go and see if I can track down Mike Rowe."

"And we," countered Constable, "will go and find out what is happening down at the gate. Please keep me posted." He turned and led the way out of the boardroom and down the stairs.

*

At the gatehouse booth at the entrance to the car park, Barry Herman stood at his post wearing an expression of mulish obstinacy, confronting a mild-looking bespectacled man in his thirties holding a briefcase. The young uniformed officer stood close by, looking slightly apprehensive.

"Ah, here he is!" cried Barry triumphantly. "Ask him, if you don't believe me. *He'll* tell you you can't go in. Inspector, I've told him what's happened, but he still ..."

Constable took charge. "Thank you, Mr. Herman. I think you can safely leave this to us." He turned to the newcomer. "I'm Detective Inspector Constable, sir – this is my colleague Sergeant Copper. I gather you're wishing to gain access to the factory, sir, which at the moment is restricted, being a crime scene. So perhaps you'd like to tell me why. And who you are."

The man produced a business card from a top pocket. "My name is Rowe – Mike Rowe." Constable perused the card – Michael Rowe, Managing Director, Mike Rowe Systems, he read. "And I have a contract with the Winker Chocolate Company to carry out some very confidential work of a highly sensitive nature."

"Mr. Rowe!" the inspector exclaimed genially. "You are the very man we need. In fact, we have just been talking about you with the company's Head of Security, who is I believe trying to get in touch with you as we speak." As if on cue, the music of a mobile ringtone sounded from the businessman's pocket. "So do please answer that."

"Hello ... yes, I'm actually here at the gate ... yes, I would, if they'd let me in. There's a police inspector here asking me questions."

"Mr. Rowe," interrupted Constable, "as you've been vouched for in advance, as it were, by Miss Lockett, I think we can let you go through. And we'll want to speak to you, but I dare say that will be no problem."

"Hello, Heidi ... yes, they say I can come in. I'll be up in a minute." Mike Rowe climbed into his car and looked expectantly at Barry Herman.

"Mr. Herman, perhaps if you would ..." prompted Dave Copper.

"Oh ... er ... right. Yes, of course." With an embarrassed look, Barry pushed the button in his booth and the barrier rose on cue. "Sorry about that, gents, but I wasn't to know ..."

The inspector brushed his excuses aside. "Never mind about that now, Mr. Herman. I'm more concerned with the events of yesterday leading up to Mr. Winker's unfortunate death. So perhaps we can concentrate on your movements in that context. Sergeant," he said over his shoulder, "if you weren't already planning to do so, it might be useful to make a few notes."

"Already on it, guv," replied Dave Copper, notebook at the ready.

"Now I think you said," pursued Constable, "when we first spoke, that you were on night duty yesterday."

"That's right." Barry now seemed eager to help, in order

to make up for his former unhelpfulness. "I was on duty here at the factory gate yesterday evening."

"Which factory do you mean?" asked Copper. "You've got two."

"Ah. Well, you see, there's what we call the factory, which is the original building this side of the road, and there's what we call the plant, which is the new one over there. And there's the two gatehouses, one for each. Now, the one the other side closes down just after five-thirty, because that's when the plant goes home, so you haven't got any more lorries and what-not going in and out and the car park that side is clear. So whoever is on at night stays this side, so they can just keep an eye on both. Do you see what I mean?" Barry looked up hopefully to make sure his explanation was being followed.

"I think that's all quite clear," Constable reassured him. "So your shift started when exactly?"

"I got here just before five-thirty and took over from my oppo."

"And, I presume, nothing untoward at that stage."

"No, not a thing. So then my mate went off, and I was left here on my own."

"So that would mean that you monitor all the comings and goings through this gate after that. And you can stop anyone going through, as you did with Mr. Rowe."

"Ah, well, it's not as simple as that, inspector. You see, all the management staff who work on this side have got their own key cards for this barrier. You see that little post there with the box on top of it?" Barry pointed to a small installation alongside the barrier. "Because the management are coming and going at all hours sometimes, they put that in, so I don't have to be here to push my little button. They just put their card in the slot, and up goes the pole, and they can get in or out whenever they want. That was one of Carson's ideas, and it makes my job a lot easier."

"And is the to-ing and fro-ing monitored?" put in Copper. "I mean, can you tell who goes through and when?"

"No," replied Barry. "I think it's going to be, with this new system, but it doesn't do it now."

"Then we shall have to rely on good old observation, Mr. Herman," said Constable breezily. "So, if you were here as of five-thirty, what can you tell us about any movements in or out?"

"I saw Heidi come in just before six – that's Heidi Lockett, my boss. She said something about checking up on security, so I thought 'Thanks a lot – what am I for?'. I was a bit miffed, to tell you the honest truth, so I didn't really pay too much attention to her."

"So then what? Do you have a particular routine?"

"I usually do a bit of a prowl around the offices about six. It all depends on whether there's anyone around or not – sometimes if they've all gone and it's all closed up, I leave it till a bit later."

"And yesterday?"

"I did my normal six o'clock rounds."

"And do you usually check in all the offices?"

"Well, yes and no. I mean, it's not as if they're all actual separate offices as such. Some of it's sort of open plan, with big screens and plants, and some of them are partitioned off with doors, but I don't really know why they bothered, because Mr. Winker had this what he called 'open door policy', so everything is usually open all the time anyway, so you can hear what goes on as you pass people's desks, even if you can't see them."

"So effectively there are no separate offices at all?"

"Apart from Mr. Winker's, of course. With him, it was more a case of 'do what I say, not what I do'. He kept his door well closed, and apart from the big bosses, if anyone else wanted to see him, they had to go through Candy."

"Yes, we've seen that Miss Kane has her own room off to the side," observed Constable. "So there were in fact two ways into Mr. Winker's office."

"Three, sir," Copper corrected him. "Don't forget he had his own private stairs down to the factory floor."

"True, sergeant. I'd forgotten that. Thank you for the reminder. So, Mr. Herman, to resume our virtual tour, you were up in the office corridor, having got as far as Miss Kane's room."

"That's right, inspector. And she came out with the post as I got there, and just then Carson came up and tapped on Mr. Winker's door, and as he went in, he said 'I need to talk to you about those papers', and then the door closed, so that was that."

"So then what? Did you carry on with your rounds? Did you see any of the other members of staff?"

"I did," confirmed Barry. "Well, not so much saw as heard.

35

And here's a thing that might be useful to you. You see, I was coming past Ivor Sweetman's section, and I heard him and Bernie Rabbetts having a right go at one another."

"And have you any idea what it was about?"

"Oh yes. It's not as if they were bothering to keep their voices down, so you couldn't really call it eavesdropping. Ivor said something about whatever-it-was being 'the latest in a long line of ridiculous ideas', and then Bernie said 'He's not going to listen to her forever, so that's you fixed.' Hammer and tongs, they were going at it." Barry started to smile at the memory, but then recollected himself and assumed a serious expression. "It's not what you expect of management, is it?" he said sententiously.

"So that's Mr. Sweetman and Mr. Rabbetts you've seen," said Constable, ticking them off on his fingers, "plus Miss Kane, and of course Mr. Laurie ..."

"Right." Barry snapped his fingers as a further thought occurred to him. "That's another thing. I was just starting off back downstairs, and Carson came out of Mr. Winker's office as Heidi was coming along the corridor, and he looked a bit surprised to see her and said 'What are you doing here?', I suppose because she was meant to be off yesterday, and she said 'Finished with Wally? Good. My turn. I'll see you downstairs later', and then she knocked on Mr. Winker's door and went in, and I carried on with my rounds, and then I came back here and put the kettle on for a cup of tea."

"Which could be very helpful, Mr. Herman, if it enables you to tell us what time people left the premises."

"Right." Barry gave it a moment's thought. "Ivor Sweetman and Candy Kane were the first to leave the car park – I remember that. He always gives her a lift. In fact," he continued in tones of heavy meaning, "I don't think there's much they don't do together, if you catch my drift." He winked.

"I think we understand," said Constable, since a reaction was obviously expected.

"I think it's very funny," resumed Barry, "because they think it's such a big secret, and I reckon practically everybody knows. Well, except for his wife and her boss."

"Yes, I've noticed how everybody usually manages to know everything in any organisation, except for the person at the top," observed Constable wryly. "So you believe that Mr. Winker was kept in ignorance of this ... arrangement? Any particular reason?"

"I don't think it would have gone down too well with Mr. Winker at all, if you want my opinion."

"We do know that Mr. Sweetman is a married man, sir," pointed out Copper.

"Exactly," nodded Barry. "Now me, I don't point the finger, because what people do in their private lives is up to them. But I reckon Mr. Winker would have seen it differently, what with the religious family background and all. Funny how religion and chocolate seem to go together, isn't it?"

"How's that?" queried Copper, baffled.

"It's perfectly true, sergeant," said Constable, "although I have to confess the thought had never occurred to me before. Yes, you've got that other big Midlands family in this industry, and there's that large firm up in York, so there seems to be a distinct puritanical streak running through the entire confectionery business. I can see how a relationship between Mr. Sweetman and Miss Kane might be a delicate topic. Anyway, I think we're straying from the point a little. Mr. Herman, you were telling us when people left the premises."

"I think Bernie Rabbetts left just after those two, and then Trixie, but I'm not absolutely sure. You see, it got a bit chilly after a while, so I was sat inside with the door shut with my cup of tea and something to eat. I always have a bit of snap around half past seven – helps the evening go by. But I know they were all gone by eight o'clock, apart from Mr. Winker's car, but he's very often still there when I knock off at ten o'clock anyway, so I didn't really think anything of it. I just thought 'Cor, he's the boss, and he's still not gone home yet'." Barry paused as a thought struck him. "Well, he won't be going home now, will he?"

*

Constable and Copper stood in the foyer of the factory building, watching overall-clad members of the forensic team as they carried the plastic-shrouded form of Wally Winker out towards their vehicle, overseen by the doctor.

"We're off, Andy," announced the doctor. "I've done all I can here, so we'll get him back to my guest suite and see if there's anything new to discover under the candy coating." He consulted his watch. "With a bit of luck, I might even make it back in time for elevenses."

"Presumably you'll be giving the chocolate biscuits a miss today," smiled Constable.

"And I thought the ghoulish jokes in the face of death were my province," retorted the doctor good-humouredly. "I'll be in touch." The foyer door closed behind him.

"Happy to carry on, guv," asked Copper, "or do we want to wait for the doctor's report?"

"I don't suppose it'll tell us much we don't already know," answered Constable, "so we may as well carry on here while we've got everybody on the premises, rather than traipsing to and fro to the station. I'm quite exercised by the possibility that there may be some CCTV footage from this security system of theirs, so let's go and see Mr. Rowe, if we can find him."

At the head of the stairs, the detectives were met by the bustling figure of Val Hart carrying two cups and saucers. She looked at them reproachfully.

"Now look, dears, here's those cups of tea I made for you, and you never even touched them. Too late now, because they've gone stone cold, but I dare say you've been busy, so I'll tell you what, I'll make a nice fresh pot and bring some new ones along to you. Going back to Mr. Winker's office, are you? Well, you just go and sit yourselves down in there, dears, and I'll be along in two shakes of a lamb's tail."

"Very kind of you, Mrs. Hart," said the inspector, slightly intimidated by the older woman's determination. "But can I just ask, would you leave out the sugar this time?"

"Well, if you think so, dear." Val sounded highly dubious. "I'm sure you know best. And I expect your boy here is probably watching his waistline, isn't he? Right, shan't be a mo." And she trundled away, leaving a slightly bemused Dave Copper in her wake, muttering 'Cheek!' under his breath.

Andy Constable failed to subdue his amusement. "There you are, sergeant – I told you all those pies in the station canteen would catch up with you in the end. Salads for you from now on, and I think I may be forced to deny you any of those biscuits from Mr. Winker's secret stash."

In Wally Winker's office, the newspaper still lay spread open on the desk. "Shall I clear this away, guv?" asked Copper.

"Yes, do. Although hold on a second. Candy Kane said

Winker liked to keep up with the local news. Let's see what was interesting him yesterday."

Copper browsed the page swiftly. "Mostly human interest stuff, by the look of it. There's a story about a three-legged dog which ran the local half-marathon – oh, look at that picture. There's something about fears of job losses at the local Job Centre. Oh, and some Scottish bloke's caused a row because he says the more water you put in your whisky, the better it tastes ..."

"Man must be mad," commented Constable, taking the chair behind the desk.

"Other than that, it's just the weekly reports from the local magistrates court. Hey ..." Copper took a closer look. "I wonder if they've got that case last week where I got called to give evidence ..."

"No time for that now," Constable interrupted him. "You can catch up with reading about your fifteen minutes of fame on another occasion. At the moment, we have better things to do."

"Righty-ho, guv," replied Copper, not at all chastened, and folding up the newspaper. "Aha! What have we here?"

"Sergeant," said Constable, "perhaps you could resist the temptation to do your impression of a comedy policeman in a bad 1950s B-movie, and tell me what we do have here."

"Memo, guv," answered Copper succinctly. "Lying here on the desk under the newspaper. A memo! Honestly!" He cast his eyes to heaven. "Has this man never heard of emails?" He glanced over the sheet of paper. "Looks like a whole load of gobbledegook to me."

"Suppose you let me be the judge of that. What does it say?"

"It's addressed '*Memo to all management staff. From: MD. To: QD, DSP, PMB, TM, HS.*' And apparently it's all about '*H & S Regulation GOV/8738/19/B Section 17 Clause 28*'. See what I mean, guv?"

"You're right," admitted Constable. "It does sound like the most appalling gibberish. Reminds me of some of the emails I get from the top brass about some sort of new target they've devised to make our lives more interesting. The curse of modern policing, and don't you dare quote me! I suppose we should at least be grateful that Mr. Winker was old-fashioned enough still to be sending out actual paper memos instead of emails and tweets. So, does it carry on in the same incomprehensible vein, or does it get any better as it goes on?"

"A bit. In fact, it's actually written in proper English. '*You are reminded that EU and government regulations require protective overalls, overshoes, gloves, and headwear to be worn at all times in food production areas. Please ensure that you adhere to this regulation without exception, and that all members of staff in your department are aware of the requirement.*' And it's signed *Wally Winker, MD.*"

"Well, there's the answer to one question, at any rate. It explains why Mr. Winker was all dressed up in the whites when he was found, instead of a proper managerial suit. That's why Val Hart didn't recognise who it was."

"Not necessarily one of the questions we needed an answer to, though, is it, guv?" objected Copper. "Isn't it more a matter of who did what and where and when?"

"You may have a point," said Constable. "So with that in mind, why don't you go and find Mike Rowe and see if he can spare us a minute. But don't ever be too ready to discard irrelevant information – sometimes doing that has a habit of coming back and biting you in the backside. Anyway, let us return to our muttons, as somebody once said. Mr. Rowe can't be far away."

"On it, guv." Copper turned and headed for the door.

Constable's attention was caught by a flash of yellow. "Hold on – what's that on your shoe?"

Copper hopped on one foot to remove the offending object. "It's just one of those little self-adhesive notes people stick on phones or paperwork to remind them about something. I must have picked it up off the floor as we've been walking around."

"Anything interesting?"

"It just says '*COLOR'S IMPOSSIBLE TO ACHIEVE!*' in big scrawly capitals, guv. Looks as if somebody was in a strop about something. Take a look." He handed the paper to Constable. "Didn't Bernie Rabbetts say something about yellow chocolate? Maybe it's to do with that. In fact, it could be ..."

"Or maybe not. There are other possibilities. Think about it. But not now!" A look from the inspector discouraged Copper from further immediate speculation. "In the meantime, I think you were about to ..." An eyebrow was raised.

"Right. Mike Rowe. I've gone."

*

Ushered in by Dave Copper, Mike Rowe took the seat across the desk from the inspector. He looked slightly distracted as he took off his glasses to polish them, and then swept a lock of hair out of his eyes.

"So, Mr. Rowe," began Andy Constable, "I'm hoping you've got some helpful news for us from your CCTV records."

Mike shook his head. "The reverse, I'm afraid, inspector," he confessed. "I can't get into the system at all. For some reason, it's decided to freeze completely, so I've had to close it down so as to run a complete scan on it, which I'm afraid is going to take quite a long time."

Constable was philosophical. "You know, Mr. Rowe, sometimes I think that the computers forget that they're supposed to be on our side. But let us not be down-hearted. We shall settle for good old-fashioned question-and-answer police work, if you have the time."

Mike shrugged. "There isn't a great deal I can do at the moment anyhow," he said, "so ask away." He shook his head. "This is really shocking news about Wally. I'm not sure I can believe it yet. So, how can I help you?"

"Just to confirm a few details, you said you're involved with work on the company's computer systems in some way. And how long have you been employed by the Winker Chocolate Company?"

"Oh, I don't actually work for Winker's," explained Mike. "I'm just free-lancing at the moment."

"Of course," said Constable. "I remember you mentioned that you run your own business. In which case, can I ask how you came to be involved with this one? Did you approach them, or did they approach you?"

"Oh, they came to me."

"Would there be any particular reason that you know of why they should decide on you rather than any of the other firms they might have chosen? Have you had dealings with Winker's before?"

"No, none at all," said Mike. "No, it was all down to networking, really. You see, I used to be with Universal Business

41

Machines over at Greenditch before I started up on my own, and I still play squash with one or two of the chaps over there every so often. I'm not very good," he admitted, "and I tend to get thrashed most of the time, but I keep going because when you're working for yourself, you never know when it's going to be useful to keep up some contacts. Anyway, to cut a long story short, one of the guys I know put Heidi, the Head of Security, in touch with me, because his wife goes to the same Zumba classes as her, or some such – it's all very convoluted – and he told me that she'd told him that Heidi had told her that they were having problems trying to de-bug this new security system of theirs." Mike let out a gusty sigh. "So I'm here on an as-and-when basis."

"And did that as-and-when happen to include yesterday?"

"It did. Heidi told me they wanted to run some sort of test, so I was here late last night when it was all happening."

"When what was all happening, Mr. Rowe? What exactly do you mean?"

"Oh, nothing violent, inspector," said Mike hastily. "I just mean there was quite a bit of to-ing and fro-ing, and because they've given me a desk between Heidi Lockett's section and Mr. Winker's office, I couldn't help but be aware of it. Not that I saw much, because I was at my keyboard most of the time, but people kept coming past me, and they're not used to someone being there so they don't pay attention to what they're saying around me."

"So it sounds as if you were perfectly placed to see, or at least hear, anyone who visited Mr. Winker's office during the late afternoon period yesterday," suggested Constable.

"Probably better than anyone," agreed Mike, "but I'm not sure that that will be much help to you, inspector, because I think pretty much everybody went into Mr. Winker's office at some time or another yesterday. The door's quite often open, unless he's got a meeting with someone."

"Let's see if we can't be rather more specific, Mr. Rowe," said Constable. "My sergeant here is attempting to build some sort of time line as to who was where and when." Copper, in response to his superior's cue, took a seat to one side and opened his notebook expectantly.

"I know Carson was in there," said Mike after a moment's

thought, "and that must have been just after six, because Val Hart was going round collecting tea things." Mike smiled indulgently. "This place is so old-fashioned in some ways – they still actually have a tea-lady with a trolley. Something about traditional values, according to Bernie Rabbetts, but he's been here forever, so I suppose it's a case of what you're used to."

"And did Mr. Rabbetts go into Mr. Winker's office, to your knowledge?"

"Ah, now, I know he went in to see Wally not long after Carson came out, because the door was left open, and I remember they were talking about some new ideas that Bernie was working on. But I don't think Wally was too impressed, from what I could hear."

"And what did you actually hear?"

Mike furrowed his brow in recollection. "Wally said something like 'Not again! How many times do we have to go through this?', and Bernie said he deserved better treatment after so long. I think they both got a bit irate, but I didn't like to eavesdrop too closely, and in any event, I didn't hear any more details because Trixie Marr turned up looking for Candy."

"Was Miss Kane not in her office at that point?"

"No. In fact, she'd just come across to me to ask me if there was anything I needed to send out in the mail, but I'd said no, so when Trixie arrived she asked me if I knew where Candy was, and I told her she'd just gone downstairs with the post."

"Did Miss Marr explain why she wanted to see Miss Kane?"

"Oh, it wasn't Candy she actually wanted," explained Mike. "Trixie said she just wanted to know if Wally was free, and I think she probably put two and two together because we could both hear the sound of voices coming out of Wally's office where the door had been left ajar. So in fact she was just about to leave when the door flew open and Bernie came out looking like thunder, and Wally shouted after him something about there being no room on the Board for failures. At which point I just put my head down and tried to get on with my work, because I didn't want Bernie to know that I'd heard any of it for fear of making him feel embarrassed."

"Did you notice where Mr. Rabbetts went?"

"No, inspector, I didn't. Sorry. I was desperately

43

attempting to concentrate on my own stuff."

"How about Miss Marr? Did she leave as well?"

"No, actually, she didn't. Now if it had been me, I would have thought that the atmosphere was all a bit heated, whatever it was I wanted Wally for, but no, I heard Trixie knock on his door, and he said 'Oh good! Another one! Come in and shut the door', so she did, and I didn't hear anything else. So I went back to what I was doing."

Constable smiled sympathetically. "Well, at least you got the chance to get some work done."

"You think so?" Mike laughed dismissively. "No such luck!"

"Why, did Mr. Winker have any other visitors to his office?"

"But of course. I was starting to think that the whole factory was forming a queue all down the stairs, because a few minutes later, Ivor Sweetman came along and knocked at Wally's door, and as he opened it I heard Wally say 'Wait for me on the factory floor. There's something I want you to explain to me'."

"Presumably," suggested the inspector, "he would have been speaking to Miss Marr."

"I think so," said Mike, "and I suppose Trixie must have gone down Wally's stairs, because she didn't come out past me. Anyway, Ivor was hovering in the doorway, and then Wally said 'Talking about explaining things, Ivor, I want a word with you', and Ivor went in and closed the door behind him. And at that point, I decided I'd had enough. I thought, I'm not going to get any work done in this madhouse, and any thoughts about this test of the security system seemed like complete pie in the sky, and Heidi was nowhere to be seen, so I started to pack up, and I went home."

"So Ivor Sweetman going into Mr. Winker's office was the last person you saw before you left the premises?"

"Yes," confirmed Mike. "Oh, except that I passed Candy coming up the stairs as I was on my way down, but that's all. Then I went home and had what I thought was a well-deserved beer, and that's all I know until I arrived here this morning. And so far today, I've got exactly nowhere."

Constable took the hint. "And I'm guessing that you would rather like to get back to your baby and see if you can

44

persuade it to talk," he smiled. "To which I have no objection, because I'm hoping it will tell us something helpful."

"Have you tried turning it off and turning it back on again?" proposed Copper. "That always works for me." He was rewarded with a withering stare from Mike Rowe.

"I think Mr. Rowe probably knows his own business best," said Constable. "So shall we just leave him to get on with it?"

*

"Seems to me, guv," commented Copper, as he closed the office door behind Mike Rowe, "that this corridor was like Piccadilly Circus last evening." He slumped in the tub chair across the desk from Constable and surveyed his notes. "I've got people going in and out of this office like a fiddler's elbow, but I can't get any sense of a pattern, if there is such a thing. And as for motives for murder, so far they seem to be a bit thin on the ground."

"What I'm beginning to get a sense of," responded Constable, "is the fact that this so-called old-fashioned family business doesn't seem to have been quite the happy family which they portray in their adverts. You've seen that one on TV where the little girl goes into her favourite chocolate shop, and the dear old gentleman dazzles her with his array of luscious goodies. Arguments between the staff, sneaky unofficial liaisons, conversations behind closed doors – this place is looking more like an episode from a Scandinavian thriller. So I have a horrible feeling that we may end up trying to find someone who *doesn't* have a motive for murder. Hmmm." He paused for a moment, musing. "Right!" He clapped his hands together and stood. "Time, I think, to emulate Barry Herman and have a bit of a prowl around. Let's see if we can absorb some atmosphere and pick up any useful snippets. Put that notebook away, see if you can possibly manage to let your mind go blank, and we'll see if anything out there sticks to it."

"Righty-ho, guv." As Copper closed the notebook to replace it in his pocket, his pen slipped from his grasp and, after fruitless attempts to catch it, fell down the side of his chair. "I'll give up on the idea of a career as a juggler, then, shall I, guv?" he remarked facetiously, as he reached down at the side of the cushion to retrieve it. "Well, fiddle-dee-dee!" A broad smile lit up his face. "What is it they say, guv – you can either be clever or lucky? I think I'll settle for being lucky."

"What are you drivelling on about, man?" asked Constable testily.

"Only this, guv." Copper held up a small piece of paper. "This seems to be my day for finding notes. I've got another one." It was another self-adhesive note, this time pink. He passed it over to his superior.

"And another one written in capitals," noted Constable. "It seems to me that, either everybody round here was off school the day they did joined-up writing, or else some person or persons are eager that their hand-writing should not be recognised."

"Why, what does this one say?"

"It's all very mysterious. It's addressed to 'T.M.', and it says '*Funny how secrets have a habit of being found out, unless ...*'."

"Dot, dot, dot? That's all a bit melodramatic, isn't it, guv?"

"As you say. And uncommonly careless of someone with, presumably, secrets they do not wish to be found out, to leave that lying around to be found. Questions would be asked."

"Ah," countered Copper, "but was it dropped, or was it left on the chair to be found and slithered down the side of its own accord? 'Who's been sitting in my chair?' said Daddy Bear."

"Oh, come along, sergeant. Do a little brain-work. It's not the most difficult thing in the world to work out. All we need to know is what this supposed secret is."

"Val Hart was going on about secrets, wasn't she, guv? Maybe she's the one we need to talk to. Do you want me to go and see if I can find her?"

"No," said Constable. "We'll stick to Plan A, and we'll both go. You never know, your talent for finding odd things lying about may come in handy. Just pop your head through there ..." A nod indicated the door through to Candy Kane's office. "... and see if Miss Kane can tell us where the lady may be lurking."

Copper tapped on the door and went in. "She's not here, guv," he called.

"Try Mr. Sweetman's office," suggested Constable drily. "If the two are as inseparable as Barry Herman seems to think ..."

"Speaking of Barry Herman, guv, come and have a glance at this." The inspector joined his colleague in the secretary's office. "As I seem to be in the mood for finding things, what about

46

these?" Copper held up two small white plastic cards, the size of a credit card. They seemed virtually identical – each bore the legend 'Wally Winker's Chocolate Factory' alongside the company's logo, with beneath it in smaller letters in the corner 'Staff Car Park'. At the top was printed a bar-code, with a long series of jumbled letters and numbers underneath. On the reverse was a simple black magnetic strip, with in the corner, in tiny letters, 'MDS' on one card, and 'MD' on the other.

"And the mystery would be …?" asked Constable.

"Well, obviously they're the cards for the barrier mechanism downstairs," said Copper. "I just wondered why she would have two."

"So speculate for me," invited Constable. "Why might she?"

Copper thought for a moment. "It could be," he said slowly, "that she might be trying to disguise her movements. I mean, if there was some sort of tally kept of who uses their card and when, she could use one which would show that she had left the premises when she was in fact still here. Thus giving her the opportunity to carry out some sort of nefarious activity on the premises."

"Such as murdering her boss?"

"It's a possibility, isn't it, guv? Or … I don't know … maybe she was involved in some sort of industrial espionage. In her position, she'd be perfectly placed, wouldn't she? And didn't someone say that there was a lot of spying going on in this business? And that's one of the reasons this new security system's being brought in."

"Excellent thinking, sergeant."

"Thank you, sir." Copper smiled modestly.

"Only one flaw in it," continued the inspector. "According to Barry Herman, the present system doesn't monitor the car park ins and outs. The new one will, but the current one doesn't. So I'm afraid you're one technical revolution short of a theory."

"Rats!"

"Plus, you haven't got a motive. Unless you'd care to magic one of those out of thin air as well."

Copper sighed. "Sorry, guv. Well, it was just a thought."

"Do not be discouraged, sergeant," consoled Constable. "I enjoy your flights of fancy. Sometimes, without them, we would get nowhere. Think of yourself as a human catalyst – you stay the same, while all the reactions occur around you."

"Thank you for that, guv," said Copper, faintly embarrassed. "Anyway, you wanted to get on. If Miss Kane can't tell us where to find Val Hart, shall we go a-hunting?"

"Let's."

As the detectives proceeded along the corridor, they could hear a faint murmur of voices coming from Ivor Sweetman's office.

"You were right, guv," mouthed Copper. "Sounds as if she's in there with him. Want me to pop in and break up the party?"

"No, leave them to their tête-à-tête," said Constable. "Perhaps, if people are having quiet conversations in odd corners, it might mean that someone's getting jumpy. Carry on with Plan A and the great Val hunt."

"Here, look at this, guv." Copper indicated a display case containing various chocolate items, together with a large poster captioned 'Proposed Easter Promotion'. "This must be one of Bernie Rabbetts' projects." The illustration showed the Mad Hatter's Tea Party in full swing, with Alice, the Hatter, and various creatures, including the Dormouse peeping out of the teapot. Chocolate cakes and biscuits provided the fare. And in front of the poster were various of the products which were obviously under consideration – a large rabbit in a collar and tie, a number of Easter chicks in varying shades of yellow, and a chocolate teapot.

"Hmmm. I suppose at a stretch you could get away with casting the Easter Bunny as the March Hare," remarked the inspector. "But I'm not absolutely convinced about the rest of it."

"Onwards and upwards, then?"

"Downwards," corrected Constable, and started down the stairs. The foyer stood deserted, with only the silhouette of the uniformed officer standing guard outside the frosted-glass front doors as the sole sign of human presence. The detectives joined him on the front step.

"Any activity to report, Collins?" asked the inspector.

"No, sir, it's all gone quiet," reported the young P.C. "All the SOCO team have gone now, and there's been nobody out or in. And the barrier man has gone over the road to have a chin-wag with his mate in the other booth, so I thought I'd just take station out here to keep an eye on things."

"Very resourceful," commended Constable. "Keep up the good work. We're off for a walk around the factory – if anything occurs, that's where we'll be."

"Right, sir."

The factory floor stood eerily deserted. In a space which would, Constable assumed, normally be filled with the hum of equipment, the clank of machinery, and the exchange of human voices, nothing was to be heard except a subdued rumble which appeared to be coming from the ventilation system. A pool of congealed chocolate on the floor, marking the position of Wally Winker's body, was the only indication of anything untoward. Suddenly, at the far end of the factory floor, Dave Copper caught a momentary glimpse of a white-clad figure moving behind the machines.

"Hey, you!" he cried, launching himself in the direction of the unknown person as the inspector followed in his wake at a less frenetic pace. "What are you doing here?" He rounded a piece of packaging machinery and came face to face with his quarry.

"What's up, dear?" asked a familiar voice. "Were you looking for me?" The features of Val Hart looked up at him amiably from beneath a white hair-netted hat.

"Er, yes, Mrs. Hart, we were, as it happens," replied Copper in slightly disconcerted tones, as Constable joined the pair, making a strenuous effort to keep a smile off his face at his junior's discomfiture. "I ... I didn't recognise you for a moment."

"Oh, what, you mean all this lot, dear?" Val indicated the white coat and shoe-covers she wore. "No, I'm not surprised. It's all a rigmarole, I know, but rules is rules, and Mr. Winker does insist – did, I should say – that everyone wears them on the factory floor at all times, so we all have to do it. That's why there's these rails all over the place." She pointed to what the detectives had not previously noticed – at each point of entry to the factory floor, by the doors from the foyer, at the foot of the stairs leading up to Wally Winker's office, by a large metal roller shutter which Copper surmised led to a loading bay, and at various other locations, stood a clothes rail bearing a number of white coats and sets of over-trousers, while in bins alongside appeared to be heaps of overshoes, gloves and headwear identical to those which

Val was wearing. "I don't really know why I bothered to put them on now, what with all the to-do this morning, but it's force of habit, isn't it? Anyway, dears, what can I do for you?"

Constable took over. "We wanted to have a chat about things in general, Mrs. Hart. You said you had things to tell us, over and above what you saw when you arrived this morning, and we wondered if this might be a good time."

"No time like the present," agreed Val promptly. "I was on my way to get my cleaning things to see if I could clear up the floor where they'd put poor Mr. Winker after they pulled him out from where I found him, but I dare say that can wait. Tell you what, dears, you come and have a sit down in my little cubbyhole, I'll put the kettle on for a nice cup of tea, and then we'll have our chat." As Copper wondered whether his system was up to coping with what Val evidently believed to be the British policeman's standard capacity for cups of tea, she led the way through a door into a small store-room filled with cleaning equipment, with one end fitted out as a kitchenette with a table and a couple of elderly armchairs. "Sit yourselves down, dears, and I'll sort myself out." Val busied herself removing her protective clothing and preparing the tea things.

"I think I gathered from what you said earlier that you may have some confidential information for us, Mrs. Hart," began Constable. "Do you mind if Sergeant Copper makes some notes? I mean, we wouldn't want to make any mistakes as a result of remembering things incorrectly."

"Oh, you go right ahead, dear," said Val comfortably. She looked Copper up and down. "You seem a nice reliable young man – I'm sure you're not the sort to go repeating things out of turn."

"Oh … er … right. Thank you." Copper seemed unsure how to take the compliment.

"I suppose you'll want my full name for your records, dear, won't you," said Val, plonking three cups of tea on the table and seating herself in an upright chair alongside, as Copper opened his notebook. "My actual first name is Beatrice, so when I was a child the family all called me Beattie. Now that was all very well, but when I married my husband, I changed it."

"You surname, you mean?" queried Copper.

"No, dear, I was talking about my first name. Because of course I was marrying Mr. Hart, and I couldn't go around with a name like Beattie Hart, could I? I mean, people would laugh. So then my husband George, God rest him, suggested that I could use my second name, which is Valentine. I think Valentine Hart has a much nicer sound to it, don't you? But everyone calls me Val anyway."

"And you've been with the company for a considerable time?"

"Oh, forever and a day, dear. I remember the old days, going back to old Mr. Winker – that was Wally's dad. Oh, a right tartar, he was. Wouldn't ever stand any nonsense. Now Wally was a much nicer man, but for all that, he still had a bit of his old dad in him."

"We were talking about the possibility of you having some information for us," prompted Constable in an effort to bring Val back on track. "You said something about secrets."

"I did, dear. And I have. When you've been here as long as I have, there's not much you don't know about people. In fact, I think the only one who knows more about that lot upstairs would be Heidi, but then she would in her job, wouldn't she?"

"Ah." Constable was intrigued. "So Heidi Lockett has a lot of information on people, has she?"

"Well, it stands to reason, doesn't it? I mean, Head of Security and all that, she'd want to know all the ins and outs of people, wouldn't she? And I happen to know for a fact that she keeps files on the staff – I've seen them." Constable's eyebrows went up in enquiry. "Oh, I don't mean I've been snooping in the actual files," explained Val hastily. "I'd never do a thing like that. But, you know, when I'm taking the teas round or collecting cups and so on, sometimes I've seen things lying about on her desk. But I'd never look inside," she concluded virtuously.

"But dossiers do exist," mused Constable, half to himself. "Hmmm."

"In fact, dear," continued Val, "I'd have thought if anyone was going to get bopped on the head, it would be Heidi – it just goes to show, doesn't it? But I can't really think why anyone would want to kill Mr. Winker. Unless they wanted to stop him finding out something, of course. He didn't like people not being honest. He was a bit like his father in that respect."

"How do you mean?"

"Now, here's an example. I was going around collecting

the tea things yesterday teatime, and I was in Candy's office when Carson went in to see Mr. Winker."

"Yes?" said Copper in encouragement.

"Well, it just so happened that Candy's door through into Mr. Winker's office was ajar, so I couldn't help overhearing, could I?"

"And what was it that you couldn't help overhearing?" asked Constable.

Val leaned forward and unconsciously lowered her voice. "Carson said he wanted to make a confession."

"Which was ...?"

"That he'd been done for speeding." Val seemed conscious of a slight anticlimax. "Ah, but you see, it wasn't the first time, and because of that, he'd been up in court for it ..."

"*That* must be what Mr. Winker was reading about in the newspaper," broke in Copper. "I said you should have let me go on reading the court reports, guv."

"Let Mrs. Hart finish, sergeant," said Constable sternly. "This is her evidence, not yours. So, Mrs. Hart, was there more?"

"Yes, dear. Because Carson said, he had so many points now that he was going to lose his licence."

"So the company was about to have a transport manager without a driving licence. I imagine that wouldn't go down too well. How did Mr. Winker react?"

"Actually, Mr. Winker was very nice about it. He said that it would be all right because Carson had owned up, and that they'd get Carson a driver. To be honest, I think Mr. Winker had a bit of a soft spot for Carson – I think he saw a bit of himself when he was young in him, and Carson's done a very good job since he's been here. And Mr. Winker said to him, 'Never keep secrets, and you'll be quite safe here'. And I think Carson was just so grateful – he didn't seem to say much after that, and then he left just afterwards."

"So, in fact, what you might almost call a reverse motive, guv," remarked Copper to Constable. "Job secure, and every motive for keeping Mr. Winker alive."

"As you say, sergeant," agreed the inspector, "but I get the impression that isn't all Mrs. Hart has to tell us. So what other secrets are there?"

Val took a sip of her tea. "Of course, Ivor and Candy have

got their big secret affair, but I have the feeling that Mr. Winker had just found out about that from somewhere."

"I wonder who might have told him, Mrs. Hart?"

"Don't look at me, dear," replied Val, affronted. "You won't find me going around passing on gossip. Anyway, it's not as if they're that clever about things, and I'm sure pretty much everybody knows, although it's funny that it's always the one at the top who's the last to know anything, isn't it. But I don't think it would have taken much doing for Mr. Winker to find out the truth – he wouldn't have needed one of Heidi's monthly meetings for that. But I do know that he's very fond of Ivor's wife – I think he went to their wedding, so he wouldn't have stood for any nonsense from either of them, Ivor or Candy. It's that religious background again, you see – it makes some people very strait-laced."

"I see." Constable considered for a moment, mentally reviewing the list of people. "How about Miss Marr? Anything you can tell us about her?"

Val furrowed her brow. "I don't really know about Trixie. She's one who keeps herself very much to herself. The only thing is, I know she was up for promotion to the Board."

"But I seem to remember her telling us that she isn't actually one of the directors."

"That's the thing, dear - she's not," confirmed Val. "It was talked about – you know how these things get about. At the time, some of her staff were quite excited about it, and someone even put up a banner on one of the machines saying 'Welcome to Marr's Bars', but in the end, it never happened. The word was, Mr. Winker refused for some reason, but I never heard what it was."

"And that, I think – correct me if I'm wrong, sergeant – that just leaves us with Mr. Rabbetts."

"That's right, sir."

"What, old Easter Bernie?" Val chuckled. "That's what they call him on the shop floor, you know. Now, if we're talking about being on the Board, it's not as if that's been a bed of roses for him. Not that he doesn't deserve it – I've seen him work his way up through the firm, and he's not been like some people you hear about, treading all over others to get to the top. No," she said firmly, "Bernie's a very nice man, and I won't hear a word said against him, but for all that, it's no secret – everybody knows Mr.

Winker was always going on at him about something or other, but I think that was just because they'd known each other for so long. A bit like an old married couple, always moaning on about each other, but I reckon he thought the world of him really."

"'*Full of sound and fury, signifying nothing*'?" quoted Constable, to be rewarded by a puzzled stare from Val. "No matter. So, coming on to the events of yesterday, it seems you were here late, like everybody else, which of course gave you the chance to see and hear what was going on."

"Oh, nothing unusual about any of that, dear," said Val. "Just another ordinary day at Winker's."

"But the fact is, Mrs. Hart," pointed out Constable, "is that it wasn't an ordinary day – far from it. Your Managing Director has been killed. So it isn't the ordinary we're concentrating on – what I'm interested in is the out of the ordinary."

"Well ..." Val hesitated a moment in reflection. "The only thing I can think of that was odd about yesterday evening was that I saw somebody go through into the factory with all the white clothes on, some time after seven o'clock."

Constable leaned forward intently. "And where was this, Mrs. Hart?"

"I was out in the foyer, dear, because I was just clearing up to go home. I'd finished through here, and I'd got my coat on and I was on my way out to wait for my bus, and then I got to the doors and it was just starting to drizzle, so I thought, 'I might as well wait here in the warm instead of out there at a draughty bus stop', because it wasn't due for another ten minutes anyway, and then I heard footsteps on the stairs, and somebody came down and went straight through to the factory. Oh, no, wait a minute, I'm lying – it wasn't one person, it was two, about five minutes apart. Funny sort of time to be going into the factory, I thought, what with there not being a night shift on or anything."

"And can you tell us who these people were?"

"Sorry, dear," shrugged Val. "I've got no idea. You see, I only saw them from behind, and in the coat and hat and whatnot, you can't tell one person from another. And let me tell you, it's no joke keeping all those coats and what-have-you clean, you know. There's so many of them. I mean, you've seen all the rails in there ..." She gestured towards the factory. "... plus everyone keeps a coat in their office, so I've got my work cut out doing all that laundry every day. That's why I said to Mr. Winker, it's no use expecting me to cope with an ordinary washing machine. I told him I needed one of those big industrial ones, and give him his due, he got one put in for me."

Constable, in an effort to stop Val straying any further from the point, intervened. "But in essence, Mrs. Hart, you can't help us with the identities of these two people at all?"

"Oh!" A thought struck Val. "I can, dear. I've just remembered. One of them must have been Trixie, because I saw her come out a couple of minutes later, and she came out and realised that she still had all the whites on, so she took them off and just popped them back through on to the rail, and then off she went. And I looked at my watch and thought, goodness, my bus'll be here any second and I don't want to have to wait another twenty minutes for the next one, so then out I went to the bus stop. And that's about it. More tea, dear?"

*

"Are you sure you won't have another cup, dear?"

"No, honestly, thanks, but two's my limit," said Dave Copper hastily, putting his hand across the top of his cup. "Any more and I'll go pop. In fact … is there a loo round here?"

"Just outside the door on the left, dear," said Val, smiling at the speed of the sergeant's exit. "Well," she continued, "I can't hang around here chatting all day – I've got work to do, you know." A polite smile of acknowledgement seemed to Andy Constable to be the only possible response. "I'd better carry on and see if I can get all that chocolate off the floor next door. No, stay where you are dear," she said, as Constable made to get up from his seat. "You finish off your tea." She gathered up a selection of cleaning materials and, with a rattle of mop and bucket, disappeared out into the factory.

When Copper returned a few moments later, he found his superior gazing unfocussed into the middle distance. "Any thoughts, guv?"

"A few," replied the inspector, "but nothing that really amounts to anything. Motives seem a bit thin on the ground. The only person we know who had a stand-up row with Wally Winker was Bernie Rabbetts, but that's just too obvious - according to Val Hart, it doesn't seem to have been anything unusual, so why would he suddenly snap now? Carson Laurie has what you might

55

call an un-motive – he expected to get the chop, and instead was on the receiving end of an act of kindness. No, it seems to me that we have to go looking among these secrets that Val has been talking about – Ivor Sweetman and Candy Kane might have been batting on a stickier wicket than they were aware, and there's something that we don't know about Trixie Marr that could be relevant. And Heidi Lockett is the keeper of the keys on all this information, so to speak – if Val knew that, how many other people did? And how afraid was someone that Winker might be about to use that information against them?"

"So back round to everyone, slam them into a chair with a bright light shining in their eyes, and bark difficult questions at them until someone cracks? Is that the plan, guv?"

Constable smiled indulgently. "We could try that technique, sergeant, but I think it would get us into a spot of trouble with the Police Complaints Commission. On balance, we'd better stick to the rule book and ask nicely. You're the one who reads the detective fiction – hasn't that Belgian detective chap got a saying about catching more flies with sweetness than with vinegar?"

"Enough sweetness round here to catch a whole gang of flies," remarked Copper.

"Then come along, and we shall see if we can add some light to it." Constable rose to his feet and headed back towards the foyer.

At the head of the stairs, he almost collided with Trixie Marr as she emerged from her office.

"Ah, Miss Marr. Just the person we wanted to see. Might we have a word?"

A light of alarm came into Trixie's eyes. "Er ... of course, inspector." She looked around. Nobody was in sight. "Do you want to come in?" She turned and led the way back to her desk, seating herself behind it, indicating chairs for the detectives, and playing unconsciously with a pen lying in front of her. "How can I help you?"

"Miss Marr," began Constable, "we've had a number of conversations with a number of people, and the impression we're getting is that there were several ... shall we say, undercurrents existing in certain people's relationships in this company. Some of these seem to have come to the surface during the meetings which Mr. Winker had with the various members of staff during the crucial period leading up to his death yesterday. But one which hasn't is yours. We know you went to see Mr. Winker. We also know that you were seen on the factory floor during the period in question. So, Miss Marr, I think we would find it helpful to know what you and Mr. Winker were discussing, and how it affected this company."

"It didn't, inspector. You have my word."

Constable smiled faintly. "I think I'm going to need a little more than that, Miss Marr."

Trixie closed her eyes for a moment and sighed deeply, but then seemed to reach a decision. "Very well, inspector. The truth. The reason I wanted to talk to Wally last night was because I'd come to the end of my tether. I knew he thought I hadn't been up to the job lately, but I wanted him to know the real reason."

"Which was ...?" prompted Constable gently.

"I'd had something preying on my mind." A pause. "It was about my daughter."

"So, you have a daughter, Miss Marr." The inspector was careful to keep his tone neutral. "But I still don't see what relevance this has to Mr. Winker. Unless ..."

"No, not what you're thinking, Mr. Constable," said Trixie firmly. "Nothing like that. In fact, nothing to do with Winker's at all. I've always kept my work and my private life well apart. I don't even think anyone here was aware that I have a daughter. The father was someone I used to know – a married man I'd worked with, and we met up again by chance, and ... well, I'm sure I don't need to draw you a picture. But the point was, someone here had found out."

"And this person would be ...?" Constable suspected that he might know the answer.

"I won't tell you who," said Trixie. "I daren't. But the point was, I was afraid for my job, what with Wally and his famous morality, so I'd paid this person to keep quiet. But yesterday, I'd had some problems with production, and suddenly it all got too much for me, so I went to see Wally in order to make a clean breast of the whole thing."

"And how did Mr. Winker react."

Trixie gave a watery smile. "I couldn't believe it. He said he would finish the whole thing."

"What did you take him to mean by that?"

"He didn't have a chance to say. Someone else knocked at his door just then, so he told me to go down his private stairs and wait on the factory floor so that I could tell him about the problems I was having with production. That's why I was down there. But I didn't see him after that. I waited for a while, but he'd obviously been held up or distracted, so in the end I went home. And now I'll never know whether he ..." She tailed off and sighed again. "Well, anyway, that's all I can tell you. And now goodness knows what will happen."

*

Ivor Sweetman raised his head as the two detectives entered his office.

"Yes, inspector? Is there something else I can help you with?" The offer was perfunctory – it was obvious that Ivor was far more intent on dealing with the mound of papers on the desk in front of him. "As you can see, I do have a great deal to do."

"Then we shall try not to take up too much of your time," replied Andy Constable in soothing tones, taking a seat across the desk from Ivor without waiting for an invitation. "But, you see, we are still in something of a quandary as regards identifying who might have a motive for wishing Mr. Winker harm. And I thought perhaps that you, as a very senior member of staff, might be able to shed some light on some of the personalities in the firm, and perhaps their relationships."

"Relationships?" echoed Ivor uneasily. "What do you mean?"

"Oh, merely the day-to-day working relationships between colleagues," said Constable, smiling blandly. "For instance, I take it that you and Mr. Winker were always on the best of terms? No causes of friction at all?" He waited.

Ivor seemed to come to a conclusion. "Very well, inspector. You've obviously heard something, although I can't imagine what. But yes, I am, as you describe it, a very senior member of staff, and Wally knew that if he tried to make trouble for me, he'd have a fight on his hands. I've got friends on the Board, and I've been here long enough to know how to stir it up if I want to. But there would of course be no cause to do so."

"Nice bluff," thought Dave Copper. "Excuse me, inspector," he said aloud, consulting his notebook, "but is Mr.

Sweetman saying that this relationship of his with Miss Candy Kane would not fall into that category?"

"Ah, thank you for the reminder, sergeant," said Constable. "Mr. Sweetman?" He looked expectantly at the man across the desk.

Ivor cleared his throat. He flushed with embarrassment. "Oh. You know about that, do you?"

"Yes, sir," responded Constable gently. "And I think we may not be the only ones. And it's possible that this might have led to a confrontation, is it not?"

"But that wouldn't be any reason to … I mean, there's no cause for …" Ivor floundered for a moment, but then marshalled his thoughts. "It would have not have come to that, inspector," he stated firmly. "This business with Candy is just a bit of fun. It's not serious."

"No, sir?"

"No!" Ivor was emphatic. "Now she might have thought it was – if Wally had found out, she might have lost her job over it, but I can't help that, can I?" He spread his hands in appeal. "I mean, inspector, I'm sure you understand my position. After all, surely we're both men of the world."

Constable gazed at Ivor steadily for a long moment. His face showed nothing. "And Mr. Winker, sir?" he said eventually. "Was he also a man of the world?"

Ivor let a brief flash of dislike pass across his features. "You should know, inspector, that Wally Winker wasn't quite such a nice man as everybody made out."

Constable raised an eyebrow. "Would you care to expand on that, sir?"

"I'll just say this, inspector. Why do you suppose that Wally made Heidi Lockett compile a full dossier on everyone? You may not have known that, but take my word for it, he did. And shall I tell you why? It was so that he would have plenty of excuses to sack anyone if he needed to."

*

"Bit of the cloven hoof showing through there, guv," murmured Dave Copper as the two left Ivor's office and closed the door behind them.

"Never fails," replied Andy Constable in similarly lowered tones. "Keep stirring the ants' nest with a stick, and something

59

always emerges."

"So where are we stirring next, guv?"

Constable smiled. "Oh, I think at this juncture, a little chat with Miss Kane might be productive."

"In the light of what we've just heard?" grinned Copper. "Now that, while we're mixing metaphors, is likely to put the cat among the pigeons, guv."

"Isn't it just?" said Constable, and tapped on the secretary's door.

"Come in." Candy Kane was seated at her desk applying a fresh coat of lip-gloss with the aid of a small hand-held mirror. She had untied her hair so that it now tumbled loose about her shoulders. The effect was striking.

"Please excuse us if we're interrupting something important," said the inspector drily.

"Oh, that's all right," replied Candy. "I haven't started yet. I was just going to begin to get in touch with all the people on Mr. Winker's confidential contacts list to tell them the news, but I thought I'd freshen up a bit first. I suppose we all have to try to carry on as normally as possible, don't we?"

"Life goes on, is that it?" remarked Copper.

Candy dimpled. "Yes, I suppose it does."

"Except, of course, that for Mr. Winker, it doesn't." Constable decided to cut short the niceties. "And my job is to find out why. And I'm starting to discover certain facts which show that there are people who might very well have a reason for fearing Mr. Winker because they believed their position could be under threat."

"I ... I don't know what you mean," said Candy. "I didn't have anything to fear from him."

Constable sighed. "Please don't take us for fools, Miss Kane. We're starting to learn that, in a place like this, few secrets can be kept for long. And one of the secrets which seems to have been more common gossip than anything else is your relationship with Mr. Sweetman. Several people have pointed out that Mr. Winker's well-known views on personal morality might easily have caused you some difficulty in respect of your affair with a married man. Any comments on that?"

Candy tossed her hair. "Oh well, if you know that ..." She shrugged. "I suppose you're right. Of course I was a little bit

60

worried that things might come out, but then, who wouldn't be? After all, Mr. Winker was very strait-laced – in some ways, anyway – and I don't think he'd have liked the idea that I was seeing Ivor. That's why we kept it such a secret."

"You think?" muttered Copper in the background.

"But, Miss Kane," said Constable. "There's a well-known saying about the things you should not do on your own doorstep. Should you not have taken that into account?"

"I know." Candy smiled helplessly. "But Ivor is such a kind man, and so generous too. He works so hard here, and so he likes to enjoy himself when he's away from work. He loves taking me out for meals and buying me presents and so on. His wife doesn't understand him, you know."

"Oh dear," said Constable. He managed to keep a straight face.

"But really," continued Candy, "even if he had found out about Ivor and me, Mr. Winker was such a lovely man, that I'm sure he wouldn't have said or done anything unpleasant."

"That's not necessarily what we've heard from everyone," countered Constable.

"Oh yes," insisted Candy. "Of course, if he'd felt that he had to give me my notice, I would just have appealed to our old friendship."

"Old friendship? I didn't realise you'd worked here for that long a time, Miss Kane."

"Long enough, inspector." Candy's smile expressed a cat-like satisfaction. "Yes, Mr. Winker and I had what you could very well call an old friendship. In fact, a very close old friendship, if you follow me."

"I think I do, Miss Kane."

Candy abandoned all pretence. "After all, when you work that closely with a rich and important man, in the end you're bound to develop a certain ... what's the word?"

"Intimacy?" suggested Copper.

"If you like, sergeant." Candy showed no sign of embarrassment. "In that situation, what can you expect? A girl has to look out for herself. So, in fact, there wasn't anything I wouldn't have done for Wally – if you see what I mean. Nor he for me."

"Even now, Miss Kane?"

Candy shrugged prettily. "Even now."

*

Back outside in the corridor, Dave Copper breathed a sigh of incredulity. "She's a man-eater!" he hissed. "Looks such a nice girl too."

"Don't judge a book by its cover," responded Andy Constable. "And take warning – watch out for nice girls in future."

"You're not kidding, guv!"

"The question is," resumed Constable, "is she a man-killer too? She certainly has a ruthless streak to her."

"Yes, but I can't see her heaving her boss bodily into a vat of chocolate."

"Remember what the doctor said, sergeant – it wouldn't have taken a lot of force to tip him over, so it could equally well have been a man or a woman. Plus, maybe Winker was actually about to chuck her out, no matter what she says, and hell hath no fury, and so on. Hidden reserves of strength? Don't rule her out."

"Fine," said Copper. "So who shan't we rule out next on our list?"

"Here's a thought," said Constable. "We've heard about nice Mr. Winker, and we've heard about nasty Mr. Winker. Let's redress the balance and give Mr. Nice another hearing."

"Not with you, guv."

"Carson Laurie. Another secret revealed, but an unexpectedly happy outcome, according to Val Hart's eavesdroppings. So let's get the man's own version."

Carson Laurie's office was half-way along the corridor, the door standing open. Carson looked up as the two detectives appeared in his doorway. "Come in, gentlemen. I was thinking you'd be around to see me at some time. Take a seat."

"Mr. Laurie," said Constable without preamble, "we've heard that you had a potential problem with Mr. Winker. You'd had something of a run-in with the law, hadn't you?"

"I ... I don't know what you mean."

"Our colleagues in the Traffic section, sir? A slight matter of speeding? We know that you might have felt yourself to be in jeopardy because of it."

"But ..." Carson attempted to interrupt.

"But we also know," the inspector pressed on, "because of a certain conversation which was overheard, that those fears were turning out to be unjustified."

"I know what you're getting at, Mr. Constable," said Carson. "You think that, because I might have been having a little … difficulty with the law, that somehow that would give me a reason to murder my boss. I can see that. Look," he continued, "if you'd come to me yesterday morning and said 'Have you got a motive to kill Wally Winker?', I'd have said 'Sure I have'. Okay, maybe not a very good motive, but when a guy's got worries about losing his job, maybe he doesn't think that straight. But that would have been yesterday, not today. I'd come clean to Wally about this driving thing, and as far as that went, he was fine about it."

"Which I imagine came as something of a relief."

"A great relief, inspector, if you want to know. Look, I'll be straight with you. I burnt my boats when I left Satsuma Motors, for reasons which I won't trouble you with. Culture clash, you might say." Carson's smile held a trace of bitterness. "Some very hard things got said, and it seemed to me that it would be better for me to get as far away from there as soon as I could. In fact, I don't think I've got many friends left on that side of the Atlantic. So when the position here sort of fell into my lap, it seemed like a whole new change for the better. A fresh start. So you can see why I had to protect my job here, and that's why I had that talk with Wally. I admit, I was worried, but it turned out okay."

"You took a gamble," smiled Constable in understanding. "Which paid off."

"Seems so," agreed Carson.

"So the only worry you would appear to have now would be the uncertainty over who will assume the reins at the Winker Chocolate Company."

"I hadn't gotten around to thinking about that yet." Carson frowned.

"Well, when you do, Mr. Laurie, I'd assume that you'll be hoping that the new managing director will adopt the same forgiving approach as Mr. Winker."

"Yeah … right." A light of concern came into Carson's eyes.

"I think that'll do for now, Mr. Laurie," said Constable, abruptly getting to his feet. "I'm sure you must have things to do,

63

so we'll leave you to get on with them." He made his way out of the office, Copper in his wake, leaving Carson sitting at his desk with a speculative look on his face.

*

"All right. I admit it. Wally drove me mad."

The two detectives had gone in search of Bernie Rabbetts and, finding his office empty, had eventually tracked him down in a corner of the factory, leafing through some engineering drawings next to what appeared to be a chocolate moulding machine.

Constable permitted himself a small smile. "I have to tell you, Mr. Rabbetts, that doesn't come as a complete surprise to us. Sergeant, I think perhaps you may have some notes to that effect?" He turned to Dave Copper.

"Yes, sir," replied Copper, swiftly leafing back through his jottings. "Not naming names at this point, but we have heard snippets concerning various, shall we say, heated conversations which Mr. Rabbetts has had with some of his colleagues. Not only Mr. Winker, although of course he is our main concern at the moment."

"Oh, don't pay any attention to me and my rantings," said Bernie. "It's true, I do get hot under the collar sometimes, but it never lasts. Just ask anyone. Although," he smiled ruefully, "I expect you probably have already. The thing is," he went on, "I know this business inside and out – I should do, I've been in it long enough – and I've done very well for myself. You see this machine here?" He gestured to the equipment looming above him. "When I started here, they apprenticed me to the tool-setter who used to jig this sort of thing up. That's where I learnt the trade. And I could still do it if I had to. That's what gets you respect on the factory floor, you see – still being able to tell these young kids how to do their jobs, because they know you can do it better. Not many people start at the bottom and end up on the Board."

"Evidently Mr. Winker appreciated your abilities, sir," said Constable.

"Perhaps, inspector." Bernie did not sound wholly convinced. "The thing about Wally was," he explained, "he was always trying to get you to prove yourself."

"In what way?"

64

"I've lost count of the number of ideas that I've come up with that he didn't like, or wouldn't authorise the finance for if there was some consumer research needed, and in the end, it gets to you. Tips you over the edge."

"As in the case of Mr. Winker, sir?" suggested Copper.

"Oh lord, no." Bernie's hand went to his mouth as he realised the import of his words. "No, I assure you, inspector, nothing could have been further from my mind. I mean ... it ... it was just an expression. Please, don't get the idea that I ..."

"I quite understand, Mr. Rabbetts." Constable stemmed Bernie's anguished stammerings with some difficulty. "An unfortunate choice of words. And if I were to tell you the number of times Sergeant Copper here has fallen into that particular trap ... So please don't worry that we're taking that as an inadvertent confession."

"Thank you, inspector." Bernie pulled himself together.

"But it does still leave us with an impression of conflict between yourself and Mr. Winker, which we have to take into account. For all your knowledge and experience, it seems that he didn't give you the easiest of rides."

"That's true, inspector. But I don't think I was alone in that. I'm sure everyone was on the receiving end of Wally's disapproval at some time or another. In fact, I remember joking to Heidi Lockett once that I wouldn't mind seeing her file on Wally for a moment, just so's I'd have something over him for a change."

"What file would this be, sir?" enquired Constable innocently.

"Oh." Bernie seemed surprised. "I thought you'd know. Apparently there is in existence a file on every senior member of staff, with goodness knows what information in it. Rumours circulate, you know. Of course, if it ever comes up in conversation, everybody treats it as a joke and professes that they're purer than the driven snow, but I expect everyone's got something they'd rather not have known, haven't they? You'd know that better than me, inspector, wouldn't you?"

Constable declined to be drawn. "And Miss Lockett's reaction to this jocular request of yours was ...?"

"Oh, she just laughed."

"But she didn't deny that such a file existed?"

Bernie stopped short and thought for a moment. "No,

inspector. Actually, she didn't."

*

Heidi Lockett's office was a paragon of neatness. Shelves held precisely arrayed box files, each neatly labelled with an anonymous alpha-numeric code. A filing cabinet, drawers secured by a fearsome-looking locking apparatus, stood behind the desk. On the desk itself, alongside the expected computer screen and keyboard, telephone and firmly-closed diary, not a scrap of paper was to be seen. On a worktop in a corner, the red stand-by light of a printer winked lazily.

"Inspector. I knew you'd be coming to see me eventually." Heidi smiled confidently as the detectives entered her office, and waved them to a sofa standing against one wall. She swung her chair round to face them. "So how are the enquiries proceeding? Or, since I'm doubtless one of your suspects, or at least persons of interest, shouldn't I ask?"

Constable smiled in return. "Oh Miss Lockett, how pleasant life would be if we could all pool our information at times like this. But you know as well as I do that sometimes we have to play our cards close to our chests. I'm afraid I'm not in a position to share with you any of the interesting facts which have come our way. But I'm hoping that won't prevent you from giving us some useful help."

"Of course I will if I can, inspector. Ask me anything. What would you like to know?"

Constable chuckled softly. "Doesn't this rather conflict with the image of a Head of Security who jealously guards the valuable information in her possession?"

"I can't imagine how you would have got that impression, inspector."

"Right, Miss Lockett." Constable's voice became steelier. "Enough verbal fencing. We can drop the pretence now. The simple fact is, you were the eyes and ears of Mr. Winker, weren't you? His pet rottweiler. He put you in a position of considerable power. We've been told from several sources that you have confidential files, gathered on Mr. Winker's behalf, on your colleagues, and goodness knows what else besides. And that information, should it come into Mr. Winker's possession, could have proved very uncomfortable for various people. That could very well provide a motive for murder. In fact someone

66

commented, not altogether seriously, that they were surprised that, as the compiler of these dossiers, you weren't the one who was killed. In the old gangster movie cliché, 'you know too much'. Any thoughts on that?"

Heidi leaned back in her chair. She pondered for a moment. "I won't make a secret of it, inspector – knowledge is power. Oh, I'm not just talking about me. It may sound absurd to say it, but the world of confectionery is an extremely cut-throat business. The amount of money that the punters spend on sweets and chocolates is unbelievable, and although in the great scheme of things the Winker Chocolate Company is quite a small fish, there are plenty of sharks out there who would be more than happy to know what we're doing and what we're thinking."

"In what way?"

"Oh, new products, new ideas in marketing," explained Heidi airily. "It's like spoiler headlines in newspapers – if you can get there first, you can cut the ground from under your competitors. If you've got information about the competition, or anything else, you stay on top."

"And Mr Winker was determined to stay on top?"

Heidi laughed quietly. "Oh yes, inspector, you can be sure of that."

"Both externally and internally." Constable's words were a statement rather than a question.

"Of course. Wally was very much in charge. There might be a board of directors nominally running the company, but Wally ruled the roost and no mistake. He was the sole share-holder, so whatever he wanted, he got. That's one of the reasons he kept me around – I could get him the stuff he needed to know."

"Helpful background, Miss Lockett, but I'm not sure how far it advances us with regard to the sequence of events yesterday. Now although you weren't in the factory during most of yesterday, you were present during the crucial period of the early evening. We've spoken to, I think, all of your colleagues, and we're building a picture of who was where and when."

"What about the CCTV system?" interrupted Heidi.

"Unfortunately, Mr. Rowe tells us that the CCTV system has frozen, and he hasn't been able to produce any results for us."

"Typical!" snorted Heidi. She got to her feet abruptly. "I can't remember how much we've been paying him, but it's obviously too much. Let me go and rattle his cage. I shan't be a moment." She paused at the door. "I'll say one thing – if you think this lot have told you everything, you're very much mistaken. If I were you, I'd check very carefully who was on the factory floor last night. I know I was, and I know Wally was, but we weren't the only ones." She left the office without another word, leaving two slightly bemused detectives behind her.

"Now there's an extremely Delphic utterance," remarked Constable. "What do you make of that?"

"Could be any number of things, guv," replied Copper. "Could be the old guilty party's trick of chucking accusations around in the direction of other people in the hope of throwing us off the scent."

"Or ...?"

"It's the 'or' that I'm still scratching my head over," admitted Copper. "I've got all this stuff I've been writing down ..." He raised his pad. "... but I'm still struggling to put my finger on one fact which looks like a specific motive for one of these people to murder their boss. It's all too nebulous."

"Because ...? Come on, sergeant – take your fine detective's brain for a bit of a walk."

Copper marshalled his thoughts. "Well, guv, technically, any one of them could have done it, because everyone had an opportunity and nobody's properly alibied. Motive-wise, there are people like Bernie having rows with Winker, people like Trixie and Carson who had secrets, but these turned out not to be as damaging as they feared, and people like Ivor and Candy who were still keen to keep their alleged secret under wraps, although we know they were on a hiding to nothing. And as for Heidi, although she's told us next to nothing about herself, maybe the fact that this new security system is not what it's cracked up to be is something that, as she saw it, put her at risk."

"Excellent assessment," said Constable. He smiled. "And you're right, it gets us precisely nowhere. Come on." He stood. "Rather than sitting here waiting like spare parts, let's go and see if she's had any luck with Mike Rowe and his box of tricks."

Entering Mike Rowe's section, the inspector was surprised to find the computer expert alone. "Oh. Sorry to bother you, Mr. Rowe. I expected to find Miss Lockett here."

"Heidi? Oh, she came and went," was the vague reply.

"Went where?"

Mike wrenched his attention from the screen in front of him. "Sorry, inspector, I can't tell you. She was asking something about the CCTV, but I didn't really pay attention to her. It's not up yet, if that's what you wanted to know, but I'd got side-tracked by this rather curious little problem...It's very odd."

"And what might that be?" Constable was intrigued.

"I'd just finished my scan, inspector," said Mike, "and there didn't seem to be anything unexpected in the system, but then I noticed that there was one strange little item which had turned up in the spam box. It's an encrypted email which had come in, addressed to the inbox of the General Accounts department – that's ga@winkerchoc.com, you see. All the departmental mail addresses go by initials here, you see, like everything else, so you have md@winkerchoc for Wally as Managing Director, and so on. And I thought, who on earth is sending encrypted emails to the accounts people? So I was curious to find out what it was all about."

"Any luck, sir?" enquired Copper.

"Well, I must admit, I quite enjoy this kind of thing, although I'm no Bletchley Park," confessed Mike. "But I've got a couple of programs I've tried, and I've made a bit of headway with the start of it. Still can't untangle the identity of the sender, but the main text looks as if it could well be something financial, which I suppose is why it was for Accounts. I'll keep on at it."

"What do you have so far?" asked Constable.

"This." Mike handed over a piece of paper. It read 'Farther to D.C.D.A. report on fraud charges ...'.

"Not more initials!" groaned Dave Copper in the background.

"And that's it?"

"I was still working on it, inspector, but I can stop if there's something else you need."

"No, Mr. Rowe – you carry on." A quiet smile appeared on the inspector's features. "You never know, something out of the ordinary like this may be just what we need. Do you suppose it will take long?"

"Just a few minutes, I hope."

"Good." Constable nodded. He suddenly became brisk and business-like. "Right, sergeant, here's what's going to happen.

You see if you can track down Miss Lockett – find out where she's disappeared to. Assuming she hasn't demonstrated her guilt by doing a runner, she'll be around somewhere. Then tell her and the rest of the management that I'd like a word with them all in the boardroom in ..." He consulted his watch. "... fifteen minutes. I shall retire to Mr. Winker's office for a little quiet contemplation. And please, Mr. Rowe, if you can bring the full text of that email through to me when you have it, I'd be grateful."

"Do you reckon you've got it, guv?" asked Copper.

"Maybe, just maybe. If I'm right. We shall see. Go on, off you go. I have thinking to do."

*

It was almost a quarter of an hour later that Andy Constable was jolted to full awareness by the tap at the door. From his reclining position in Wally Winker's black leather desk chair, eyes unfocussed as he allowed the thoughts in his mind to circulate, form, and re-form into patterns, he swung upright and resumed his normal brisk manner.

"Come in."

"Inspector Constable – I thought you'd want this as soon as possible." Mike Rowe stood in the doorway. "It's that email."

"And you've managed to decode the whole thing?"

"Not absolutely all of it." Mike sounded apologetic. "And the sender's address is still disguised, but at least I've got the geographical location – it's somewhere in America. And the main burden of what it's about. I'm afraid it's a bit untidy, but I hope it's what you want." He handed over a sheet of paper bearing a few lines, intermingled with crossings-out and corrections in his somewhat scrawly handwriting.

Constable surveyed the paper. "Yes!" he murmured almost inaudibly. His expression did not alter at all as he folded it and tucked it away in an inside pocket. "Thank you, Mr. Rowe. That's precisely what I need."

As if on cue, Dave Copper appeared at Mike's shoulder. "Found Miss Lockett, sir – she was out at the gatehouse with Barry Herman. But I've got everyone in the boardroom now, guv, if you're ready for them."

"Oh yes, sergeant," responded Constable, beginning to smile with quiet satisfaction. "Ready is exactly what I am."

Copper knew that look. "I take it, sir, that we may be

leaving before too long? And perhaps not alone?"

"You take it correctly."

"Time to point the chocolate finger, eh?" grinned Copper in anticipation but then, in response to his superior's glare, cleared his throat and assumed an almost convincing straight face. "Sorry, sir. And maybe I should ask our uniformed colleague downstairs if he would like to come and join the proceedings up here, guv? Just in case someone wants to break up the party early?"

"A very wise precaution, sergeant. And you might like to put a call in to the station and warn them to prepare the guest accommodation. Oh, and rustle up another car with a couple of chaps to come here and take over."

"Sir." Copper turned and vanished immediately.

"Er … do you want me in the boardroom too, inspector?" asked Mike hesitantly.

"I don't think that'll be necessary, Mr. Rowe," said Constable. "We'll need to take a statement from you later, but I think that will keep. So please feel free to go back to work debugging whatever you have that's bugged, and I will get on with what I have to do." He made his way along the corridor and into the boardroom, just as Dave Copper arrived at the head of the stairs, the young P.C. in his wake.

"Collins, just the man," Constable greeted him. "Come in here, close the door behind you, and just stand there, would you? I might want you later."

"Watch, listen and learn," muttered Copper into the younger man's ear. "Not many people get to see the master at work. Sorry, sir," he said aloud, in response to Constable's quizzically-raised eyebrow. "Just confirming your instructions." He took a seat in an upright chair alongside the door as Collins, with just a hint of self-consciousness, took his stance in front of it.

Constable turned to face the assembled company in the room. "Often the character of a victim provides the key to their murder," he said without preamble. Six faces regarded at him with varying degrees of apprehension, startled by the suddenness of his remark. "So what sort of man was Wally Winker? Each of you has given us some kind of insight into that. We've been told he was a strict moralist. We've heard that he was loyal to old friends. But against that, we also know that he had dossiers on his employees in order to have a hold over them." Several among those gathered around the table exchanged looks of uncertain surprise. Others studiously avoided anyone's gaze by concentrating fixedly on the table-top in front of them. "But set against that, it seems that he was also capable of surprising acts of personal kindness. Miss Trixie Marr has given us one illustration of that ..."

Puzzled looks were directed towards Trixie, who flushed and looked down at the hands twisting in her lap. "Inspector ..." she began.

"...but I do not intend to break any confidences by going into any detail," continued Constable smoothly. "Suffice to say that she was not the only person who would fall into that category. And here I think we come to the essence of the matter. Secrets. And one question is, was Mr. Winker himself harbouring a secret? A very personal one, considerably at odds with his much-trumpeted morality. I think we can probably deduce that he was, if the extremely unsubtle hints given to us by Miss Candy Kane regarding her relationship with her boss are anything to go by."

"Candy? What's he trying to say?" Ivor Sweetman turned to challenge the young woman seated next to him. Understanding began to dawn. "Does he mean that you ... you and Wally ...?"

"Please don't make a scene, Ivor," murmured Candy. "It's not going to help."

"I think perhaps you may be better advised to postpone that conversation until a more convenient time," Constable forestalled the increasingly red-faced Ivor. "There are rather more important questions to be answered here and now. And one of those is the matter of who would have had the opportunity to commit the murder of Wally Winker.

"Nobody can fully account for their movements during the period of the murder. The last we know of Mr. Winker was that he was in his office and intending to descend to the factory floor. Now we know that each of you had the opportunity to visit the factory floor during the period in question. Trixie Marr was ordered to meet him down there by Mr. Winker himself, and we have confirmation that she was there because she was seen to leave by Val Hart. But Mrs. Hart, as she was so helpfully waiting in the foyer for her bus to arrive, also saw two people go *into* the factory from the foyer, having come down the main staircase. Neither of those was Trixie, because we know she came down the rear stairs direct from Mr. Winker's office. Barry Herman, the security guard, heard Heidi Lockett arrange to see Carson Laurie downstairs – we can only presume she meant on the factory floor. Might that have been so as to be away from the offices, where conversations could be so easily overheard? It seems logical. Ivor Sweetman and Candy Kane were also together for some of the time – in fact, someone remarked to us that it was rarer for them to be apart than together." Constable allowed himself a small dry smile. "I'm not intending to speculate how much further that situation is likely to obtain. But is it feasible that they might have acted together for goodness knows what reason – jealousy? revenge? thwarted ambition? Surely all rather too 'Othello' for this situation – after which they fled the scene of the crime together? And if we're in the realms of melodrama, we know that Bernie Rabbetts had a blazing row with Wally Winker, after which Bernie disappeared. And who knew the factory better than him?"

"Now look here, inspector," interrupted Bernie, "it's all very well chucking accusations around, but you seem to forget that some of us have lost a friend here."

"I don't forget that for one moment, Mr. Rabbetts," rejoined Constable, "but it's worth remembering that sometimes an apparent friendship can conceal a deep hostility and hatred. Call 'Othello' to mind once again, just as an illustration. Not that I'm suggesting anything so convoluted here.

"So having looked at the question of opportunity and failed to come to any conclusion, we have to consider the matter of motive. What reason could any of you have for murdering Wally Winker? Again, there appear to be simple and obvious reasons, but they tend to shrivel up as soon as we shine a bright light on them. Let me take you one by one. Trixie Marr? Admittedly, her personal problems had affected her work, and not through any fault of her own, but as she has pointed out to me, Mr. Winker's reaction to her revelations had meant that her job was safe, and her persecutor looked set for retribution."

"Persecutor?" asked Carson Laurie. "Trixie, what's that all about?"

"Interesting that you should ask that, Mr. Laurie,"

73

continued Constable, "because you were in a similar situation to Miss Marr's, in that you also felt that your job might be jeopardised by what you had done."

"Okay, okay," said Carson. "Let's have it all out, if it's got to be that way. Everybody, you might as well know, if you haven't caught up with the papers already, that I'm getting a driving ban. One speeding ticket too many, and now I'm the guy with the criminal record. So you can't blame me for worrying that Wally was going to kick me out. After all, who's gonna resist a good laugh at the expense of a Transport Manager with no driving licence?"

"And the simple answer to that," replied Constable, "was that Mr. Winker was the one man who could resist that temptation. Again we have one of those unexpected acts of kindness. We know that Mr. Winker had set your fears at rest over your job, and that he intended to arrange a chauffeur for you during your driving ban. He must have held you in very high regard, Mr. Laurie – I believe he even gave you some friendly advice regarding your future with the company.

"Let's move on to Mr. Sweetman and Miss Kane, since I bracketed them together a few moments ago. Ivor Sweetman? Well, he told us himself that he has friends on the board – if ever he feels his position as senior director, perhaps even heir apparent to the company, to be at risk, he can muster enough support to cause sufficient trouble to safeguard his position, without going to the unpleasant lengths of murder. And Candy Kane had only to let slip a few details of her relationship with Wally Winker in the right quarters for his reputation as a pillar of the community to be in tatters. Hardly worth even risking breaking a nail for, I should have thought.

"So let's come back to Bernie Rabbetts – the man who had the most obvious, and the most public, conflicts with Wally Winker. This was nothing new – it had been going on for years. It seems that probably everyone had overheard rows between the two at some time or another – it was Val Hart who told us about the stormy relationship between them, but she believed there was no harm in it, and in a place like this, I'll take the tea lady's evidence every time. She always knows what's going on. So the last person we have to consider would be Heidi Lockett, who seems alone in having nothing to fear from Mr. Winker. In fact, the opposite – her knowledge of everybody else's weaknesses appears to make her invulnerable. Or at least, it did, until yesterday. Because perhaps she had misused that knowledge. Did she decide to take advantage of it to earn a little extra income? And did Miss Marr's revelations to Mr. Winker spoil her fun and put her in danger?"

Ivor Sweetman had been shifting restlessly in his seat for some time. "Mr. Constable," he said, "this lecture of yours is all very fascinating, but are we actually getting anywhere? You've called us all here, and so far all you've told us is that anybody could have been on the factory floor when Wally died, and that any one of us might have had some sort of reason to kill him, or not, as the case may be. And I have to say that some of your reasoning is highly debatable. Not only that," he blustered on, "but I for one take a dim view of you repeating unsubstantiated gossip about people's personal lives which has no bearing on the matter at all. Aren't you supposed to be looking for some sort of evidence?"

"I'm very grateful to you, Mr. Sweetman," returned Constable calmly, "because you've put your finger on the very point I was intending to raise next. Evidence is the key. And not necessarily the sort of concrete evidence you probably mean – the overlooked fingerprint, the tell-tale lipstick on the wine glass, the suspicious blonde hair on the jacket. We tend to leave those to the realms of detective fiction. In the real word, evidence is very often what people tell us, even though you may dismiss it as 'unsubstantiated gossip'. And here, I believe that it is the evidence we heard from Val Hart which is crucial, and I don't believe she was even aware of it herself. She saw the truth when she said that she was surprised that it wasn't Heidi Lockett who was murdered."

"Me?" Heidi was startled. "But why would she say that?"

"Bear with me, Miss Lockett," said Constable. "All will become clear. Because what if Mrs. Hart was right? What if we'd been looking at the case upside-down? What if Wally Winker wasn't the intended victim?"   Murmurs of puzzlement arose around the table. "And what if the murderer's target was in fact Heidi, because of what she knew about someone – knowledge that made it too dangerous to let her live? Do we come back to those famous investigations of hers? I think we do. Now, we know that, as far as Mr. Winker was concerned, Trixie Marr had nothing left to conceal. Ivor Sweetman and Candy Kane were the subject of gossip all round the factory, and they have both shared with me their thoughts regarding the strengths of their own individual positions, so what real danger were they in? And Bernie Rabbetts' habit of coming up with ideas which were, let's face it, not one hundred percent thought through, was well-known too – indeed, his bumbling approach was viewed with some affection - so how could he hope to conceal that? But what about Carson Laurie?"

Carson's head shot up. "Inspector, surely we've covered all this already. I'd told Wally all about this court case business – you know that. And now I've told everybody here as well, so it's not as if I've been trying to keep secrets. So why would I have anything against Heidi?"

"As to that, Mr. Laurie," continued Constable, "we know that you and Miss Lockett were not exactly friendly. The words you were heard to exchange at the door to Mr. Winker's office tell us that. And we also know that you were to meet on the factory floor in the aftermath of this little confrontation. And now I'm going to move into the realms of speculation, but please, feel free to correct me if you think I've got anything wrong. What if the two of you did in fact meet on the factory floor, both dressed in the white overalls, hat and all the other all-concealing paraphernalia which made it difficult to distinguish one person from another? And what if Miss Lockett revealed that she had further information regarding your past – information which would destroy you, and which could lead to ruin, prison, and expulsion from the country?"

Carson Laurie gazed at him mutely.

Heidi Lockett spoke up. "But inspector, I didn't have any such thing. I never got a reply to the ..." She tailed off.

"To the email you sent out seeking additional incriminating information, do you mean, Miss Lockett? Information which you could have held over a second victim, and perhaps increased your own income from personal extortion? Is that what you mean?"

Heidi's eyes were wide with apprehension. "No ... I mean I ..." She stumbled to a halt.

"No, Miss Lockett, you never got that reply," said Constable. "And the reason is, I have it here." He held up Mike

Rowe's sheet of paper. "And it's all down to the simplest of reasons – human error. Because the email was sent to you, but it never arrived. The person who sent it intended to address it to you as the Head of Security at Winker's – hs@winkerchoc.com – but they mis-keyed. They typed in one character to the left, so in fact it went into the General Accounts files - **ga**@winkerchoc - which led to Mr. Rowe's accidental discovery of it while he was checking through his systems. Such a trivial error, but without it, no doubt that email would have disappeared into your files, and we should have been none the wiser. Not that you needed it to issue your threats to Mr. Laurie, but it would have been useful confirmation of the facts which he probably already knew. Shall I read it to you?" Silence answered him. "I'll take that as a yes. '*Farther to earlier D.C.D.A report on fraud charges, confirm Carson Laurie being sought regarding embezzlement of research funds at Satsuma Motors. International warrant to be issued. Thanks for tip-off.*'

"So let me continue my speculation. Somehow Heidi Lockett had come across a hint of this in her constant searches for information on her colleagues. And although she didn't have this absolute confirmation, she had enough to confront Carson Laurie with what she knew and demand substantial hush-money. He made some sort of excuse to leave, promising to return shortly, and in fact did so – but in the meantime Trixie Marr, and then Wally Winker, had come down the back stairs to the factory floor. Heidi had to make herself scarce. Trixie and Wally had their conversation, and then Trixie left – Val saw her go. Carson returned, saw Wally leaning over the chocolate vat, mistook him for Heidi because of the all-concealing clothing and, on the spur of the moment, and with only self-preservation on his mind, came up behind the unsuspecting man, grabbed him, and killed him by dunking him in his own product."

"You were ready to kill me?" Heidi was aghast. She jumped to her feet. "Then I hope you get what you deserve, you murdering b..."

"Don't think I was the only one!" snarled Carson over the top of her. "I reckon if I had, it would only have been doing everyone else a favour. I'd have gotten a round of applause!"

"That will do!" Constable's voice over-topped the rising volume and halted the two in their tracks. "Carson Laurie, I am arresting you on a charge of the murder of Mr. Walter Winker. Sergeant Copper, would you please take Mr. Laurie in and have him formally charged. Leave me the car keys – I'll follow on. I still have one or two things to deal with here. Collins will drive you."

Carson gave a gentle smile as he calmly held out his hands for Copper to apply handcuffs. "Money. That's all it was. But it sure makes you do dumb things. It even makes you kill the guy who turns out to be your best friend in an ugly world." He raised his head and looked at the people assembled around the boardroom table. "And for what it's worth, I am truly sorry that it all went so wrong." He turned and followed Copper from the room.

"Miss Lockett." Constable addressed the rather shaken-looking Heidi. "I think you had better come with me. We need to have a conversation about some of your activities which are not completely connected with your security duties for Winker's. There is a very unsavoury odour of blackmail in the air. And in the light of what we know, I shall be applying for a search warrant covering the material in your office and the data on your computer. You seem to have had one lucky escape so far, but I don't believe that you should rely on your luck continuing to hold." He surveyed the rest of the company. "Ladies and gentlemen, I think this has been a very instructive instance of the dangers of concealment. Without wishing to sound too sententious, learn the lesson. Let some of the secrets out. As St. John said, the truth will set you free. You'll probably sleep better. Miss Lockett, shall we go?" He took Heidi by the elbow and led her towards the door.

*

"So come on, guv – cards on the table. How did you figure it out?" Dave Copper sat at his desk, his notebook open in front of him. "I've been ploughing through all my notes, and I can't see what it was that made you put your finger on it. I mean, I know about the email, which pretty much gave it away, but you were on the track before that, weren't you?"

"That was certainly one of the things that set me thinking. Right at the start of it, the use of the word 'farther'. We don't usually say that – in the U.K. we normally say 'further'. So that drew my eye to the American connection. But there were various indications, sergeant. I'd have hoped you might pick at

78

least some of them up."

"Well, there were a few things that caught my eye, sir. I've highlighted a couple of them."

"Such as?"

"For a start, I couldn't figure out why Candy Kane had two identical pass cards for the car park barrier on her desk."

"Then you should have looked at them a little more closely. They weren't identical at all. One had 'MD' on it – the other 'MDS'. Obviously, as Mr. Winker's secretary, she looked after his card, the one with 'MD' on it, whereas her own, the one with 'MDS', was completely surplus to requirements, since she always got a lift with Ivor Sweetman. Like so much else, the initials are crucial."

"'Managing Director's Secretary' – got it!" Copper leafed through his notes. "Like that memo – everything was addressed to people by their job title rather than their name, so you had DSP for Bernie Rabbetts and HS for Heidi Lockett, and so on. By the way, what's happening to her?"

"At the moment," replied Constable, "the lady is cooling her heels downstairs doing a little thinking. 'Helping with our enquiries' is the way we're putting it. I've left her to consider whether it might be to her advantage to tell us everything we need to know, rather than having to crowbar it all out of her computer files. Let's carry on with this, for the moment. Where were we?"

"The memo, guv."

"Which of course told us two things. Firstly there was the obvious conclusion we could draw from the contents, which was that when they were on the factory floor, everyone was dressed the same, giving the possibility of mistaken identity. You proved that yourself when you went haring off after dear old Val Hart under the impression that she was some sort of sinister intruder."

"Well, anyone can make a mistake," said Copper, but then, anxious to redeem himself, went on, "but I've just realised the other thing the memo told us with the initials business. It was about that unsigned note which was addressed to 'TM'. It wasn't to Trixie Marr at all, which is what I thought it was, first off – it was to Carson Laurie as Transport Manager."

"Exactly. Like the other note you picked up inadvertently."

"The one that said something about colour. I thought it must be something about those yellow Easter chicks that Bernie had been going on about."

"And it might have been," replied Constable, "except for one thing. 'Color' was spelt the American way, without the 'u'. It was probably something to do with the project to turn all the company vehicles into various manifestations of chocolate, but it was another straw in the wind which drew my eye towards Carson Laurie. Like that newspaper on Wally Winker's desk. It was a reminder that Winker kept a close eye on wrong-doers within the company, and in the end, their sins would probably find them out."

"So Bernie and his yellow chicks were never in the frame?"

Constable chuckled. "Oh, they were in the frame, all right. The display frame that we saw in the corridor with the proposed Easter products – don't you remember? Dear old Bernie Rabbetts – I could get quite fond of him, with his Mad Hatter and his March Hare, and his equally hare-brained ideas for yellow chicks. But how could you take seriously as our murderer the man who invented the chocolate teapot!"

*   *   *

THE DEAD OF WINTER

"Lord Ellpuss."

"Who?" enquired Detective Sergeant Dave Copper.

"Lord Ellpuss." Andy Constable replaced the telephone on his desk as he repeated the answer to his junior colleague's question. "Found dead in suspicious circumstances, which is why our services are required. Get your coat – it's bloody freezing out there."

"That'll teach me to come in on a Saturday instead of staying nice and snug in bed."

"That reminds me," said Constable casually, "how is that lovely girl you were foolish enough to introduce to the chaps in the pub the other week? She seemed very smitten with you."

"Charlene? Alas, guv, smitten no longer, I'm afraid. Probably something to do with me being called away in the middle of what was supposed to be a romantic dinner at home for that all-nighter surveillance job in the drugs case. Came home to find a rather short note and a very congealed Chicken Kiev. Anyway, enough about me," said Copper, anxious to change the subject, as the two detectives made their way towards the police station car park. "Who is this Lord Ellpuss anyway? I've never heard of him."

"I'm not entirely surprised, sergeant," replied Constable. "He's one of those alarmingly powerful men who prefer to pull the strings of everyone around them while keeping their own light hidden firmly under a bushel. He's chairman of MegaMedia Worldwide."

"Still doesn't help, sir."

"Television, publishing, all that sort of thing. In this country, they own the 'Splash' group of newspapers."

"Oh, right." Copper caught on. "Not that I read the 'Splash', of course," he continued. "Some of the neanderthals used to leave the odd copy lying around in the locker room at the station until the W.P.C.'s took exception to the fact that they always seemed to have fallen open at the Page 5 picture of 'gorgeous pouting Chenisse, 17', so that put a stop to that. I do buy the 'Sunday Splash' sometimes, but only for the ..."

"Football coverage," chimed in Constable with a smile. "Yes, where have I heard that before?"

"Plus they do a very good magazine of the week's television programmes," added Copper defensively. "If I ever get a chance to watch them," he muttered under his breath.

"But why would you bother with all that fictional detective rubbish on TV when we have the pleasure of dealing with the much more fascinating real thing?" teased Constable. "It's far more enjoyable," he said, as he boosted the power of the car's heater and switched on the windscreen wipers to clear the sporadic flurries of snowflakes.

"So what's this all about, guv? And where are we going anyway?"

"Over to Camford. It seems His Lordship has been found dead in the quadrangle at one of the colleges."

"What's he doing there?" wondered Copper. "You'd think he'd have been a bit old to be a student?"

"Apparently he was the Master or Chancellor or some such thing. We shall no doubt find out in due course."

The University of Camford was one of the three oldest educational establishments in Britain. Founded in medieval times by breakaway students from one of its rivals, it had grown over the centuries to become an architectural as well as an academic gem, and was worthily nicknamed 'the City of Aspiring Dreams'. The streets of the town, some the narrowest of twisting alleys, some broadening out into stately squares, were lined with college buildings from all periods ranging from the Gothic to the Regency, the vast majority in the local red sandstone, while on the outskirts, more modern cathedrals of glass and steel had arisen to house the upstart disciplines of science and technology.

The group of emergency service vehicles, blue lights flashing, parked in the street outside a monumental Tudor building left no doubt as to the detectives' destination. The gatehouse of Ewell Hall, with its bands of contrasting stone and brickwork, adorned with terracotta roundels of Roman emperors and a huge coloured coat of arms, was one of the most photographed buildings in the town, and appeared on many guidebook covers. The college itself had been founded in the 1500s by one of Henry VIII's ministers who had worked his way up from the reputed back streets of Bermondsey to the dizzy heights of the nobility, only to lose his head as the result of a spectacular misjudgement regarding one of the king's many

82

marriages. Sadly, the founder's estates had gone to the king, leaving very little in the way of an endowment, and the college had struggled along through the centuries, relying on its reputation for excellence in the study of theology and classical Greek literature, until modern times, when a spectacular offer of monetary support had been seized with both hands by the outgoing authorities. In deference to the benefactors, an American pharmaceuticals conglomerate whose president, having fallen in love with a picture of the gatehouse, had decreed the gift on a whim, Ewell Hall had been officially renamed Harde-Knox College, although nobody in the town ever referred to it as such.

Detective Inspector Andy Constable drew to a halt between a plain black van and a rather battered-looking Volvo. "I see the doctor has beaten us to it once again," he remarked with a smile. "That man is drawn to dead bodies like iron filings to a magnet." He looked up through the windscreen at the graphite-grey clouds roiling overhead. "So, let us see what the fates have brought us this bright and sunny day." He climbed out of the car, Copper following, nodded to the uniformed P.C. standing guard, and stepped through the small open wicket in the massive and forbidding iron-studded oaken gates, only to find his way blocked by a small officious-looking man wearing a neat toothbrush moustache and sporting a bowler hat.

"You can't ..."

"Oh yes we can." Dave Copper gave him no chance to get any further. He produced his warrant card. "Detective Sergeant Copper ... this is Detective Inspector Constable. I'm sure you can work out why we're here, so let's not mess about."

"Will this be the officer in charge, then?" responded the man eagerly. "Oh good," he continued, assuming a reply in the affirmative. "Because I've been waiting for someone senior to arrive, so that I can tell them all about it. You see, what happened was, I was opening up ..."

"First things first, sir." Copper interrupted once again. "You are ...?"

"My name is Lisson, officer – Colin N. Lisson. I am the lodge-keeper of the college." He puffed himself up. "That's my little office in there." He indicated a small hatch window overlooking the entry passage. "Now that's very important, you see, because it means that nobody can come in or out without coming past me, so you'll want to be knowing what I can tell you, won't you? Vital evidence, and all that."

"So you're on duty here at the gate all the time?" Copper sought to clarify.

"Indeed I am." The self-satisfaction was overwhelming.

"In that case, sir, I wouldn't dream of dragging you away from your duties for a second." Copper could hardly restrain a smile at the deflationary effect of his words.

"But I was the one who called the police in the first place," bleated Colin. "Surely you want to speak to me?"

"Of course we do, sir. Later. And we shall know where to find you, shan't we? So perhaps if you'd like to point the way for the inspector and myself, we can go and find out what's actually happened."

"If that's what you wish, sergeant." Colin, with the slightly huffy air of a thoroughly ruffled hen settling back on to its clutch of eggs, stood back and pointed to a stone arch on the opposite side of the snow-dusted grass quadrangle. "It's at the end of that passage, in the Vice-Chancellor's private quad. You'll find all the other police gentlemen through there." There was the faintest of pauses before the word 'gentlemen'.

"Thank you so much, Mr. Lisson," said Constable affably. "We shall be back. In the meantime, sergeant, to work." He led the way across the large open space, its centre adorned with a rather straggly Christmas tree whose lights lent a sort of melancholy cheer to the scene, and into the darkness of the passageway.

Emerging into the wintery half-light of a late-December morning, the detectives were met with the unusual sight of the police doctor standing somewhat nonplussed, viewing a dead body from a distance. The reason was easy to guess. The Vice-Chancellor's quadrangle was a modest space, scarcely ten yards square, a miniature version of the main quad with a paved path running around all four sides, a further arched exit opposite the entrance, and a grassed area in the middle. The grass here likewise bore a light coating of snow, unbroken save for the body of a man who looked to be in his sixties, lying in the centre, his features contorted in a grimace.

"This is a turn-up for the books, Doc," Constable greeted the doctor, as flash after flash from the police photographer lit the scene. "Normally when you beat me to a crime scene, I expect to find you up to your armpits in the victim, full of helpful information for me."

"Cheeky young whipper-snapper," retorted the doctor good-humouredly. "As it happens, I am standing here freezing my nether regions off in order to help you do your job better. I didn't wish to be accused of contaminating your evidence by trampling in there to look at him, when there isn't much doubt that the gentleman in question is not terribly likely to be joining the party any time soon. And even the daftest plod – no offence, sergeant ..."

"None taken, doctor."

"... will have picked up the fact that we have a dead body lying in the middle of a patch of snow with no footprints leading to him. So I thought that I would let the photographer get on with it until you turned up."

"Very considerate of you, Doc. So, that is the late Lord Ellpuss."

"So I'm told. And now that you've seen him, I propose to have my minions load him on to a stretcher and haul him away to my nice cold examination room, which is probably a damn sight warmer than it is here. If that's all right by you?"

"If that's what you think best."

"Frankly, Andy, the only thing I can do here is try to establish some sort of time of death by sticking my thermometer somewhere unmentionable, and in these temperatures, that's not necessarily going to be too reliable. I can't see any obvious injuries, but that look on his face is none too pretty, so if you want a back-of-the-envelope opinion, I'd say that in the absence of strokes or heart-attacks, he's consumed something that didn't agree with him. That's the first thing I shall look for."

"You're the expert. Tell us when you know anything." The inspector nodded to two officers standing by who, under the doctor's supervision, began the process of gathering up the body to be taken away. Constable turned to Copper.

"Right, we've seen the scene and we've seen the body. And so far, I've got nothing to tell me that this is a suspicious death."

"Other than the fact that His Lordship doesn't look as if he was having a thoroughly good time when he dropped off the twig, guv," commented Copper. "And the doc said he might have a bit of trouble sorting out time of death, but I reckon we can get a pretty good idea from the weather. I looked out last night just as I was going to bed, which was around midnight, and it was coming on to snow then. Not too hard, but a bit. And when I came out this morning, there was only about as much as there is here, so I don't think it snowed for long. So Lord Ellpuss must have been in position by midnight, or else there'd be footprints."

"Good thinking, sergeant. Keep going."

"Ah. Right, guv." Copper took the point. "Either his footprints, or if he's been done unto by somebody else, their footprints bringing him here and dumping him."

"For which we have not one iota of evidence," said Constable. "So I suggest we go and see if we can find some. Chummy at the gatehouse was bursting to spill the beans about whatever he had to tell us." He looked around the quad, to see the little procession of doctor and stretcher-bearers disappearing towards the exit. "Nothing much else to do here, so let's follow this lot and ask a few questions in the warm."

"Righty-ho, guv," agreed Copper. "People like that always have a kettle stashed away in their cubbyhole. If we can't get a cup of tea out of him, we're in the wrong job."

*

A brisk knock on the hatch at the gatehouse brought an immediate response, as Colin N. Lisson appeared in the adjacent doorway.

"I thought you'd be back," he said knowingly. "I knew you'd be needing to find out what happened. You'd better come inside." He stood back to allow the detectives to enter.

"Do I understand from what you said earlier, Mr. Lisson," began Constable, "that you were the person who discovered the body?"

"That's right."

"Then perhaps you'd like to tell us exactly what happened. My colleague here will make a few notes."

"Thirsty work, note-taking," pointed out Dave Copper, casting an extremely meaningful look at a tray on a cabinet which bore a kettle, mugs, a box of teabags, and a bottle of milk. "And it's not that easy to write, sir, when your fingers are chilled to the bone."

"Point taken, sergeant," said Constable comfortably,

settling into the only available armchair, a slightly shabby item with a floral print cover. "I'm sure if we ask nicely, Mr. Lisson will be kind enough to furnish a couple of frozen policemen with a warming cuppa."

"That'd be great, Mr. Lisson," enthused Copper, seating himself into the only other chair, an upright chair next to the small dining table squeezed into a corner of the room. "Milk, no sugar, thanks."

As the slightly startled Colin Lisson found himself rail-roaded into the rôle of host, filling the kettle and clattering mugs, Constable continued with the questioning. "I think you mentioned that nobody can get in or out of the college without passing your lodge. So this is the only entrance to the precincts?"

"It is, inspector. That's why my job is so important, you see. Now, what happens is, the gate's open all day, but I go around last thing every evening to check all the open areas, and then I lock the gate for the night."

"And what time do you call last thing?"

"That'd be about half past eleven usually. I go round the quads and the cloisters, and then I lock up and go up to my little flat upstairs for the night." He pointed to a spiral staircase visible through a small door in a corner.

"So you live on the premises?"

"Well, I have to, don't I, otherwise there wouldn't be anyone to answer the night bell," said Colin reasonably. "Sometimes one of the dons who live on the premises stays out past curfew, so I have to let them in."

"How about the students?"

"Oh no. If they're late, they have to stay out. I don't stand any nonsense from them." The words were filled with a smug self-satisfaction. "But there aren't any students here at the moment anyway."

"And last night, nobody went in or out after curfew?"

"No, inspector. It was all quiet until this morning. And then I did my usual – I got up about half past seven, had my bit of breakfast, and then I did my usual walk-round just before I open up the gates at eight o'clock. And that's when I found him. Gave me a turn, I can tell you, seeing the Master all stretched out in the snow with that horrible look on his face. I could tell he wasn't right, and I didn't want to touch him, so I came back here and phoned 999 straight away."

"And here we are," said Constable. "So, then, a bit of background, if you don't mind, Mr. Lisson. Some information about the set-up here yesterday would be useful. Am I right in thinking that the college students have all gone down for the Christmas vacation?"

"That's so, inspector," answered Colin. "They all disappear pretty promptly after the big do."

"Sorry, sir, what 'do' would that be?" asked Copper.

"The Ewell Hall Yule Ball," explained Colin. "They have it every year just before Christmas, on the last Thursday of the Michaelmas term. Black tie event in the Great Hall, with a band and everything. It's quite the social event of the season." Colin seemed happy to bask in the reflected glory. "And then as soon as that's over, everyone disappears the next day, and my job gets a lot easier, I can tell you."

"So let me see if I've got this right," said Constable. "The Ball was two days ago, since when the college has been deserted?"

"Well, not completely, no. I'm still around, of course, because I have to be, and there's one or two of the college servants stay on over Christmas – you know, cleaners and so on. And some of the academic staff live here. But it was mainly just the people for the meeting of the Trust yesterday."

"Which Trust is this, sir? I'm afraid we're not *au fait* with the workings of the college."

"Camford Academy Strategic Holdings, they call it," said Colin, placing mugs of tea in front of the police officers. "C.A.S.H. for short. They set it up – oh, quite a few years ago now, because Ewell Hall has never really had two halfpennies to rub together, so the former Master set up a trust to try and manage the finances a bit better and get gifts from donors and what-have-you. It was all a bit haphazard, to be perfectly honest, but then the old Master passed on and Lord Ellpuss took over, and he became Chairman of the Trust as well and really gingered things up, and then they got all that money from the American company and things started to much rosier. Mind you, that's when they started all this 'Harde-Knox' nonsense." Colin looked and sounded thoroughly grumpy. "Trying to change the name of a place with our history. It'll always be Ewell Hall to me."

"So you said something about a meeting of the Trust, Mr. Lisson," said Constable, trying to bring the lodge-keeper back on track. "This was yesterday?"

"Friday, that's right. Yesterday at seven, it was."

At last, thought Constable, we're getting somewhere. "And can you tell us who was involved with that? Lord Ellpuss himself, presumably?"

"Yes, he stayed on with his family after the Ball."

"Family?"

"Yes, his wife and their son."

"They were also on the premises last night?"

"Yes. The Master's House is just round here to the left in the main quad, before you get to the chapel. Lord Ellpuss stays there whenever he comes to Camford. And the Reverend Grey lives in the apartment on the other side of the chapel. He's another one of the trustees - he's the college chaplain," explained Colin, in response to a quizzical look from Dave Copper, his pen poised in mid-air.

"And you mentioned other dons who live inside the college, Mr. Lisson. Who would they be, and were they also involved with this meeting of the Trust?"

"There's Professor Plump, of course – he's the P.V.C."

"Sorry?" Copper looked baffled again.

"Pro-Vice Chancellor," explained Colin. "He lives in the Vice-Chancellor's House, which is on one side of the Vice-Chancellor's quad where I found the Master."

"Does the professor also have a family?" asked Constable.

"No, inspector. He's a single gentleman. He says he likes to think of the staff and students as his family."

"Any more residents within the college?"

"Well, yes and no. There's Miss Scarlatti, who's the Dean of Modern Languages. She's got rooms on the opposite side of the main quad, just round to the right, but she doesn't often use them to stay. She's got a big house out on the edge of town. Fancy modern place, it is – must have cost a fortune."

"And is that all of the trustees?"

"Oh no," said Colin. "It's a right mix of Town and Gown. There's also Mrs. Pocock, who's Financial Secretary to the Trustees; we've got Colonel Muskett – he's Vice-Chairman of the Board of Trustees; and then naturally there's Mrs. Wright, of course."

"Mrs. Wright?" Constable furrowed his brow. "The name rings a bell. Who's she?"

"She's the Lady Mayoress of Camford, inspector. I'd be surprised if you didn't know a thing or two about her," added Colin with a meaningful look.

"Of course! I knew I knew the name. She's on one of the Chief Constable's committees for something-or-other, I think. And that's the lot who were here for yesterday's meeting?"

"That's right, inspector. Everyone arrived about six o'clock or so for the meeting – ah, now, I tell a lie, because Mrs. Wright was late. She'd phoned up earlier to speak to Lord Ellpuss, and it came through here to my switchboard." Colin indicated an ancient-looking contraption next to the hatch, with an old-fashioned headset and a cats-cradle of wires and jack-plugs leading from socket to socket, which looked as if it might have been installed by Alexander Graham Bell himself. "She's never been good at punctuality at the best of times, and I thought, she's going to trot out all the usual excuses, so I put her through to the Master's House. It's amazing what you overhear sometimes, isn't it? Anyway, where was I?"

"People arriving?" Constable reminded him. "Mrs. Wright?"

"Yes, well, if you've heard anything about her, I dare say I don't need to go into details."

"Let's assume I haven't, Mr. Lisson. It probably depends on which newspapers I read, I imagine. So perhaps you'd better remind me."

"Let's just say she's got the reputation as a bit of a good-time girl, if you see what I mean, inspector." It was hard to tell from Colin's expression whether he approved or not. "Three husbands, she's had, and there have been rumours, but I'm not one to repeat gossip, of course. Let's just say that I was told by somebody who ought to know that she used to be in the profession."

"Does that mean what I think it means, sir?" enquired Copper.

"Does it, Mr. Lisson?"

"It means," said Colin, with heavy emphasis and a half wink, "that she used to be in West End shows in London, and

90

don't you go saying I said anything else. But yes, she used to be on the stage, and then she married the composer of the musical she was in – you know, that odd-looking bloke with the sticky-up hair. Made a lot of fuss, that did, what with his wife kicking up and everything. But then the next thing you know, she's divorced him, picked up a bundle, moved up here and married old Lord Camford. Dear old soul, he was, and well-liked around here, too. That one caused a lot of gossip, but everybody reckoned it suited them both – he got a pretty young wife, and she got herself a title. Then, blow me down, he pops off not long afterwards, and they say she did quite well out of the will. Not the title and the house, of course, because they went to some cousin or other, so she was left at a bit of a loose end, so to speak."

"And did the end remain loose for long?"

"Not so's you'd notice, inspector. Being a bit of a local celebrity, as it were, she managed to get herself elected to the local council, and before you know it she was getting married to old Joe Wright, the Lord Mayor. Not that he lasted long – heart attack, they said, but my opinion is, she wore the poor old devil out – but by then she had quite a few friends on the council, as you might say, so they made her Lady Mayoress in his place."

"That certainly is an interesting career," remarked Constable. "Three husbands!"

"Yes, and I've heard tell she's on the lookout for the next one already. I reckon Lord Ellpuss's papers would have had a field day if they'd known about her history."

"So back on the subject of this phone call, Mr. Lisson, you mentioned overhearing something. I assume you left the loudspeaker connected by accident, or something of the kind?"

"Oh, er, yes, that's what happened, inspector." Colin reddened, plainly thoroughly embarrassed at being caught out in his eavesdropping. "She rang up, and told Lord Ellpuss that she was going to be late for the meeting because she'd got tied up with one of the University rowing team – her 'personal trainer', as she called him. I've seen him – six foot four, and built like a ..." Colin recollected that he was posing as a man unwilling to spread gossip. "Anyway, she told His Lordship that she'd make it up to him somehow, and that she was worth waiting for."

"And that was the end of the conversation?"

"Yes, because she was finishing just as everybody arrived

91

– those that weren't here already, that is. Mrs. Pocock put her head around my lodge door to ask if there was any post for her, so I had to get off the line, and she asked who it was, and I told her, and she said it was time Lord Ellpuss knew the sort of people he was dealing with. Then she took the post from the tray – loads of it, there was, because she gets all the Trust financial stuff to do with the C.A.S.H. appeal – and she went on up."

"So that's Mrs. Pocock out of the way, then."

"Yes. The only time I saw her later was in the quad when I was doing one of my patrols. She was over by the chapel, and I just nodded, but I don't think she saw me."

"And all the others you mentioned had gone through to the meeting, you say? The colonel and the other academics? Professor Plump, and so on?"

"The professor was already on the premises, inspector. Oh, but I did take a call for him later on in the evening. I wouldn't normally have bothered to find him at that hour, but it was from America, and the chap seemed very insistent and said it was important, and the Professor was expecting the call, so I put it through to him in the Master's study."

"And do you by any remote chance have any idea as to the nature of the call, Mr. Lisson?"

"Certainly not." Colin bristled at the implication. "I hope you aren't suggesting that I would listen in on a private call."

"Not at all," returned Constable soothingly. "Just a thought." He downed the remainder of his tea. "Well, we shan't keep you from your duties any longer. Thank you for the information."

"If I find out anything else, I'll let you know." Colin seemed eager to assist.

"That would be kind." Constable stood. "Come along, sergeant – the game's afoot."

*

The detectives stood sheltering under the arch of the gatehouse, as a brisk breeze whipped the occasional snowflake around the quad.

"Right then, sergeant," said Constable, "what did you manage to garner from all those ramblings? Who's on our list, and where do we begin?"

Copper consulted his notebook. "There's half-a-dozen or

so names, guv, but as for where you want to start, I don't have a clue, do I? There's Professor Plump, Miss Scarlatti, and the Reverend Grey – they seem to be what you might call the insiders – and after that I've got Mrs. Pocock, Colonel Muskett, and Mrs. Wright, who are somewhere out in the big wide world. I suppose it's easier to start here and work outwards, wouldn't you say?"

"I agree," said Constable. "And don't forget the wife and the son. We'll need to speak to them, but I think I'd rather leave that until we've got a little more information. I suppose we may as well start at the top with the Professor, who I assume we'll find in his house next to the crime scene."

"If crime it was, sir. I mean, it's not as if Lord Ellpuss was hit over the head with a piece of lead piping or something obvious like that. We still don't know for certain."

"And shan't until we hear from the doctor. But my detective's nose tells me we're not wasting our time, so let's be about it. Start at the top and work down."

The pair skirted the small lawn in the Vice-Chancellor's Quadrangle, where the outline of Lord Ellpuss's body still stood out from the surrounding snow, now trampled by footprints, and a small team of overall-clad SOCO officers were beginning to erect a small white tent. Constable rapped on the sturdy timber door with its shiny brass letterbox engraved 'Prof. E. Plump'. The knock was answered by a heavily-built man of about sixty, with quivering jowls, small eyes, a red-veined nose, and thinning grey hair carefully arranged across the top of his head.

"Professor Plump? Good morning, sir. Sorry to disturb you. I'm Detective Inspector Constable, and this is Detective Sergeant Copper." The two officers presented their warrant cards. "We'd like to ask you some questions about the death of Lord Ellpuss. May we come in?"

The professor wheezed his way up the creaking oak staircase and showed the detectives into a cosy low-ceilinged sitting room with a fire blazing in the brick hearth. He waved his visitors towards a large chintz sofa, took a seat in a matching wing chair, and looked expectantly at the inspector.

"May we have your full name, just for the record, please," began Constable.

"Of course, inspector. It's Edwin Samuel Plump, and I'm the Pro-Vice Chancellor of Ewell Hall – sorry, I haven't yet got used to calling it Harde-Knox College. I suppose I shall in time."

"And I'm afraid I'm a bit hazy as to titles and responsibilities, what with Chancellors and Masters and so on. Can you clear that up for me?"

"I'm sure it must be very confusing if you're not from our world, inspector." The professor's patronising tone and the accompanying smile set Copper's teeth on edge, but Constable seemed untroubled. "The actual Chancellor is the Countess of Sussex, but of course that is purely ceremonial, and Her Royal Highness doesn't have anything to do with the running of the establishment. The late Master was also the Vice-Chancellor, and that meant that when he unfortunately died, the position of Vice-Chancellor was left vacant, and because there are so many considerations to be taken into account in selecting a new V.C., I was appointed as Pro-Vice Chancellor in the interim."

"So effectively, you're the man in charge, sir."

"Indeed so," said Professor Plump comfortably. "And it is a big responsibility, being at the helm of an establishment such as this, with all its history and traditions, but of course an academic background like mine is the perfect foundation for such an important job." He waved a casual hand in the vague direction of a wall of highly impressive-looking framed diplomas. "Needless to say, I delegate a great deal. One is so lucky to have good colleagues around one."

"And Lord Ellpuss, sir," pursued Constable. "The position of Master seems to have been filled far more quickly than that of Vice-Chancellor. Why would that be?"

"Money, inspector," replied the professor. "The world of finance moves a great deal faster than the world of academe, and evidently those in a position to make the decision felt that swift action was appropriate. And I have to say that his presence has been a godsend. I have had a huge amount of help and support from His Lordship – he has been very much a hands-on Master in terms of monitoring our activities and placing us all on a sound footing, albeit that he's done everything from a distance. It's such a shock that he's died so suddenly like this."

"Which brings me to my next question, professor, which is to ask when you last saw His Lordship? I gather there was some sort of meeting of trustees yesterday evening, which you attended. Would it have been then?"

"Well, yes, then, and of course at the party afterwards."

"Which party would that be, sir? We don't know anything about a party."

"Oh, it was a very small-scale affair, inspector – hardly worthy of the name, really." Plump smiled deprecatingly. "But as it was so close to Christmas, there was a little get-together in the Master's house for a few drinks. I of course attended, as I believe did all the other members of the Trust." He nodded in recollection. "Yes, I think we were all there, plus of course Lady Ellpuss. She is a most gracious hostess."

"And Lord Ellpuss was well when you last saw him?"

"Oh, most certainly, inspector. He seemed to be thoroughly enjoying himself. In fact, one might say the Master was having the time of his life."

"Which perhaps is just as well, considering how little of it there was left to him," remarked Constable drily. "So you can think of nothing unusual about the events of yesterday? Nothing to disturb the smooth running of the evening?"

"No, not at all, inspector."

"What about the phone call, sir?" prompted Dave Copper.

Professor Plump looked momentarily puzzled. "Phone call, sergeant? I don't understand."

"The college gatekeeper said he put a phone call from America through to you, sir," said Copper. "He said it sounded important. Was that anything to do with the Trust meeting?"

The professor's brow cleared, and he gave a chuckle. "Oh dear me no, sergeant, nothing like that. Well, only in an oblique way. We have approaches all the time from large companies who want to offer some sort of support or sponsorship for us. It's all in the aftermath of the arrangements we made with the Harde-Knox Corporation. Mostly it's a hen-pecked company chairman wanting a lecture theatre renamed in honour of his wife – I've become very adept in finding ways of accepting their generosity while saying no."

Constable glanced at Copper, who gave the smallest of shrugs. "Then I think that will do for the moment, sir," said the inspector. "Except that we need to speak to the other people present last night, and I believe that some of your academic colleagues are among them. Could you perhaps tell us where we might find Miss Scarlatti or the Reverend Grey?"

"If Miss Scarlatti is here, she may be at her apartment in the main quad, and as for the chaplain, you'll normally find him somewhere around the chapel."

*

In the quad, the detectives surveyed the array of identically-studded oak doors in the ranges of two-storey buildings around the periphery.

"Well, I'm not going hammering door-to-door like some over-age trick-or-treater," said Constable.

"Why don't I knock up Colin Lisson and ask, sir? Much quicker."

"I knew I brought you along for a reason, sergeant. Well, don't just stand there, get on with it."

In response to Copper's enquiry, Colin emerged from the fug of his den into the chill of the quad and pointed to a door in the middle of the range.

A thought struck the sergeant. "While I've got you here, Mr. Lisson, can you tell me where I might track down Mrs. Pocock, Colonel Muskett, and the Lady Mayoress? I'm assuming that as they are none of them resident here, they would have left the college last night."

"That's right, they did," confirmed Colin. "Now Mrs. Pocock, she's got a little house just round the corner from the college in Cutpurse Lane. That's where all the low-class drinking dens used to be in the eighteenth century," he explained in response to Copper's quizzical look. "It's all gentrified now. Number 17, she lives at. As for the colonel, you'll usually find him propping up the lounge bar of the Camford Arms Hotel, boring everyone stiff with stories of his time in the army. And you could try the Town Hall in the Square if you want Mrs. Wright – I think there's something going on today with children and carols round the Christmas tree, so she'll probably be there."

Details noted, Copper rejoined the waiting inspector and knocked at the door indicated by Colin. A light, visible through a tiny lancet window, went on in the hall, and a brisk clack of approaching footsteps was heard. The door opened.

"Yes?" The woman who opened the door was tall and striking-looking. A glossy black bob framed a face with piercing eyes and dramatic cheekbones, and the slim body was dressed in a bright red blouse and elegant black pencil skirt. The ensemble was completed by red stilettos. Late forties, estimated Constable, and looking good on it.

"Miss Scarlatti?"

"I am. And you two, if I'm any judge at all, look very like policemen. I assume you're here to talk about Lord Ellpuss. You'd better come in out of the cold." She passed through a door into a sitting room furnished with a mixture of comfortable tradition and stylish modernity, seated herself in an expensive-looking leather and chrome armchair, and nodded the detectives towards a similar sofa. "How can I help?"

Constable introduced himself and his companion. "We're given to understand, Miss Scarlatti, that you are involved with the Trust whose meeting was being chaired by Lord Ellpuss last evening, so I'm hoping you can give us some information surrounding yesterday's events."

"I'll do what I can, inspector."

"I suppose it's first things first. Your full name, if you wouldn't mind, just for my sergeant's notes."

"Of course. It's Donnatella Immaculata Scarlatti, sergeant. Donna for short." A slight pause as Copper's eyes widened. "That's with two 'n's, two 'l's, two 'm's, and two 't's."

"Thank you, madam," said Copper in relief. "I'm not terribly good with foreign spellings. Italian, is it?"

Donna smiled. "A very long time ago, sergeant. The family is originally Sicilian, of course, but we're as English as can be now."

Constable resumed the questions. "And you're one of the leading academics of the college, I believe? Dean of something, I think?"

"That's correct, inspector. I'm the Dean of Modern Languages. And to think that I used to be a mere student here, but of course, that's more years ago than I like to remember. They were very happy days, and I've loved this university ever since, but who would ever have thought that I would end up as a don?"

"Quite an achievement, Miss Scarlatti," agreed Constable.

"Of course, I would never have got here but for the support of my family," continued Donna. "That's why I feel so sorry for Lord Ellpuss's wife and son. Family is so very important, isn't it?"

"Which brings us very neatly to the matter in hand. Now,

97

you were present at the Trust's meeting yesterday – is there anything you can think of that we ought to know about that? Any tensions, for example? Any controversial subject matter?"

"Not that occurs to me offhand," replied Donna. "I seem to remember everything was fairly routine. There was a great deal of talk about money, of course, but that was hardly surprising, since that is the main purpose of the Trust. I suspect that I am like most people – too much talk of money, and I'm afraid my attention begins to wander."

"And then there was a small party after the meeting, I'm told. Which you attended?"

"Yes, I was there for a while."

"And did you have any contact with Lord Ellpuss during the course of the party? Or were you conscious of any conversations which the other guests may have had with him?"

"I chatted with him, certainly, inspector, but I really can't recall exactly what about." Donna's eyes assumed a wary expression. "Inspector, I'm starting to wonder where these questions are leading. Are you implying that there may have been something suspicious about Lord Ellpuss's death?"

"It's a possibility that we have to consider, Miss Scarlatti, in the light of certain information in our possession." Donna's eyebrows rose in enquiry. "Which of course I'm unable to share with you."

"I quite understand, inspector. Well, in that case, all I can tell you is that Lord Ellpuss was alive and well when I saw him last, and when I left the party I came straight back here and knew nothing further until the lodge-keeper gave me the news this morning. So, if there's nothing else ..." Donna Scarlatti stood, an unmistakeable signal that the interview was at and end.

"If there should be anything else, Miss Scarlatti, will you be here later on?"

"Possibly, inspector. Possibly not. I simply use this apartment as a *pied-à-terre* when I'm kept late on college business. Otherwise, I have a house outside Camford."

"And the address, madam?" Copper noted the details.

"Thank you for your help," concluded Constable. "We'll come and find you if we need you." On that slightly ominous note, he led the way back towards the front door.

*

"So where, next, guv? Chapel, is it, as it's just across the way?"

"Mmmm?"

"I said, do we go for the chaplain next, guv?"

"What? Oh, yes, I suppose so."

"You seem a bit distracted, sir. Is something the matter?"

"Scarlatti ... Scarlatti," murmured Constable under his breath, and then came to and focussed on what his junior colleague was saying. "No, it's just that that name is ringing a bell somewhere in the back of my mind. Don't worry – it's probably nothing important. And the lady herself didn't seem to have anything important in the way of information to impart, so let's bash on to our next port of call, which as you suggest, ought to be the chapel. To hell with 'Keep Off The Grass' – I'm taking the short route." He set out across the pristine whiteness of the snow covering the grass of the quad, heading for the chapel entrance on the opposite side.

The thud of the door closing behind the two detectives seemed an almost sacrilegious disturbance of the serene calm of the dimly-lit building. Subdued, the pair gazed around them. A subtle light filtered down from high multi-coloured stained-glass windows, and mute carved stone faces looked down on the visitors from the tops of soaring pillars. The ceiling was an arresting cobweb of tracery, with details picked out in red and gold. A tiny red light flickered above a purple-draped altar. In response to the sound of the door, a figure, cassock-clad, appeared from a door behind the choir stalls.

"I'm afraid there's no service this morning." The voice was unexpectedly high-pitched, the intonation that of a BBC radio announcer from the 1950s. The figure moved forwards into a pool of light which revealed it to be a tall thin man with a slight stoop, whose age could have been anything from thirty to fifty-five. Bright eyes of an odd light colour looked out from a smooth pink face beneath a shock of untamed hair whose colour in daylight might have been somewhere between silver and pale gold. "Can I help you gentlemen?"

"Would you be the Reverend Grey, sir?" began Constable, approaching nearer.

"That's right. Petroc Grey, D.D., college chaplain, for my sins." A slight chuckle. "Were you looking for me?"

"We were, sir. We're police officers..." The two proffered their warrant cards and introduced themselves. "... and we're looking into the death of your late Master."

"My Master? Oh, of course, Lord Ellpuss. Sorry ... so silly of me. Yes, Mr. Lisson gave me the sad news. I'm afraid that in here, one feels so very distant from the troubles of the world that it's easy to forget the unpleasantness of reality. I'm sure you must feel that – I could see you admiring my chapel."

"It's a very fine building, sir," agreed Constable.

"Lovely, isn't it?" Grey's eyes strayed up to the exquisite carving of the ceiling. "It's Early English Horizontal, you know. One of the finest examples in the country, I believe, and blessedly untouched by the Reformation. You should experience the atmosphere by candlelight – it's quite magical, the way the darkness and the light seem to feed off one another. I have to confess, I do spend a great deal of time here at night."

"You're evidently a firm devotee, sir."

"Indeed I am, inspector. But then, church buildings are a speciality of mine, from even before I was called to the cloth. In fact, I've even had a little treatise published on the subject of lightning-conductors on medieval rural ecclesiastical buildings. Of course, I doubt very much that you would have read it."

"You never know, sir," said Constable. "I surprise myself sometimes at some of the things I take it into my head to read. Odd information never comes amiss."

"Tell me about it," murmured Copper at his side. He had on more than one occasion been the unwilling recipient of one of the inspector's impromptu lectures on the most arcane subjects.

"Oh, well, in that case, perhaps you are familiar with my work. I called it, 'Grey's *Energy in Country Churchyards*'."

Constable shook his head. "Sorry, sir, not one I've come across." He reacted to Copper's meaningful throat-clearing alongside him. "However, that isn't really why we're here, sir."

"No, of course not," said the chaplain. "I'm so used to people coming here seeking the truth that I'm sure you must have questions of your own."

"Copper?" The inspector handed the questioning over to his colleague.

"Right, sir. Yes, Reverend, if you wouldn't mind. You are one of the members of the Trust whose meeting was held last night, I think."

"Yes, sergeant, that's right."

"At which matters of finance were discussed."

"As of course you would expect, sergeant, since that is the Trust's chief function."

"Just recapping the main facts, sir. After the meeting, there was a small drinks party, which you also attended?" The chaplain nodded. "Were you aware of any circumstances or events which struck you as unusual during any of this?"

"Not in the slightest, sergeant. Why should there be? No, of course, I spoke to Lord Ellpuss during the course of the evening, but there was nothing out of the ordinary that I recall." A cautious light came into Reverend Grey's eyes. "I don't quite understand why you're asking me these questions, sergeant. Am I to take it that you believe that His Lordship's death was other than a natural occurrence?"

"We must consider that possibility, sir."

"Oh heavens!" Reverend Grey appeared shocked. A thought seemed to strike him. "But how? And what does Lady Ellpuss say about this?"

"We haven't spoken to Her Ladyship as yet, sir." Constable resumed control of the conversation. "We didn't wish to trouble her until we had a slightly clearer picture of the situation."

"Oh, the poor woman," said the chaplain. "I must go to her. I must offer her whatever consolation I can. I'm sure you'll excuse me, inspector. Needs must when the devil drives." Without waiting for further permission, Grey dived back through the door by which he had first entered, reappearing seconds later, prayer-book in hand, throwing round himself a voluminous black cape. The cape billowed behind him as he swooped down the nave, and the door to the quad closed after him with a hollow echo.

*

Back under the gatehouse arch, where the chilly breeze did not swirl quite so penetratingly, the detectives took stock.

"Halfway down my list of trustees, guv, plus there's still the family. What about the grieving widow and her son?"

"I think we'll do best to leave Her Ladyship in the tender care of the chaplain for the moment," replied Constable. "We don't know what sort of state she's in, and the last thing I need is

101

a hysterical woman to cope with. So on down the list, and since there seems to be a lot of money talk sloshing around, let's get some information from the horse's mouth."

"Best not let the lady hear you call her that, sir," commented Copper, "if by that you mean Mrs. Pocock."

"Which I do. Just around the corner, I think the very helpful Mr. Lisson said."

17 Cutpurse Lane was a delightful Georgian cottage with sash windows and a tiny portico – 'that's worth a pretty penny', thought Constable to himself. The door was opened by a stout middle-aged woman with greying hair dressed back into a pleat, and wearing a cardigan, tweed skirt, and sturdy shoes of the type which are invariably described as sensible. Introductions effected, she preceded the police officers into a cosy drawing room, a fire burning in the Regency grate, the walls adorned with prints of eighteenth-century rural scenes.

"I hope this won't take long, inspector," said the woman briskly. "I was just about to go out to the shops. As I'm sure I don't need to tell you, if I leave it too late on the last Saturday before Christmas, there won't be a sprout to be had."

"We'll be as quick as we can, madam. Now, it's Mrs. Pocock, that much we know – first name?"

"Elizabeth."

"And is there a Mr. Pocock?"

"No, inspector. He died some years ago. He'd been ill for a long time."

"I'm sorry to hear that, madam. And you are employed by the college Trust, I understand."

"That is not quite correct, inspector. I am Financial Secretary to the Trustees, but it's an honorary position. There is no salary."

"Perhaps you've heard about the reason we're here."

Mrs. Pocock nodded. "I have, inspector. One of my neighbours knocked on my door earlier to tell me there were police cars at the college gate. And when she went up to ask what was happening, she came back and told me that the Chairman had been found dead. I told her, I could scarcely believe it."

"I'm afraid it's true, Mrs. Pocock. And because there is a serious possibility that Lord Ellpuss's death may not have been natural ..." A startled look swept across Mrs. Pocock's face. "... we have to look into all the circumstances surrounding the meeting of the Trust which took place last night."

"This is all very worrying, inspector," said Mrs. Pocock. "I suppose you know all about the Trust?"

"A certain amount, madam."

"Camford Academy Strategic Holdings," enthused Mrs. Pocock. "Such a great benefit! And Lord Ellpuss managed to work wonders with it, but of course, with all his connections, he was perfectly placed to do so. And I have to say, the money keeps rolling in. We receive donations from wealthy individuals as well as commercial organisations, you know – those who haven't already given all their money to political parties, that is." There was definite disapproval of the latter, signalled by the pursed mouth of the speaker. "And the benefits have been enormous – financing of research projects, new buildings, and so on." Her face fell. "Goodness knows how we'll manage without His Lordship."

"May I take it that you were on good terms with him?"

"Oh, very much so, inspector. We worked very closely together, but of course, he had so many other interests that he was entirely happy to leave all the routine matters of finance in my hands."

"And that would have included the matters discussed at last night's meeting?"

"Naturally." Mrs. Pocock preened a little. "Lord Ellpuss relied on me to present all the latest details of new donors to the Trust. Of course, some of that information is of a highly confidential nature, inspector, so I'm afraid I couldn't divulge any details to you, even if I wished to."

"No, I quite understand, Mrs. Pocock. So may I take it that all went smoothly at last night's meeting, and at the party following it?"

"So far as I know, inspector. I didn't stay late, because the weather forecast was not especially promising. So I popped into the chapel on my way home, because I always like to spend a few moments there every day, and then I came back here. Actually, I had quite an early night. And then I awoke this morning to the snow and the awful news. And now, I hope you'll forgive me, but I really must get on."

"Of course. And no doubt you'll also be extremely occupied, once this unpleasant business is over, with dealing with

103

all the financial implications."

"I'm sure Lord Ellpuss would have agreed," said Mrs. Pocock comfortably, "that matters will be quite safe in my hands."

*

"Fancy a drink, guv?" suggested Dave Copper. "Or a coffee? Something to warm us up? Something tells me they probably serve a decent cup of coffee in the bar at the Camford Arms."

"What an extremely cunning plan, sergeant," said Constable approvingly. "And you never know who we may run into there. Two birds with one stone. Lead on. You're buying."

"... but you see, when they were in Afghanistan for the second time, the Russians made exactly the same mistake as they had in the nineteenth century." The only occupant of the bar, a white-haired man in his late sixties wearing a bilious yellow tweed jacket and sporting a striped tie, was perched on a bar stool, evidently expounding at length to a terminally bored barman. "Damn fine fighter normally, your Afghan, but the trouble is ..."

"Excuse me, sir, while I serve these two gentlemen." The barman seemed enormously relieved to have an excuse to escape, and rapidly busied himself with Dave Copper's order for a pair of cappuccinos.

In no way daunted, the speaker turned his attention to the newcomers. "Now, you, young chappie – you've got a bit of the squaddie look about you, so you'll know what I'm talking about. As I was telling this feller here, when you're up against it, the last thing you want ..."

Andy Constable felt no qualms about interrupting. "Would you be Mr. Muskett, by any chance?"

"Colonel Lewis Muskett, D.F.C., (Retired), to be exact. Got to be exact in this game, you know. Who's asking?"

"My name is Constable, sir – Detective Inspector Constable, since we're being exact, and this is my colleague Detective Sergeant Copper."

"Aha!" declared Muskett. "Well, a nod's as good as a wink to a blind horse. You don't need to tell me what brings two members of the County Constabulary sniffing round here at this hour of the day, and it won't be the smell of coffee! The little matter of a deceased peer, eh? Am I right?"

104

Constable smiled. "I can see we've no hope of pulling the wool over your eyes, sir. Yes, of course you are right, and I'm taking it from what you say that you are aware of what has happened."

"Course I am," said Muskett. "You can't keep a thing like that quiet. It'll be all over the town by now. Something funny about it, I've heard. Got it from the hotel concierge – ever want to know anything, keep in with the hotel concierge, that's my motto! Amazing what those fellows can find out."

"I'll bear it in mind, sir," said Constable mildly. "But at present, I'm more concerned with finding out what you can tell us about the events of yesterday, particularly concerning the meeting of the Trust. I gather you hold quite a senior position there."

"True, inspector, quite true. Vice-Chairman of the Board of Trustees is the precise title, since I see your young chappie here is doing his best to take down the details surreptitiously, and to be frank, not making a very good fist of it. But yes, old Ellpuss appointed me Vice-Chairman not long ago, a while after he took over as Master. Chappie I knew from another college recommended me. Needed someone with a good head on their shoulders to take things forward when he wasn't around, d'you see? That's where the military training comes in, you know – nothing like an army background when it comes to organising this Trust business."

"Were you in the forces long, sir?" enquired Copper.

"Lord, yes," replied Muskett. "Made a career of it. Now you won't remember this, sergeant, because you look far too young to me, but we used to have National Service in this country. Well, I was one of the lucky ones – I was included in the last ever group to be called up. Worked my way up through the ranks – not too many people get made up to officer from that sort of start, you know, but the Army will always recognise talent. Same with the Trust. That's why they like an army chap on the board, you see. After the Falklands, anything's a piece of cake."

"You were there too, sir?" said Copper admiringly.

"All the right people were, laddie," said Muskett. "Walked all over the other lot, but of course, one doesn't like to brag."

"Fascinating though all this may be, sir," said Constable, "I'd like to come back to the events of yesterday. The meeting,

105

and the party which followed it."

"Don't know that I can tell you much, to be honest, inspector," said Muskett. "There was a lot of talk about money at the meeting, but to be honest, all these financial details bore me stiff. Can't fathom what they're on about half the time. I'm more your practical man. And as for the party, well, nobody's going to turn down the chance of a free drink, are they?" He gave a meaningful look at the empty whisky glass before him, which Constable chose to ignore. "I had a drop or two of Lord Ellpuss's single malt, and I had to pull out all the stops to get that, followed by a couple of rather uninspiring vol-au-vents, after which I wended my way home, duty done. And that's pretty much it."

"Is that man for real, guv?" asked Copper, as the detectives stood sheltering from a sudden squall beneath the hotel's porch. "He's like a cartoon character."

"Let nobody tell you that we don't meet all-sorts in this job, sergeant," intoned Constable. He chuckled. "The trick is to pick out the ones with the tasty bit in the middle of the liquorice."

"Isn't 'lickerish' an old-fashioned term for 'randy', guv?" quipped Copper. "How dangerous would it be to link the words 'tasty bit' and 'Lady Mayoress'? Since I assume that's where we're heading next."

"You might very well think that, if Colin Lisson is to believed," responded Constable. "I of course couldn't possibly comment. Let's go and find out."

*

The detectives climbed the stairs of the Town Hall, in accordance with an extremely surly 'Up there' from the taciturn individual in a peaked cap at the inappropriately-named Welcome Desk in the foyer, and pushed open the door marked 'Mayoral Suite'. Perched on the front of a desk in the reception area, long fishnet-clad legs crossed, sat an attractive woman with blonde hair in an elfin cut, liberally high-lighted, wearing an abbreviated fur-trimmed Santa costume with a dangerously revealing neckline.

"... and if you're a very good boy, Justin, I'll bring your present round for you to unwrap tonight," she breathed into the mobile phone held to her ear. She turned and noticed the newcomers. "Whoops! Got to go, darling. See you later." She looked expectantly at her visitors. "Yes?"

"Excuse us, we're looking for the mayor," said Constable.

"Well, you've found her." She registered amusement at the detectives' evident surprise. "Lady Mayoress, if you want to be more correct about it, but I'm not surprised you don't recognise me without the official robes and chain." She gestured to her outfit. "This get-up's all in aid of the kiddies' Christmas Carols later on. I don't normally dress like this – well, unless it's a special occasion. So why were you looking for me?"

Constable introduced himself and Copper and explained their presence. "So if you can spare us a few minutes..."

"You'd better come into my parlour, hadn't you?" She opened a door to a lofty chamber, part-office, part-sitting-room, and arrayed herself on one of a pair of leather chesterfields, waving the detectives to the other. Dave Copper took the opportunity to study their hostess a little more closely. Mid-forties, but a very plausible attempt at a playing age of mid-twenties, he judged.

"So, Madam Mayor ... -ess." Constable fumbled for an appropriate form of address.

"Oh, don't bother with the formalities, inspector – save those for the Council Chamber. It's Isla ... Isla Wright ... Mrs., although my husband's gone now, bless him, but he was a lot older than me. Well, they all were."

"So I understand, Mrs. Wright."

"Oh, I expect you've heard all the gossip," said Mrs. Wright cheerfully. "People can say what they like, and what they don't know, they usually make up. But if you want the official version, here it is. Born Isla Egg in nineteen-hundred-and-never-you-mind, changed my name when I went on the stage – well, wouldn't you? - so then I was Isla Skye; married André while I was in one of his shows when his marriage fell apart - that was just after he got his knighthood - but then that didn't work out either, so I decided to leave the profession and turn respectable."

"Which is what brought you to Camford?"

"That's right. I'd met Quentin – that's Lord Camford – when he came backstage after the show one night. A real old-fashioned gentleman, he was, and he seemed very taken with me. And after all, what girl can resist a title and a lovely house in the country? No, that's not fair – I was very fond of him, but nothing lasts, does it, and he died. But by then I'd already met Joe – that's

107

Joseph Wright, the former Lord Mayor, in case you didn't know. Sweet man, and not so old, really. He was a widower, and he persuaded me that it was no good sitting around moping, and a Lord Mayor needed a Lady Mayoress, so we sort of fell into it, as it were. And after he passed away last year, the council asked me to step into his shoes."

"It's quite a mixture of good and bad fortune," remarked Constable.

"Well, it gives people something to talk about," replied Mrs. Wright. "I've even heard people calling me the Merry Widow when they think I can't hear them. Jealousy's a terrible thing, but it's all water off a duck's back to me. Here I am, and here I stay!"

"And one of your official duties," said Constable, bringing the conversation round to the purpose of his visit, "is to serve on the board of the Camford Trust, I think."

"Oh yes. Camford City Council have very close dealings with all the University bigwigs, not just the ones at Harde-Knox College - that's why Lord Ellpuss invited me on to the board of the Trust. And sometimes people prefer to make a more indirect approach when it comes to offering donations, just in case they get rejected for some reason, and then it's humiliating for them. That's why very often they like to go through me. And I do know a lot of very wealthy people in show business."

"Very helpful, I'm sure. Which brings us round to the meeting yesterday evening, which you and the other trustees attended."

"Yes, over in the college." Mrs. Wright giggled at the memory. "Yes, that was fun."

"Really?" Constable was surprised. "We'd got the impression from the others that it was a fairly routine meeting."

"They told you that, did they?" laughed Mrs. Wright. "Honestly, the lies some people tell! No, you take it from me, inspector, the fur was really flying. Lord Ellpuss really had his dander up, and he went all round the others at the table. Mind you, a lot of what was said was just hints and innuendo – I dare say it meant more to the people concerned than to the rest of us." She noticed the inspector's growing interest. "Now you're going to hate me, but I don't think I can say anything about what was said. Lord Ellpuss swore us all to secrecy, because he said that if anything were revealed prematurely, it would do a great deal of harm to someone's reputation. He wanted to keep control of the whole thing."

"Something of a strained atmosphere, then?"

"Well, yes and no. The funny thing is, it all seemed to pass off, and then we moved on to the little party – well, I say party, if you call a warm glass of sherry and a few limp sausage rolls a party – and everybody seemed to be quite normal again. Well, normal for Camford, anyway."

"So nothing was said after the meeting closed – nobody did anything unexpected – no odd tensions from anyone in particular."

"Not a thing that I can think of, inspector. Sorry to disappoint."

Just as Constable drew breath to attempt to carry the questioning further, there came a knock at the door, and a young woman with serious glasses and a serious demeanour to accompany them put her head into the room. "The children are just starting to arrive, Madam Mayoress," she said severely, completely ignoring the two detectives. "I'm sure you won't want to keep them waiting."

Mrs. Wright got to her feet. "Well, I'm afraid I have to go, inspector. My city needs me, and all that, and Janet here never lets me forget it. Ah, the burdens of civic responsibility!" She smiled in mild self-mockery. She gazed Dave Copper up and down in frank assessment. "Do let me know if there's anything else I can do for you – anything at all. I'm quite easy to find." With a flash of teeth, and adjusting the neckline of her costume to a more modest level, she tripped from the room.

"Well!" said Copper, somewhat taken aback by the entire performance. "That was a whole lot of something and nothing, wasn't it, guv?" He rose from the sofa, along with Andy Constable, and the two began to make their way down the staircase, under the beady eye of the mayoral secretary.

"On the contrary, sergeant," countered the inspector, "it was quite a lot of several things. For a start, on one hand we have a lady with several dead, or at the very least disposed of, titled husbands in her past, and on the other, we have a dead titled gentleman whose demise is at the very least fishy. Not that there's the slightest reason to link the two facts at the moment, but I've always been very uneasy about coincidences. Secondly, she told us that there was a great deal more to this meeting than we've been told. Everybody's tried to tell us that the whole thing was very dull, and all about columns on a balance sheet. Now we learn that Lord Ellpuss, as Mrs. Wright put it, went round the table having some sort of a go at everyone."

"And you'll have noticed," put in Copper, "that she carefully excluded herself from that list."

"So she did. But apart from that, she was very up-front about everything."

"As you might say," grinned Copper. "Justin, whoever he may be, seems to be a lucky boy."

"I shall ignore the unsavoury implications of your remark," said Constable loftily, as the two emerged once more into the square, where a group of rather pinch-faced children, huddled in coats, could be seen posing for a photographer in front of the Christmas tree in the company of an exuberant Lady Mayoress, her bright smile undimmed by the chilly weather. "I have more important things on my mind. Let us return to the *locus in quo*."

"The which, sir?"

"*Locus in quo*, Copper. You really are going to have to pay closer attention next time you're giving evidence in court. It's Latin – lawyer-speak for 'the place in which'."

"Or, if you're a normal human being, 'the scene of the crime', I assume," said Copper. "You'll have to forgive me, sir – we never did Latin when I was at school."

"*O tempora! O mores!*" riposted Constable with a wicked smile. "Look it up! Perhaps you need to go back to college. In fact, let's both do exactly that." He headed for the Harde-Knox gatehouse.

*

Copper's mobile rang as the two climbed through the door and entered the arch. "Yes ... oh, hello, doc ... yes, he's here. Hold on a second while I put it on speaker." He handed the phone to his superior.

"Hello, doc. What can I do for you?"

"*It's more what I can do for you, Andy,*" came the voice from the other end. "*A piece of information which may help you in your endeavours.*"

"And what may that be?"

110

"I've got Lord Ellpuss's stomach on the bench in front of me." Constable grimaced in distaste. *"Never seen anything quite like it. It's heavily inflamed – almost looks as if it's being eaten away by something. No idea what – the contents don't respond to any of the obvious instant tests."*

"But you're saying it's definitely a poison of some kind?"

"Stake my reputation on it," boomed the doctor cheerily. *"Not the foggiest what it is at present, but I thought you'd appreciate an update."*

"Thanks, doc. Much obliged." Constable handed the phone back to Copper. "You heard that?"

"Certainly did, sir. Puts us on a bit of a firmer footing, doesn't it?" The sergeant had been idly browsing the contents of a noticeboard mounted on the wall, dotted with flyers on every subject from holistic healing to a planned rugby club drinking contest. String quartets vied for attention with the forthcoming offering of the university Shakespeare society. A suggested bridge tournament looked likely to clash with an open lecture on 'Yoga and its place in Education'. Bicycles were offered for sale – obscure reference books, unobtainable from the library, were sought. A highly-coloured art-nouveau-themed poster for the recent Ewell Hall Yule Ball was still very much in evidence. "It's all a wild social whirl for these students, eh, guv?" he remarked. He indicated the selection of events advertised. "I'm surprised they have any time left to study. Mind you, some of these gigs I wouldn't mind going to." He pointed to a modest black and white handbill, marked 'Special Event', which read 'Black Sabbath! Sunday 3.00! Don't miss out!'. "I must say, I do enjoy a good rock band."

"Sadly, sergeant, you do not have the leisure for frivolous pursuits at the moment," the inspector reminded him. "In case you've forgotten, we have what now definitely looks like a murder to solve, which I'd like to get on with, before Lord Ellpuss is spread all over the doctor's lab in little bits."

"You and me both, guv. Yuk!"

"So I suggest we see if the family are in any fit state to be spoken to." Constable turned left into the quad and made for the door bearing a shiny brass plate which carried the simple words 'The Master'. The jangling doorbell was answered by an elderly woman, overall-clad, with eyes which looked to be red from

111

weeping – perhaps a housekeeper, guessed the inspector.

"We'd like to see Lady Ellpuss, if that's possible," he said gently.

"I'm afraid she's with the chaplain at the moment, sir," said the woman. "I don't really like to disturb her."

"No, of course not, we wouldn't want to do that, Mrs. ...er ...?"

"Maggs, sir – Eileen Maggs. I come in to do the cleaning for Her Ladyship." The soft Scots burr was gentle on the ear.

"We're police officers, Mrs. Maggs." The detectives showed their identification. "And we're looking into the events of yesterday."

"Oh, sir, isn't it awful." Mrs. Maggs pulled a handkerchief from her sleeve and seemed inclined to begin weeping afresh. "Oh, what am I thinking of? You'd better come in. I suppose you could wait, or of course there's always Mr. Ellpuss – what about him?"

"What?" Copper was startled. "But I thought ..." He gestured wordlessly in the vague direction of the exterior.

"No, sir, I mean young Mr. Ellpuss – His Lordship's son. He's upstairs. I could get him if you like."

"I think that would be very helpful, Mrs. Maggs."

"If you'd like to wait in here, gentlemen, I'll go and tell him you're here." The housekeeper showed the detectives into a book-lined study, and then disappeared towards the staircase, closing the door behind her.

Constable browsed the shelves. "The late Lord was obviously one for his biographies," he commented, running a finger along one section of books. "'*Tolstoy*' by Warren Peace ... '*Emile Zola*' by Jack Hughes ... '*The Works of Landseer*' by Monica D. Glenn ... evidently something of a polymath."

"Not quite in keeping with his position as big boss of things like the 'Splash', is it, guv? Bit of a contrast of cultures." Copper was prowling around a large partner's desk towards one end of the room. "Oh, hallo! Here, guv, there's something here which is a bit more relevant in terms of reading matter."

"And what might that be, sergeant?"

Copper held up a piece of paper. "It's all about last night's Trust meeting, sir. Note from Lord Ellpuss to all the other members of the Board of Trustees. Calls them to this special meeting yesterday, and then goes on about '*a particular matter which has come to my attention concerning the status and reputation of C.A.S.H., which I believe will have severe effects on our financial standing, particularly with reference to donations*'. Aha! What do we make of that, then, sir?"

"Well done, Copper. Good find. And that all connects in with what Mrs. Wright was saying about gifts from her wealthy contacts."

"Here, you don't suppose the lady has gone a little too far in her schmoozing in order to bring in the goodies, do you, guv? Now that would be something to interest your average 'Splash' reader. Because it goes on, '*I have asked the Financial Secretary to provide a detailed list of donors and cheques received for discussion at that time*'. Cheques! That's all a bit antediluvian, isn't it, sir? I would have thought everything was done by direct transfer online these days. That's how I pay my bills."

"Yes, sergeant, but you are a child of modernity. Don't forget that places like this are probably operating in some sort of time-warp. And donors can't get much kudos out of the public presentation of an online transfer, can they?"

"Suppose not, sir."

"Well, don't stop there, man. While you're exercising your considerable talent for snooping, is there anything else lurking around that desk that relates to the task in hand?"

"I hope you're going to carry the can for me if somebody comes in and discovers me conducting an illegal search without a warrant, guv," said Copper, beginning nevertheless to leaf through the various papers in the stationery tray on the desk. "Nothing that jumps out at the moment ..." His speech slowed, and a grin spread across his features. "Except for this, of course." He exhaled gustily. "Were you saying something earlier about your detective's nose, sir?"

"I may have made mention. Why?"

"I don't know how you do it, guv. Have you got a document signed in blood stashed away somewhere or other?"

"Stop rabbiting, man, and cut to the chase. We haven't got all day. What is 'this'?"

"'This', sir, is a letter which was lurking *underneath* the tray of papers. And it's not just the 'what' – it's the 'who' as well. This letter is addressed, not to Lord Ellpuss, but to Professor

Plump, so what's it doing here?"

"Is it Trust business? Maybe the professor brought it here to show to His Lordship."

Copper scanned the letter. "Doesn't read that way, sir. And this may be the answer to one of the questions we were asking earlier on. It's from some university in America – '*Collegiate University of Gary, Indiana*', whatever and wherever that may be. And apparently, they have literate furniture, guv," laughed Copper, as he read on. "This one's from a desk – '*From the Desk of Yukon E.Z. Lee, Dean for Academic Awards*', to be precise. Don't you just love American names?"

"And? I assume there is actually some meat in this sandwich."

"All very corporate blah, as far as I can see, guv," said Copper. He quoted, "'*We have been conducting researches through our files, and have noticed that it is some time since we received our customary renewal fees as laid out in our original terms and conditions upon conferral. We would respectfully remind you that these are due upon every third anniversary of the event in question in order to prevent any inconvenient lapse of entitlement*'. Whew! What's that all about?"

"All rather oblique, isn't it? Any more?"

"More of the same, sir, if that's what you really want. '*At the same time, we are happy to advise you that, as a client of long standing, we are able to offer you additional certification from associate bodies at preferential terms, which we are sure you would find highly advantageous in any future career progression. My secretary will take the liberty of telephoning you* ... oh, that's what it's doing here ... *telephoning you within the next few weeks in order to discuss your farther requirements. Yours, etc, etc*'. So, this is all to do with that call the professor had. He knew it was coming, so he had it with him when he took the call in here."

"But why do you suppose it's been left here?"

Copper shrugged. "Search me, guv. And what is all that drivel about anyway?"

Constable was denied the opportunity to answer by the sound of the door opening, while Copper by some miracle succeeded in being found standing several feet away from the desk, a picture of innocence, as the newcomer entered the room.

"Are you Inspector Constable? Eileen said you wanted a

word." The young man standing in the doorway provided a vivid injection of brightness into a dull winter's day. The floral shirt, with its colourful pattern of hibiscus and parrots, would have felt entirely at home on a Caribbean beach, and the white jeans appeared to leave no room for expansion. A heavy lock of dark brown, almost black, hair fell across his brow, and was frequently swept back with a shake of the head. He advanced towards Constable, proffering his hand to effect a rather limp handshake. "Evan Ellpuss."

Ignoring the slight snort from Dave Copper standing behind him, Andy Constable gave a welcoming smile. "Lord Ellpuss's son, I believe, sir? My condolences on your loss, Mr. Ellpuss."

"Thank you, inspector. Do please sit down." Evan sank into an armchair, tucked his feet up under himself, and left the detectives to make their own arrangements. "You want to talk about what happened yesterday, Eileen said."

"That's right, sir. If it's not too delicate a subject."

"Oh, you go right ahead, inspector. I'm not some Victorian maiden who swoons at the mention of murder. And it may be murder, according to the chaplain. Is that so?"

"I'm afraid it is, sir. We had grounds for suspicion earlier on – I have to tell you that we have had confirmation, so this is a murder enquiry."

"Well then, you ask me anything you want. If somebody's done the Old Man in, I'd want to know who as much as you do."

"Thank you, Mr. Ellpuss." Constable nodded to Copper to deploy the customary notebook. "Now, I understand that your whole family was here in Camford for the meeting of the Board of Trustees."

"Oh no, inspector," Evan contradicted him. "Mother and Father came up specially from London, but I'm here all the time. I'm a student at the university."

Constable looked Evan up and down. "Oh yes, sir?" There was an echo of doubt in his words.

"Of course. A mature student, I should say."

"Can I ask how mature, exactly?"

"Twenty-nine," said Evan, with a perfectly straight face. Copper, in the background, reflected that it was normally considered a very serious offence to lie to the police, but wisely

115

kept his thoughts to himself.

"And yesterday," continued the inspector, "everyone was gathered here for the meeting of the Trust?"

"Yes. Of course, I'm not actually on the board of the Trust – neither is Mother, but we've got a pretty good idea of what goes on."

"Are you aware of what went on yesterday?"

"I do know that there was some sort of financial crisis, so they wanted to talk about that. But I suppose they must have sorted it out, because I heard my father tell my mother at the start of the party that he was going to call the editor of the 'Splash' first thing this morning with a new lead story for Sunday's paper."

Constable leaned forward. "Did you hear any more details of exactly what he meant?"

Evan shook his head. "Sorry, I'm afraid I can't help you there. You see, I was rather on the move last night, because my mother had me circulating with the drinks. Honestly – sherry! Who drinks sherry these days? Another one of these fusty old university traditions, I suppose."

"So as far as you were concerned, the party was all rather dull?"

"Well, actually, inspector, no, not really. In fact, everyone seemed a bit jumpy."

Constable's interest was awakened. "Can you think of any particular instances?"

Evan cast his eyes up in thought. "Oh, I do remember one moment which seemed a bit tense, for some reason – there was a bit of a frisson. My father was saying something to Miss Scarlatti about money not being able to buy everything, not even silence, but nothing was set in concrete yet, and she said that all sorts of things can be set in concrete, and her family are the experts. I didn't even know she was interested in buildings, but I suppose she could have been speaking about one of the Trust development projects. I think there's talk of a new library."

"Was that all of the conversation that you heard?"

"Almost. Miss Scarlatti said something about having to go soon. I think she may have been planning to spend the night with friends off-campus, because she mentioned sleeping with the Fishers, whoever they may be. Somebody at another college, I expect."

Constable mused for a moment, quietly filing facts away at the back of his mind. "Did your father speak to anyone else that you know of?"

"Oh, everyone at some time or another. I did hear him talking to the Reverend Grey about the chapel. I've heard a rumour that something pretty amazing has been discovered. Mind you, you never know what to believe in a place like this – the whole college is a hotbed of rumour and gossip. It's great fun sometimes."

"And this amazing discovery – have you any idea what was found, or by whom?"

"Sadly, no, inspector. That bit of the story hasn't got to me yet, but I expect it will. Perhaps," speculated Evan with sudden enthusiasm, "it's another medieval wall-painting! They discovered one a few years ago in the chapel crypt underneath some whitewash when they were doing some restoration. It's all about damnation and the casting of souls into hell – it's very graphic, with all those writhing bodies. Maybe it's another one of those. Anyway, my father said it couldn't stay covered up for ever, and he wanted to make sure that the whole world knew the naked truth, and then he cracked some joke about getting Ozzy Osbourne in to sing at the chaplain's next service. And I thought, big respect, dad, getting down with the kids!"

"How did the chaplain react to his remarks?"

"It was very funny, really," giggled Evan at the memory. "The Rev. Grey lost it a bit and said that my father was really getting his goat, but for some reason that made my father laugh even more. But then the Rev went off looking a bit sick. Overdosed on that cheap sherry my mother was serving, I expect, or else he'd had too much of his home-brewed communion wine."

"Home-brewed wine?"

"Yes, he's always concocting something in that little lab of his in the crypt, but everyone knows that."

"And what about the rest of the evening?"

"Not the faintest, inspector," said Evan airily. "I'd had enough by then, so I sneaked off. I thought, I'm not going to waste the whole evening hobnobbing with all these dreary people. Actually, Mrs. Wright's quite fun – you can have a laugh with her, but we're not really each other's type. So I escaped to the pub."

117

"And that would be which pub, sir?" intervened Copper, pen at the ready.

"The Rose and Rainbow, sergeant."

"I don't know it, sir."

"It's just the far side of the Square. It used to be the old 'Rose and Crown' before somebody bought it up and turned it into a cocktail bar. The barman Damien does some absolutely super cocktails there – everyone loves his 'Between The Sheets'. And I spent the rest of the evening there until about midnight or so. The first thing I knew anything was wrong was when Eileen brought me my tea this morning."

"Can anyone confirm that, Mr. Ellpuss?" asked Copper.

"Loads of people. All the crowd were there."

"Just one will do, sir," said Copper stolidly.

"Well, if you absolutely insist on checking up on me," said Evan a touch waspishly, "I suppose you'd better ask my friend Toby."

"Toby, being ...?"

Evan sighed irritably. "Tobias Wheat, sergeant."

"And where will we find this gentleman, should we wish to do so?"

"He works at Sofas-4-All in the Square. I'm sure if you rush there now, he'll confirm what I've told you."

"Just a thought, Mr. Ellpuss," interrupted Constable. "You say you stayed out until after midnight, but the lodge-keeper told us he locks up long before that. So, how did you get back in?"

"Ah." A sly look came over Evan's face. "You've discovered the other secret of Ewell Hall, inspector. Yes, the gates do get locked up, but I'm sure you know what students are like. You can't get us to obey the rules if there's a way round them. So each student year passes the secret down to the next." Evan unconsciously lowered his voice. "There used to be a little gateway leading from a yard at the back of the chapel vestry out into the lane behind. Now, it was all walled up years ago, but there is a tree in the lane, and if you're agile, you can climb up, clamber over the wall, let yourself down into the yard, and come out through the chapel. In fact, there was even supposed to be a secret passage from the chapel through into the Master's House, but I've never found it. Anyway, generations of us have got in that way, and the bulldogs have never found out how."

118

"Bulldogs, sir?"

"Yes, inspector. The chaps in bowler hats, like Mr. Lisson at the gate. Of course, no ex-student would ever become a bulldog, so the secret's pretty safe, I should think. Oh!" A sudden realisation came to Evan. "That's as long as you don't give us away."

"I think that your secrets, if secrets you have, will be quite safe with us," replied Constable drily.

Evan uncoiled himself from his chair. "So is that all?"

"I think so, sir. If you don't mind, we'll just wait for your mother here. Although ..."

"Yes?"

"I wonder if we might take a look at the room where last night's party took place?"

"Just to get an idea of the *locus in quo*, you understand, sir," said Dave Copper with an admirably straight face.

"Of course. It's just across the hall in the dining room." Evan led the way and held open a door. "Mind you, I don't suppose Eileen's had a chance to clean in here this morning yet, so it's probably still a bit of a mess."

"So much the better, sir. Just leave it with us." With a smile Constable closed the door, politely but firmly, in Evan's face.

*

The unlit dining room was long and low-ceilinged, with dark oak beams and mullioned windows. A dining table, which looked as if it would have been at home in a monastic refectory, was prominent in the centre of the room, while around the walls were ranged various cabinets, chairs, bureaux and console tables. Trays bearing bottles and plates with the remains of a finger buffet formed an untidy centre-piece on the table, while sherry glasses and the occasional whisky tumbler stood abandoned on various surfaces about the room. At the end opposite the door a large carved stone fireplace, its mantel supported by a pair of sturdy caryatids, presided over the room.

"Hey, guv," said Copper, "what about all these bits and pieces left over from the party? If the doc's pretty sure that Lord Ellpuss was poisoned, shouldn't we be getting the SOCO team in to bag everything up? Maybe we're looking at vital evidence."

"Extremely sound thinking, sergeant. With a bit of luck,

119

they'll still be fiddling about where the late Lord was found. Nip out and put this on their agenda."

"Will do, sir." Copper trotted smartly from the room.

The sergeant had only been gone a matter of moments, as Constable stood surveying the room and seeking somehow to absorb the atmosphere of the previous evening, when he was aware of another presence. Turning, he was met with the sight of a woman silhouetted in the doorway.

"Inspector Constable? May Ellpuss. Lord Ellpuss was my husband." She switched on the light and stepped into the room. Constable saw a woman of mature years and middle height, dressed in an elegant ensemble of purple dress and black court shoes. Pearls gleamed discreetly in her ears and in a single strand around her neck. The complexion was pale but flawless, with merely a hint of sombre red lipstick. The eyes were grey and clear, and the hairstyle, with its immaculate sweep of carefully-lacquered ash-blonde hair, was positively prime-ministerial in its authority. "I understand that you wish to speak to me."

"If that isn't inconvenient, Lady Ellpuss. And may I offer my condolences." These were accepted with a grave nod of the head. "And I am sorry to distress you, but I have to ask you some questions."

"Naturally, inspector – we all have to do our duty," said Lady Ellpuss. "But I think I'd prefer it if we didn't talk here. After all, this room is the place where I last saw my husband, so ..." A small lace handkerchief was drawn from her sleeve as she dabbed at the corner of her eye. "Perhaps we could go through to the drawing room." Constable followed her into the hall, just as Copper, with a brief murmur of "Just caught 'em, guv. They're on their way", returned and fell in behind them.

"So, how may I help you, inspector?" enquired Lady Ellpuss, as she seated herself with a ramrod back in a Queen Anne chair by the fireplace and invited Constable to another opposite.

"I would like, if I may, to ask you about the individuals who were at the party last night."

A flash of distaste lit up Lady Ellpuss's face. "Of course, none of these dreadful people are what they pretend to be. Frauds, all of them. I mean, they're all posing as members of the great and the good, just because my husband appointed them to the Board of the Trust, but most of them are nobodies. They have no idea how to behave."

The inspector was slightly taken aback by the firmness of May Ellpuss's expression. "I was under the impression that several of the Trustees were of quite long standing," he ventured.

"That's as may be," said May darkly, "but when my husband took over as Master, most of them had to be re-appointed. He could sometimes be very naïve, you know – took people at their own valuation, in fact far too often for his own good on occasion. But woe betide them if he found himself let down."

"You said something about their behaviour, Your Ladyship. I don't quite understand."

"Well, look at what happened when Elizabeth Pocock spilt my husband's drink all down him. All of a flutter she was, blushing and dabbing at him with her handkerchief, and gabbling on 'Take mine, take mine, I can easily get another'. Nobody with an ounce of breeding would have caused such a scene."

"Do I gather that you don't much like Mrs. Pocock?"

"Ridiculous woman!" The pose of grieving widow seemed to have been forgotten, and had been replaced by a formidable virago. "She may be Financial Secretary of the Trust now, but she used to be an accountant with Ladhill's Bookmakers, and according to Eileen Maggs, before that she was just a cashier at one of their betting windows. Always keep in with your servants, inspector – you'll be amazed what they can tell you."

"I shall try to bear that in mind, madam," said Constable solemnly. "Ladhill's Bookmakers, eh?"

"I think she may still be involved with them, because I saw her in deep conversation with my husband right at the start of the evening, and he said something like 'Lost a great deal of cash? You bet!'. And then she scuttled away, and he turned to me and said, 'Honestly! Losing a fortune because of a useless old nag!', and then he stamped off."

"Your husband not a betting man then, Your Ladyship."

"Oh no, not from a horsey background by any means, inspector." Lady Ellpuss smiled fondly. "A dear man, but no seat on a horse at all. No, my side of the family are the ones with riding in the blood. Now my brother, for instance, when he was serving with the Household Cavalry, he used to ... oh, that reminds me."

"Yes?"

121

"I don't know if it's at all relevant to what you want to know, inspector, but it's just another instance of the sort of people we were having to mix with. Now, one of my husband's new appointments, Muskett – oh, I beg his pardon." The voice was heavy with irony. "He always insists on the full 'Colonel Muskett, D.F.C., (Retired)', but I think we can all see what's going on there."

"Yes, Lady Ellpuss," smiled Constable, "we have met the colonel. So where does your brother come in?"

"Well, dear Gerald was on the staff at Sandhurst, and I happened to mention Muskett one day, and he'd never heard of him. And it's not the sort of name you'd forget, is it?"

"To be honest, madam, I'm not sure that the colonel is the sort of man you'd forget," agreed Constable.

"And the army are normally so good at keeping records, aren't they? But according to Gerald, the only time he'd ever come across the name was in connection with Aldershot, and he thought that might have been the Catering Corps, so that would have made no kind of sense, would it?" Lady Ellpuss shrugged dismissively. "Not, I have to say, that I'm particularly concerned one way or another."

"So all in all, not exactly your kind of people?" summarised Constable.

Lady Ellpuss leaned forward confidentially. "To be frank, inspector, I have as little to do with these persons as I can, commensurate with supporting my dear husband in his work, of course. Oh dear!" She broke off for a moment and wiped away a tear. "For a second I'd forgotten ..." She took a breath. "Forgive me, inspector. Do carry on."

"We were speaking about your guests at the party."

"As far as that was concerned, I contented myself with making sure that Evan kept the sherry glasses filled, but I saw some people just helping themselves. So rude! Ah! I've just remembered – that was another thing. My husband was never a one for sherry - he had one or two at the start of the evening, but he was always partial to a rather fine single malt whisky in preference, so he changed over to that later. But when he saw him with a whisky tumbler in his hand, Muskett came up – Muskett again! - and virtually insisted on a whisky for himself. Such bad manners! But anyway, by this time, the decanter was virtually empty, so I had to go through to the study to fetch another bottle,

122

and as I went in, Professor Plump was just coming off the phone."

"Yes, we had been told that the professor received a telephone call during the evening."

"Did you happen to catch anything of the conversation?" intervened Dave Copper. "Oh, purely for corroboration, of course," he added, at a look from his superior.

"Of course, one doesn't like to eavesdrop," responded Lady Ellpuss primly. "But as it's in the course of your investigation … It was obviously something medical, because he was saying something about 'not wanting to buy another, the one he had was enough, and he didn't want the Doctor, and not to call again'. He flushed when he saw me, fiddled about with something on the desk, and then sloped off looking rather embarrassed. So then of course I collected my husband's whisky bottle and returned to the dining room"

"Is there anything else that occurs to you concerning the events of the evening?" asked Constable.

May shook her head. "Nothing, inspector. Some people left earlier, some hung on a little longer, but I think everybody was gone by eleven or quarter-past. And I felt quite tired, so I went straight on up to bed. But my husband said he was feeling rather headachey, so he said he'd pop out for some air. And that was the last time I saw him." The handkerchief was discreetly wielded once again.

"You weren't aware that he hadn't returned?"

"I went to sleep very quickly, inspector. And we have separate rooms."

"I see." Constable rose to his feet. "I won't take up any more of your time, Your Ladyship. I'm sure you have far too much on your mind."

"Indeed so, inspector. I have a great deal of thinking to do. My life will be so very different in future." As Lady Ellpuss showed the detectives to the door, there was a speculative look in her eye.

*

Outside in the quad, the SOCO team were packing away the items they had gleaned from the dining room into capacious plastic chests.

"Anything tasty?" Constable greeted them. "Other than stale sausage rolls?"

"Funny you should ask, sir," said their leader. "Mostly fairly ordinary plates and glasses, which we'll give the once-over to in the lab. We've dusted for prints, and most of the glasses seem to have just the one set, although one of the sherry glasses looks to have two, so we'll take a closer look at that. But there is one little oddment which struck us as a little strange. It's this." He held up a clear plastic evidence bag. Within it nestled a small miniature cut-glass decanter, only about two inches high, with a tightly-fitting glass stopper, such as might be used to contain a precious perfume. The facets gleamed a warm rose in the watery daylight.

"And what do you find strange about it?"

"Only the fact that it was lurking at the bottom of a waste-paper basket, sir. It looks like Venetian Merano glass to me, probably quite expensive, so not the sort of thing you'd throw away idly. It just gave me a sort of itch in the brain."

"Any contents?"

"Not really, sir. There's a remnant of whatever was in it coating the bottom. No colour, no obvious smell from a very tentative sniff, so no idea what it is at present."

"Here's a suggestion," said Constable. "When you get back to the lab, have a chat with the doctor. You may find it mutually beneficial."

As the two detectives stood back to allow the investigation team to finish their task, Dave Copper looked expectantly at Andy Constable. "Next step, sir?"

"For no reason at all, sergeant, I am filled with a sudden desire to take a look at this fabled wall painting in the chapel crypt. Why on earth do you suppose that might be?"

Copper shrugged. "Couldn't begin to imagine, guv. Maybe you feel some sort of affinity with the purveyors of the final judgement, meting out justice to sinners – isn't that sort of what we do?"

"That, young David, is an alarmingly profound philosophical comment for this hour of the day. I prefer to think that I just have a healthy amateur's interest in medieval history."

"You're the boss, sir." Copper held open the chapel door and allowed the inspector to pass through.

Silently descending a narrow stair to one side of the altar, the detectives found themselves in a shadow-filled crypt whose

124

only light came from two black pillar candles on stands to either side of the end wall, where the expected fresco was displayed. The flickering candlelight seemed to impart the effect of movement to the swirling flames of hell and the bodies which writhed within them. The colours of the work were still strong and vibrant, the expressions on the faces of those depicted ranging from glee to despair. Constable stood contemplating the work for several moments, and then shivered. The chill he was experiencing, he felt, could not wholly be ascribed to the temperature.

"Take a look at this, guv." Andy Constable's mood was broken by an excited exclamation from Dave Copper. "This lot is obviously what Evan Ellpuss was going on about." The sergeant drew his colleague's attention to a bench in the corner of the crypt, where a selection of scientific apparatus was laid out. Retorts, test-tubes and beakers mingled with stands, burners, and lengths of glass and rubber tubing, with jars on a shelf bearing labels echoing the style of an eighteenth-century pharmacy, containing liquids and powders of various colours and unknown properties. "And here's an interesting thing." At one end of the shelf stood an assortment of fancy glass bottles ranging in size from the tiniest phials to substantial flasks. One medium-sized vessel at the front, containing a clear liquid, was prominently labelled 'Grey's Eliminator'.

"Got an evidence bag about you, by any chance?" asked Constable.

"As always, guv." Copper reached into a pocket for bag and gloves.

"Right. Bag that, and then on your toes and see if you can catch SOCO before they escape. I want to know what's in that bottle."

As Copper disappeared at speed, Constable cast one last lingering look at the vivid portrayal of the harrowing of souls, and then followed the sergeant back up the stairs at a more leisurely pace. He met his colleague returning through the arch of the gatehouse, puffing slightly.

"Just caught them as they were pulling away, sir. They said they were off now, before we find any more work for them and completely ruin their Christmas," grinned Copper.

"Whereas we, unlucky devils that we are, have to soldier

on through until we're sorted," rejoined Constable.

Attracted by the sound of voices within his jealously guarded domain, Colin N. Lisson appeared at the door of his lodge, evidently prepared to chase away any interlopers. "Oh, it's you. I thought your lot had all gone," he grumbled.

"Not quite all, Mr. Lisson," said Constable cheerily. "We're still here."

"Well, I hope you're not going to be cluttering up the place all over Christmas, making my life a misery."

"I would have thought that the dead body of Lord Ellpuss deserves a rather more respectful description than something 'cluttering up the place'," observed the inspector mildly.

"And look at this." Colin bent down and picked up a crumpled scrap of paper. "Your lot chucking down litter without so much as a by-your-leave. Some of us try to keep this place tidy, you know."

"I cannot imagine that our Scene-Of-Crime colleagues would do anything of the sort, sir," said Constable. "May I see, please?"

Constable held out his hand for the paper, which the lodge-keeper handed over. He smoothed it out, and his eyebrows rose. "I very much doubt if this belonged to one of our team, Mr. Lisson," he remarked. "If it did, I suspect we may be paying them too much."

"What is it, guv?" asked Copper, intrigued.

"It's a betting slip from Ladhill's. Listing bets on a couple of horses at race meets last week."

"So, what about it? Obviously, if it's been chucked, the horses didn't come home."

"Evidently not, sergeant. Because if they had, this thing would have been framed and enjoying pride of place on a wall somewhere. One of these bets is for three thousand pounds, and the other is for a mere thousand quid. And at very tasty odds, I might add."

"Hell's bells, guv!" Copper sounded impressed. "Who's got that sort of money to be bunging on the back of some long-odds runner?"

"We know not," replied Constable. "There's no name on the slip. Just an account number."

"'EP108'," read Copper over his shoulder. "We could go

and ask them who that belongs to," he suggested.

"Or, sergeant," retorted the inspector, "we could pretend to be detectives, and try and use our little grey cells to work out possibilities. I think, with the various snippets we have in our possession, it wouldn't be a bad idea to go hawking these around our jolly contestants."

"Starting out or in, sir?"

"Why don't we reverse our direction of travel, just to add a bit of interest? Let's go and see if Mrs. Wright has finished her cavortings for the photographer and the children. You never know, she may have put some more clothes on by now."

"Doubt it, guv," muttered Copper, "but you never know."

Colin N. Lisson had been standing by, listening intently during the exchange. "Well, if you're going to see Mrs. Wright ..." He dived into his cubicle and reappeared holding a note. "You could give this to her. I noticed it in the post tray last night, but she came through at such a speed when she did arrive that I never got the chance to give it to her. And this morning, what with everything, I clean forgot about it."

"We'll pass it on, sir," said Copper, taking the folded sheet of yellow paper and, as soon as Colin had disappeared back into the interior, unfolding it to peruse the contents.

"What's this then, sergeant?" said Constable in mock reproof. "Reading the contents of what we assume to be somebody's private correspondence?"

"I cannot tell a lie, guv," answered Copper. "I have to confess, I am as curious as the next man."

"Yes, well, in case it's escaped your notice, I *am* the next man! So, what does it say?"

"'*I don't see why I should be the only one under pressure*'," read Copper. "'*I'm sure all the 'Splash' readers would love to know all about your 'activities' – so I think a little help is indicated! See you at the meeting.*' All in slightly wobbly capitals. And it's signed '*P*'."

"Well, well," ruminated Constable. "A dainty little attempt at blackmail. And which of our candidates, I wonder, is so coy as to go by initial only? Professor Plump? Mrs. Pocock?"

"Or Petroc Grey?" suggested Copper. "Oh, one thing I forgot to point out, sir – the thing's addressed to '*L.M.*' on the outside. Lewis Muskett, do we assume? And if so, why does Colin

Lisson think it belongs to Mrs. Wright?"

"I propose we do the sensible thing, which is, instead of standing here speculating, to go and ask her."

*

"Oh yes, that's addressed to me, all right." Mrs. Wright, now seated fully clothed behind the mayoral desk, and completing the effect of a sharply-tailored business suit with a pair of heavy-rimmed spectacles which gave her an air of intellectual glamour, was perfectly happy to confirm the identity of the addressee. "Everyone calls me 'L.M.' for Lady Mayoress – all part of the Town Hall love of bureaucracy, I dare say. Haven't you seen the mayoral Rolls Royce? Registration 'LM 1', of course."

"Would you have any idea who has sent this?" enquired Constable.

Mrs. Wright glanced over the note again. "No, not a clue. I don't recognise the handwriting. It all looks a bit childish to me."

"And yet evidently your help was expected in one way or another," pointed out Constable. "Perhaps some sort of approach was intended immediately before the meeting of the Trust, which never took place because your arrival was delayed. But there is a definite threat expressed."

The Lady Mayoress burst into peals of laughter. "And that, inspector, is the most childish thing of all! I don't care a bit whether I end up all over the papers or not. Actually, Lord E knew all about me – you don't run a Sunday paper without having your ear to the ground, and he was perfectly well aware that I've never claimed to be a saint. But he thought like me – as long as you don't do anybody else any harm, what's to stop you enjoying yourself?"

"I believe Voltaire had something to say on the same subject," smiled the inspector.

"I don't know that I'd call this the best of all possible worlds," replied Mrs. Wright, surprising Constable by her recognition of the reference, "but I try not to make it any worse. And Lord Ellpuss was quite sweet about the whole 'scandalous past' thing, really. We laughed about what his old sour-puss of a wife would have said if she'd known it all." A sombre shadow swept across her face. "It's sad really. I did think of trying my luck with him – he'd have had much more fun with me, and I miss not having a real title these days, but it's a bit late now. Oh well, never

128

mind."

Descending the stairs of the Town Hall, Dave Copper wore a small frown of puzzlement. "Not exactly what you'd call a red-hot motive, is it, guv? Killing His Lordship to stop his paper revealing what he knew all about anyway. She didn't exactly seem fussed."

"Two things you should bear in mind, sergeant," said Andy Constable. "One, the lady used to be an actress. Two, when they're on stage, magicians use distraction techniques to make you look at one thing so that you don't notice another. I'm ruling nothing out. But feel free to keep chewing things over – you never know what inspiration may strike. Meanwhile, on to the next."

*

"So, you see, when you've got incoming fire, what you must never do is give the other johnnie an easy target." Lewis Muskett was still holding court at the bar, this time to a group of three businessmen whose eyes seemed to be glazing over in unison. "Now General Montgomery, he knew a thing or two, and what he used to say was ..."

"I do apologise for butting in, sir," said Constable, "but we wanted a further word with you, and since you're on the subject of military history, it seems a perfect opportunity."

"Oh, join the party by all means," said Muskett expansively. "I was just telling these chaps ..."

"It's rather more a matter of personal military history, sir. Perhaps it would be more convenient if we were to sit down." The inspector led the way to a group of club chairs in a bay window, as the businessmen signalled their thanks and ordered fresh drinks to celebrate their delivery from their ordeal.

"We've been having a chat with Lady Ellpuss," began Constable, "and she seems to be prone to some slight confusion concerning you, sir." He related the earlier conversation regarding the colonel, as the latter's eyes assumed a steadily more wary expression. "Now, I wonder if you can straighten things out for us."

"Of course I can," blustered Muskett. "No problem there, one officer to another, eh? This business about the Catering Corps – simple mistake - very easy to explain. Obviously the chap was thinking about a cousin of mine who was at Aldershot. Distant cousin, of course – much younger, d'you see – didn't really know

129

him. Nothing to do with me at all. Mind you, apparently, in photographs, he did look a bit like me – family resemblance, and all that, so perhaps that's why they're confused."

"That would certainly explain it very well, sir," said Constable. "But you must agree, it's still rather puzzling that there should be such an inconvenient gap in the records. I suppose that must happen from time to time, even in the best regulated organisations, and after all, the British Army is a pretty huge undertaking."

"Course it is, course it is," agreed Muskett eagerly. He pointed to a row of colourfully-banded ribbons adorning the breast of his jacket. "But you don't get these medals for nothing, you know. So you can see that I had no reason at all to worry about Lord Ellpuss and his Sunday rag."

*

"That was fun, sir," smiled Copper.

"Yes, sergeant," replied Constable, "and an object lesson in making sure that you keep your records up to date, and that all your notes in that little book are watertight."

"Tighter than a duck's whatnot, guv," said Copper contentedly. "Quiz me any time you like."

"Far too busy quizzing murder suspects to play games with you, young David," retorted the inspector, as the two made their way into Cutpurse Lane and headed for Mrs. Pocock's front door. "As far as I can see, the only guilty secrets in your past consist of a procession of young ladies who, for some unfathomable reason, fail to remain captivated by the Copper charm for longer than it takes to say 'emergency call-out'."

"I blame you for everything, guv," grinned the sergeant, "but it still doesn't get me anywhere."

"Well then, here's a treat for you. I'll stay in the background, and you can exercise your considerable talents to charm some more information out of the lovely Mrs. Pocock. In fact, it looks as if we've got the timing just right. Is that not the lady herself now?" Constable nodded towards Mrs. Pocock's house, where the owner could be seen letting herself in. The detectives speeded up and caught her on the doorstep.

"Mrs. Pocock," Copper hailed her cheerily. "I'm glad we've caught you at home. We wanted a quick word, if you have the time."

"Oh, sergeant, it's you." Mrs. Pocock seemed rather put out. "As you can see, I've only just come back. Oh yes, come in if you must. Let me take my coat off and put the shopping in the kitchen. You can go into the drawing room if you like." She disappeared along the hall towards the rear of the house.

"Now, what is it you want?" she asked on her return, seating herself in her customary chair to face Dave Copper, while Andy Constable remained standing just beyond her eye-line.

"We've been gathering a little more information about what happened last night, madam," continued Copper, "including a lengthy conversation with Lady Ellpuss."

"Oh, poor dear woman," interrupted Mrs. Pocock. "And I haven't had a moment yet to go round and express my condolences to her. I absolutely must do so. How is she taking it? She must be utterly prostrated with grief."

"Um … not so's you'd notice," said Copper. "I think Her Ladyship is holding up surprisingly well."

"She was always a strong woman."

"Well, she certainly seemed capable of expressing some strong views, Mrs. Pocock, particularly on the subject of some of the other members of the Board of Trustees."

"Really? What sort of views, sergeant?" A tone of reserve entered Mrs. Pocock's voice.

"I'm afraid she did mention the word 'fraud', madam. Oh, I believe she was speaking generally," continued Copper hastily, seeking to stem the sudden reaction from the other. "It was a question of behaviour and social graces, I think."

"Yes, well, she would say that, wouldn't she," retorted Mrs. Pocock, all trace of sympathy now vanished from her words. "Her and her much-trumpeted county up-bringing. She always looked down on everyone else. I'm sure if she'd been invited to a Buckingham Palace Garden Party, she would have criticised the catering. But for Lady Ellpuss to suggest that some of us are frauds is most offensive. Let me tell you, I happen to be a very good accountant, and Lord Ellpuss and I had a perfectly happy working relationship. In fact, I think it's fair to say that he relied on me for all the financial matters relating to C.A.S.H."

"As witness his request for you to provide a full list of cheques and donors for the meeting."

"Exactly, sergeant. And of course, I would be only too

131

delighted to prove that to you, except that I don't happen to have those records to hand immediately, and I'm not sure it would be appropriate, even if I did. Matters of confidentiality, you see. But I can assure you, everything balanced perfectly – I made quite sure of that."

"I believe Lady Ellpuss did mention that you were an accountant with Ladhill's Bookmakers at one time. No doubt that helped you to develop your skills."

"Perhaps, but I don't quite see the point of your question. The fact that I used to work for Ladhill's is no secret."

"No, no, I'm sure it isn't," said Copper. "I was just hoping that you might be able to shed a little light on something which has come into our possession." He fished from his pocket the betting slip, unfolded it, and passed it across.

Mrs. Pocock surveyed it for several moments, her face devoid of expression. "Yes, sergeant, that comes from Ladhill's. I must have seen thousands of those in my time. I can't see that there's anything unusual about it."

"It just seemed to me, madam, that what was unusual was the size of the sums being staked."

"I'm sure it's no crime to enjoy a little flutter from time to time," said Mrs. Pocock with a light laugh. She stood. "And now, if you will excuse me, sergeant, I have a great many things to do. And I really must go to see Lady Ellpuss – despite her rather disparaging words about me and my colleagues. Some of us," she concluded, "do have a sense of obligation."

*

"Left or right, guv?" enquired Copper as the detectives re-entered the main quad. "Grey or Scarlatti?"

"The lady said she might not stay around all day. We'll try her first."

"Righty-ho, guv – right it is."

"Concrete??" Donna Scarlatti's reaction to Constable's opening remark was a burst of incredulous laughter. "What on earth did he mean by that?" She frowned in a puzzled fashion.

"All I am doing," said the inspector, "is repeating a remark which Evan Ellpuss believed he overheard during a conversation between yourself and his father. 'Nothing was set in concrete yet' is the way he put it, I think."

"Oh, that!" Miss Scarlatti's brow cleared. "Oh, no, Mr.

132

Constable, that was perfectly innocent. Of course, it was all in the aftermath of what we'd been talking about at the Trust meeting, wasn't it? You see, as it happens, some members of my family have building interests – you've probably seen the signs along the roadsides. Very often it's just the foundations for motorways and flyovers, so not exactly the glamorous side of the business. But there were plans afoot to change all that."

"I don't quite see what that would have had to do with the Trust, madam."

"Absolutely everything, inspector. You see, what Mr. Ellpuss must have overheard was talk of a proposal concerning the possibility of tendering for the construction of some new buildings for the college, financed by the Trust's money. Which would have meant such a beneficial boost to the reputation of the family."

"As well it might, Miss Scarlatti. I can understand that."

"I'd invited Lord Ellpuss to my house to see the sort of work my family can produce. That was a family project, you see. And an impressive new science building would have enhanced everyone's prestige," continued Donna, warming to her theme. "Of course, the sums involved could be enormous, but I was very anxious to do whatever I could to help, and I said that I would ensure that my nephews who are in day-to-day control of the firm made Lord Ellpuss a very attractive offer – one that he'd find hard to resist. That's the beauty of family relationships – my nephews usually do as I suggest. But for some reason, Lord Ellpuss's reaction seemed very dubious, and he said he would make sure that the matter was thoroughly looked into."

"That all seems very clear, madam. I just hoped that your final conversation with Lord Ellpuss might have revealed some detail of which we were unaware." Constable turned to leave. "Oh, just one thing before I go, Miss Scarlatti. Was there some talk of you leaving the college precincts after the party last night?"

"No, inspector. I told you, I spent the night here last night. I haven't been off the premises."

"Obviously some sort of misunderstanding," said Constable easily. "Well, we'll keep you no longer. We'll see ourselves out." As the front door closed behind the detectives, a calculating look came into Donna Scarlatti's eyes, and she reached for the telephone.

133

"All very plausible, guv," remarked Copper, as the two trudged across the quad once again in the direction of the chapel.

"Oh, highly so," agreed his superior, "except for possibly one tiny inconsistency. I'm not quite sure how we square talk of a financial crisis within the Trust with talk of an expensive new building programme. Something is jangling quite loud bells in the back of my mind."

"It's the ecclesiastical influence," grinned Copper, as he pushed open the chapel door.

"Oh, inspector! Sergeant! I didn't expect to see you again so soon." The Reverend Grey looked up in surprise from his position on his knees in front of the altar, where he seemed to be hard at work imparting an impressive shine to an already gleaming memorial brass of a medieval knight set into the floor of the nave. He scrambled to his feet, wiped rather grubby hands on the front of his cassock, and advanced to meet the detectives. "Were you looking for me, or were you hoping for some sort of divine inspiration in your efforts?" He chuckled.

"Isn't that a rather risqué joke for a man of the cloth, Reverend?" commented Constable. "But yes, as it happens, we did want a further word with you, in the light of various pieces of information which have come our way."

"Ask away," said the chaplain. "My life is an open book."

"How pleasant to meet someone with nothing to hide, Reverend. Do you know, that's very rare in our profession. In yours too, I imagine. I would think that a lot of your time would be taken up with the business of confession. Being good for the soul, and all that."

"Oh no, inspector. You're thinking of our friendly rivals in the Catholic chapel at St. Ethelburga's College around the corner. Confession isn't really very big around here. We're not all that given to revelations."

"More's the pity," muttered Copper under his breath.

"Except the Book of, I assume," said Constable. "Number of the Beast, final judgement, and all that. Which reminds me, Reverend, that is an extremely fine wall painting you have in your crypt."

"Oh. You've seen that, have you?"

"Sergeant Copper and I were admiring it a little earlier,

sir. And it puts me in mind of something which you were heard talking to Lord Ellpuss about at the party which followed the Trust meeting. I think there was mention of a new discovery, and young Mr. Ellpuss had an inkling that it might be another painting here in the chapel. Was he right?"

Reverend Grey shook his head. "Sadly not, inspector. When the restoration of the chapel was carried out and the first painting was found, the archaeologists conducted a very thorough investigation, but concluded that there was nothing else concealed. But for a medievalist like myself, the one treasure is more than enough. It provides me with constant inspiration. I feel myself so much in tune with those who built this place."

"Really, sir?"

"Oh, indeed, inspector. The intellectual activity of the middle ages is fascinating," enthused the chaplain. "The philosophers investigating alternative religions, and the alchemists with their experiments. Did you know that the word 'science' wasn't used at all – they called it 'natural philosophy'. In fact, and here is a confession if you like, I have been tempted to dabble somewhat myself. I've set up a little laboratory down in the crypt, and I've attempted one or two of the recipes I found in an ancient *Grimoire* in the university library." He gave a little snort of mirth. "I haven't actually managed to turn lead into gold yet, though. The best I've managed is a rather neat little weed-killer which I use on my allotment out by the river. That's where I grow all the herbs for my concoctions, you see," he explained.

"And is that where the goat comes in?"

"The goat?" Reverend Grey seemed considerably taken aback at the question.

"Yes, sir, the goat. A goat has been mentioned. Have you any idea why?"

"Oh, *that* goat." The chaplain gave a nervous laugh. "Sorry, inspector, but I didn't quite understand you for a moment. Yes, as luck would have it, some friends in my congregation do keep a goat, which they graze on my allotment from time to time. I happen to be allergic to cow's milk, you see, so they let me have the goat's milk in exchange. Nothing strange about it at all." He laughed again. "So, was there anything else, gentlemen?"

"I don't believe so at this stage, sir," said Constable. "Oh, speaking of stages, did I hear aright that you sometimes hold

135

concerts here in the chapel?"

"Concerts?" Reverend Grey seemed baffled. "The occasional choir recital, but I'm not sure you could actually call them concerts. Why do you ask?"

"Oh, it was just some remark that was made about the possibility of Ozzy Osbourne coming to sing here, sir." A blank look was the chaplain's reaction. "He's a singer, sir, with what I believe is known in judicial circles as 'a popular beat combo' – quite a famous one."

"Sorry, inspector," smiled the chaplain. "I know nothing about pop culture. Sorry I can't help you there. But do please come back if there's anything else you require."

"I'd like to do that, Reverend. I'd be quite keen to take a closer look at your famous fresco, but perhaps next time I'll bring a torch. Those black candles in your crypt don't give out a great deal of light, do they?"

"Those? No, you're right, inspector, but they were simply ordered by mistake. One of the many things on my to-do list." Continuing to smile, the Reverend Grey escorted the detectives to the door, closed it behind them, and then leaned against it with a huge sigh.

*

"Listen to that." Andy Constable halted unexpectedly as he and Dave Copper entered the small private quadrangle, and stood stock still.

The sergeant obediently cocked an ear to his surroundings. "What, guv?" he said, after a few seconds' pause. "Can't hear a thing."

"That's just it. Not a sound. No people, no traffic, no aircraft, nothing. Not a hint of the twenty-first century. These walls shut it out completely. We might as well be standing here when this place was first built, four or five hundred years ago. Just soak up that atmosphere."

"Take your point, guv," replied Copper. "Love to and all that, but my problem is that this atmosphere is starting to freeze the end of my nose off. Isn't there any chance we could absorb some historical atmosphere indoors, where I stand less chance of developing frostbite?"

"You have no soul," growled Constable, but nevertheless made for the front door of the Vice-Chancellor's House, where he

136

delivered a resounding knock. After a few moments, Professor Plump stood again in the doorway.

"There have been a few questions thrown up during the course of our investigations, sir," began the inspector, ensconced once again in the professor's sitting room. "And there have been suggestions that, shall we say, not everyone and everything are as they seem."

"I'm afraid I don't follow you, Mr. Constable. What exactly are you driving at?"

"Well, let me illustrate it with a particular instance. We know you took a telephone call from America, and you were kind enough to relate the gist of its contents to us. But that conversation was in part overheard by another person, and seems to have had an entirely different meaning. And at the end of it, we were told of a certain discomfort in your demeanour - one might almost say furtiveness. I'm troubled by the inconsistency, sir."

"Lady Ellpuss!" exploded Professor Plump. "I knew that blasted woman was snooping! Pretending she had business in the study while I was engaged in a private conversation." The professor was beginning to sound monumentally offended. "Let me tell you, inspector, that it is outrageous for Lady Ellpuss to suggest that I have anything to hide. I have had a long and distinguished career in academic administration, and for you to imply otherwise is utterly intolerable!"

"The implication doesn't come from us, sir," Constable pointed out. "We're merely seeking to clarify a few points."

"Of course, I have never actually taught," said Plump, calming down a little, "and my title of 'Professor' is an honorary one, but my qualifications are impeccable."

"I did notice that you have quite an impressive selection of diplomas and certificates," said Constable, rising and strolling across the room to examine the framed documents on the wall. Behind him, the professor began to fidget. "And from some pretty far-flung institutions. 'The English Academy of Dhaka'," he read, "'Institut Internationale Anglophone de la Republique Malagache', 'British University of the Federation of Micronesia' – very impressive indeed, sir." He scanned the display once more. "I don't see anything from the Collegiate University of Gary, professor – do you not have some sort of a link with them?" He turned to face the professor with a bland smile.

Edwin Plump cleared his throat. "Ah, yes, as it happens, inspector, my first degree was awarded by an American establishment, but with the passage of time, one forgets details so easily. But as you can see, I have had relationships with colleges all over the world since then – Nigeria, India, Romania – all of them perfectly respectable institutions."

"And after all those travels, your journey has finally come to an end amongst the ancient traditions of Camford. Come home to roost, as one might say."

Professor Plump looked uncomfortable. "I suppose you might say that, inspector."

"Sorry if I'm being thick, guv," said Dave Copper, as the detectives slowly made their way back to the main quadrangle, "but I don't quite see what all that was about. If I had all those qualifications that he's got, I wouldn't be slogging my brains out behind a desk at the station as a humble sergeant."

"You're right there, Copper," smiled Andy Constable grimly. "You'd find yourself somewhere entirely different."

"So what now, guv? Back to the station to chew over what we've got?"

"I've got quite a few thoughts swirling about at the moment, but I can't say they're forming a completely coherent pattern yet," said Constable. "Although some of the fog is starting to clear. I just need a little while on my own in a darkened room. But I suppose we ought to check in with Lady Ellpuss before we go, just to say goodbye as a matter of courtesy."

The door to the Master's House was opened once again by Eileen Maggs. "Oh, you've just missed them both," she said in response to the detectives' enquiry. "Master Evan's gone off to that bar where he meets all his friends, for a good gossip no doubt, and Lady Ellpuss has gone out to buy a new hat."

"A hat?" echoed Dave Copper, bewildered.

"For the funeral, sir," explained Eileen with a disapproving downturn to her mouth. "Said she didn't have a thing to wear that was suitable to go with her black Russian sable coat. She likes to be well prepared for everything, does Her Ladyship. And look at me, keeping you talking on the doorstep, and you both look absolutely perished. Come in and have a cup of tea in the kitchen."

"That is an offer nobody could refuse," said Constable, and followed the housekeeper as she bustled towards her domain at the rear of the house.

As the detectives began to thaw in the copper-gleaming warmth of the kitchen, a thought occurred to Andy Constable. "Mrs Maggs," he ventured, as she placed a steaming mug before each of the officers, "do you suppose I could take this through to your dining room? I'd like to have another look around in there, if I may."

"I don't see why not, inspector," she replied. "If I know Her Ladyship, she won't waste the opportunity to play the tragic widow for all she's worth in every shop in town, and as for Master Evan, I'll expect him when I see him. I don't know if you'll find whatever it is you're looking for, because I've been in there and put everything to rights, but you go ahead and help yourself."

"Do you want me too, sir?" asked Copper.

"No, you stay where you are. I dare say Mrs. Maggs can bring you up to date with any of the local gossip we've missed."

"Away with you. As if I'd do such a thing," protested Mrs. Maggs, but there was a twinkle in her eye which indicated that the inspector's prediction might not be so very far from the truth.

After some thirty minutes, fortified by two mugs of impressively strong tea and a pair of home-made buns to accompany them, Dave Copper began to wonder as to the whereabouts of his superior. Entering the dining room, lit only by the modest glow of a single table-lamp in the gathering gloom of the afternoon light, already beginning to fade, Copper found his colleague seated in a carver chair at the head of the dining table, his eyes closed, his tea gone cold at his right hand.

Copper cleared his throat. "Only me, guv. It's a bit dark in here, isn't it? Do you want a bit more illumination?" He reached for the light switch.

Constable opened his eyes and smiled slowly. "Do you know, sergeant, I really think that I have just about enough."

Copper recognised the expression on the inspector's face. "You're not talking about the light level at all, are you, sir? You've done that thinking-things-through thing of yours again, haven't you?"

"I have."

"And I don't need to ask what you want next, do I, sir?"

139

"Probably not, sergeant." Constable got to his feet, and his manner became immediately brisker. "But let's go through it anyway. No time like the present, no place like here. I don't suppose Lady Ellpuss will object if, in their absence, we use her dining room."

"The *locus in quo*, sir, as you were no doubt about to say," grinned Copper.

"I can see that you are intending to drive me mad, quoting that against me at every opportunity," replied the inspector with a smile. "But yes, exactly that. So, off you go – round up our group of party guests, and tell them I'd like a further word with each of them here in, say, thirty minutes. With a bit of luck, none of them will have gone far. Don't take no for an answer. And let them believe I want a one-to-one - don't let on to them that everyone's invited to the party. We'll keep that as a little surprise for when they arrive. Off you go."

Without another word, Copper headed off on his mission.

*

Andy Constable entered the dining room, to find a group of people seated in silence around the dining table, under the watchful eye of Dave Copper. Six faces viewed him with varying degrees of puzzlement and apprehension.

"I still don't see, inspector, why you have called us here in this fashion." Professor Plump seemed to have elected himself spokesman for the group. "Your sergeant asks me if I can spare a moment to speak to you, but gives no clear reason as to why. Then when I arrive here, I discover that you have summoned all these other people as well, and again your sergeant declines to provide any explanation of what is going on. Why all this secrecy?"

"Secrecy," mused Constable. "Do you know, professor, that is an excellent choice of words. In fact, secrecy is at the heart of this whole matter. Because each of the people seated around this table has a secret which, if exposed in a sensationalist Sunday newspaper, could ruin their reputation, or worse. They may have hoped to conceal these secrets, but some secrets are not to be hidden so easily."

The level of unease around the table increased palpably, and sidelong glances were exchanged.

"And since the professor chose to speak up," continued

140

the inspector, "why don't I begin with him? The position he holds is a very lofty one – he is a thoroughly respected academic in a thoroughly respected institution. But there is such a concept as too much of a good thing, and that highly impressive and highly colourful array of certificates displayed on his wall made me wonder just a little. That, put together with a letter which came accidentally into our possession, from an overseas college of which I personally have never heard, couched in rather oblique terms on the subject of qualifications, made me wonder a little more. And I have no evidence at all for my supposition, but what if Mr. Plump's career were based on the fact that his first dubious qualification was not earned, but purchased from an extremely dubious foreign establishment? What would be wrong with a good old-fashioned British degree? Or perhaps the alleged professor does not have one. Could he not succeed in getting a degree in the U.K.? Why might somebody fail their exams? Incompetence? Cheating?"

Edwin Plump had grown steadily redder in the face as Constable had proceeded. Now he rose to his feet, quivering with emotion. "Inspector, this is intolerable. You do not have the slightest justification for these ludicrous assertions."

"Not at the moment, sir. You're absolutely right. Everything I have said is the wildest speculation. How fortunate then that my sergeant here enjoys nothing more than conducting a little research on the internet. And when we return to the station, I have no doubt that some further investigation will reveal the truth. I imagine you'll be quite happy with that arrangement, sir?" Constable held Plump's eyes steadily, as the latter slowly subsided into his seat.

The inspector turned to the woman seated alongside Edwin Plump. He smiled in a friendly fashion. "Do you know, when I first heard the name Scarlatti, I couldn't place it. I knew it rang a bell, but it was too far in the back of my mind, and certainly nothing to do with this university. Obviously just a coincidence, I thought. Then suddenly, a little earlier, as I was sitting quietly, something clicked. I'm sure you all have instances where you are trying desperately to remember something, and then, when you're thinking about something entirely different, it comes to you unbidden. And this afternoon, for no absolutely no reason, I suddenly remembered a case which was in the headlines

141

when I had only just joined the C.I.D., younger even than Sergeant Copper here.

"I think, Miss Scarlatti, that it was the fact that in our conversations, you so often referred to your family. The word was obviously circulating in my brain. And, all unexpectedly, the thought popped up, what if she is spelling that with a capital F? What if she is related to the infamous Don Luigi Scarlatti, the head of one of the most notorious crime families in Sicily, who was eventually captured and imprisoned some years ago? The case became extremely celebrated, particularly because there was considerable mystery over who had assumed control of his organisation. So again, I speculate without a single shred of evidence, but remembering Miss Scarlatti's remark that her nephews usually do what she suggests, I simply wondered if perhaps the lady might be the heir, perhaps the granddaughter, of the notorious don. And if that were so, and the facts somehow became known to Lord Ellpuss, the news story which that would fuel might have had spectacular benefits to his newspaper's circulation."

Miss Scarlatti displayed not a flicker of emotion. "I really think, inspector, that you should be very careful what you say," she said calmly. "My family has access to some extremely talented lawyers."

Constable declined to be intimidated. "I'm sure they have, Miss Scarlatti. In fact, I should be highly surprised if they hadn't. So perhaps I should have prefixed my remarks with an all-embracing 'allegedly'." His voice hardened. "But the sort of activities such organisations specialise in are often best conducted in the dark, and we in the police have some very powerful spotlights. Which we may well now employ. Just a piece of friendly advice, you understand."

The Reverend Grey was beginning to squirm with discomfort, even before the inspector's attention fell on him. "I really hope this isn't going to take very much longer, Mr. Constable. My time is not unlimited, you know, and I do have services to prepare for."

"I have no doubt that you do, Reverend," replied Constable. "And in fact, the services which you conduct in your chapel would, I am sure, have been of great interest to Lord Ellpuss. We have heard from Evan Ellpuss of hints of some kind of revelation regarding the college chapel, and you yourself have told us of your fondness for unconventional medieval practices. So I think we have a number of very interesting jigsaw pieces which, when put together, provide a fascinating picture. And speaking of pictures, all in the context of an extremely graphic fresco of the last judgement of sinners, we have the black candles on the altar in your crypt – the fact that some of your friends keep a goat, the mention of which caused Lord Ellpuss considerable mirth – His Lordship's reference to 'the naked truth' – and an advertisement which my charmingly innocent sergeant here took to refer to a forthcoming performance by rock band Black Sabbath, lead singer Ozzy Osbourne. I don't believe that particular group will be appearing in your chapel any time soon, Reverend – but I have a strong suspicion that you and your acolytes might well be enjoying the celebration of your own Black Sabbath."

The chaplain clutched at the chain around his neck as if seeking reassurance. "There's not a word of truth in it," he protested. "My friends and I, we were simply dabbling in historical theory – it's harmless research into medieval popular belief, that's all – surely you couldn't think that I ..." His voice died away under the astonished gaze of all those seated around the table.

"Ah, but it's not what I think that matters, is it, Reverend?" explained Constable. "It's what Lord Ellpuss believed. And with a journalist skilled in innuendo, the sort which thrives on the staff of the 'Splash', putting the above elements together, it is clear that here is a front page story beyond the wildest dreams of most newspaper proprietors. The scandal would have been immense. You might even have ended up being unfrocked – that is to hope that there is not even more to discover, and to assume that you were actually frocked in the first place."

Andy Constable took a deep breath, and moved on to the individual sitting across the table from the chaplain. "And so we come on to you, sir. Colonel Lewis Muskett, D.F.C., Retired. A pillar of the community, and a man with a military anecdote for every occasion. Oh dear, oh dear, sir. You weren't very good at this, were you? Because although Lord Ellpuss may have been initially deceived by your self-generated reputation locally, his wife with her family military connections was not, and I imagine she would have been happy to point out the truth to her husband. And it's not as if you didn't make it easy for her. Even the most amateur impostor ought to know that army colonels do not normally get decorated with the D.F.C. - the Distinguished Flying Cross. So perhaps you should have stuck to peeling spuds at Aldershot."

Muskett seemed about to protest but, crimson with embarrassment, instead subsided in his seat, eyes flicking from side to side, harrumphing ineffectually and muttering under his breath.

"Mrs. Wright." Constable looked at the glamorous woman seated alongside Muskett, her head held high, her eyes sparkling, a coat with a deep white fur collar thrown back from around her shoulders. He smiled broadly. "Lady Mayoress, I suppose I should say. Mrs. Wright, I have to say, speaking in a strictly personal capacity, I like you very much." The inspector was conscious of a barrage of curious stares from around the table. "And I get the impression that so did Lord Ellpuss."

"He was a sweet old boy," agreed Mrs Wright. "And I've never been afraid of gossip. Goodness knows, there was enough of it when my two husbands died suddenly, but they held a post-mortem on both of them, thank goodness, and both of them were proved to be natural. That should have been enough to silence the wagging tongues, but you know how unpleasant some people can be." She cast an accusing look at her companions. "But people can say what they like – I plan on carrying on in my own sweet way."

"I wish every suspect in every case I have to investigate were like you." Constable could not prevent himself chuckling. "And the reason for that is that, although I spoke earlier of secrets, you are a woman whose secret is that you do not appear to care whether you have any secrets at all. Your life is an open book – in fact, if I might suggest, if you were to turn it into a book, you could very possibly end up with a best-seller. Perhaps entitled 'Fifty ...' - well, I'll leave the choice of title to you. And as you told us, Lord Ellpuss knew all about your history, and was highly amused by it. In fact, if the possibility of becoming an author doesn't appeal to you, a woman with as many men in her past as you seem to have had would probably stand more chance of getting her own television talk show series than being shamed in the Sunday papers. The loss of a powerful friend like Lord

Ellpuss has dimmed rather than improved your prospects."

Mrs. Wright shrugged philosophically. "A girl can always make her way, Mr. Constable," she twinkled roguishly. "Watch this space."

"Which brings us to our final person, Mrs. Pocock," said the inspector. "Ostensibly one of the most responsible here, since she is charged with handling considerable amounts of money as Financial Secretary to the Trust. An honorary position, she helpfully informed us – one which carries no salary. Here again, we had to assemble a jigsaw puzzle of various small pieces of information. There was a snippet of overheard conversation which seemed to relate to horse-racing. That went hand-in-hand with the fortunate discovery of a discarded losing betting slip for a very large stake – an anonymous slip, it is true, but the holder of account 'EP108' was not hard to guess, and could be easily confirmed with the firm of bookmakers concerned. And with no income to finance the losses of what is evidently a significant gambling habit, what better way to fund the activity than a constant supply of cheques made out to Camford Academy Strategic Holdings – or, as it is so often referred to, C.A.S.H.?"

Mrs. Pocock looked haughtily at Andy Constable. "Well, inspector, you seem to have made a very successful job of intruding into the private life of each of us. I'm sure that all of us are appropriately embarrassed. But I cannot see that all of this has brought you any closer to identifying whoever was responsible for Lord Ellpuss's murder."

"Oh, I think I know that very clearly," responded the inspector. "And I'm sorry to have to say that the person who was the means of the death of His Lordship was in fact you, Reverend Grey."

"Me?" The chaplain goggled with incredulity. "Inspector, you don't know what you're saying. As if I could possibly have killed Lord Ellpuss ... I'm a man of peace ... I could never ..."

"Relax, sir." Constable cut short Reverend Grey's expostulations. "I am not accusing you of being a murderer. But I do say that you provided the means whereby His Lordship was poisoned. That little bottle which we found in your crypt when we went visiting, the week-killer labelled 'Grey's Eliminator', is my short-priced favourite as the culprit. Our lab will soon confirm my guess. But did you administer it? No, I don't think so.

145

"Granted, you and the others here all had a secret and, as Mrs. Pocock pointed out, each of you could be considerably embarrassed, with careers or reputations put in jeopardy. But for one of you, the risk was more immediate – prison. Because that is where a person convicted for fraud will usually end up. And as Mrs. Pocock is only too well aware, she has perpetrated a monumental fraud, and was on the brink of discovery. Clearly, by some means or another, Lord Ellpuss had stumbled on the truth. We can only speculate how – perhaps a conversation with one of his many wealthy contacts concerning a donation which had somehow never reached its intended destination. But for whatever reason, Lord Ellpuss had demanded that an account of the Trust's funds be made available for the meeting, and Mrs. Pocock was simply unable to provide this. Perhaps she managed to stave off the reckoning at the meeting by some sort of obfuscation as a delaying tactic, but this was only temporary. Judging by Lord Ellpuss's words after the meeting, the story was about to reach the media, and therefore the police. She was doomed, and she had to act quickly after His Lordship started to drop ever broader hints at the party.

"We are told that everybody knew about the Reverend Grey's little scientific experiments in the chapel crypt. He was obviously proud of his weed-killer – he was perfectly happy to tell us about it. I imagine that Mrs. Pocock was also aware of it, and believed that it might provide a solution to her problem. We know that at some point she slipped out of the party, since she was seen in the vicinity of the chapel by the college gatekeeper. I'm guessing that she made her way to the crypt and quickly helped herself to some of the week-killer, which she poured into the smallest of the various ornamental glass bottles to hand. Concealing this about her person, she returned to the party and added the poison to her own glass of sherry. She then entered into conversation with Lord Ellpuss and, with a sudden clumsy gesture, contrived to spill His Lordship's drink so that she could replace it with her own glass containing the poisoned draught. That was the point at which everyone else in the room was witness to a murder." A muted collective gasp greeted his words. "And then all Mrs. Pocock could do was wait, and hope that her plan would work. And tragically, it did."

All eyes fell on Elizabeth Pocock. "I was so sick of people

146

looking down on me," she said quietly, almost reflectively. "Particularly Lord Ellpuss, and that viperish wife of his. He was quite content to use my abilities with figures, but she never liked me, and she never took the trouble to conceal the fact. And when my husband died, I was left very badly off – his pension died with him, and I would have lost my house, my position, everything. I hoped I could make my way by gambling – that was the start. But of course, only a fool relies on beating the odds – I should have known that from my previous job - but I was a fool. I and my money were soon parted. I was drawn steadily deeper. So I thought, those people with everything won't miss a little of so much, and with my easy access to the C.A.S.H. Funds, the temptation was simply too great. And then when I was faced with discovery and utter humiliation ..." She took a deep breath and turned to Constable. "Oh, inspector, I'm sure all this isn't necessary. Can't we just get it over with?"

Constable took a decision and addressed the group seated at the table. "Ladies and gentlemen, I don't think that I need to keep any of you any longer. I'm sure that you all have some thinking to do, and perhaps in some cases some phone calls to make or letters to write. You are all free to leave." He held the door open in an unmistakeable indication of dismissal, and those present rose uncertainly and, each seeking to avoid the gaze of the others, sidled from the room The front door closed behind them. In the ensuing silence, Constable nodded to Sergeant Copper.

"Elizabeth Pocock, I am arresting you on suspicion of the murder of Lord Ellpuss." While the sergeant recited the customary formula, the inspector watched through the window at the dispersal of the departing group, observing that fresh heavy snow was falling on the quadrangle outside and beginning to blot out many of the traces of the day's activities.

As Copper completed the formalities, the front door was heard to open again, accompanied by a ringing cry of "Eileen, I'm back. Tea, please, I think," and Lady Ellpuss appeared in the dining room doorway.

"Oh. Inspector, I didn't expect to find you here."

"I'm afraid we took advantage of your absence to make use of your house, Lady Ellpuss," explained Constable. "I hope you don't mind. Copper, would you please take Mrs. Pocock out to the

147

car, while I have a word with Her Ladyship to explain matters. Perhaps we could go and sit down in the other room, madam," he suggested. "And under the circumstances, I think a cup of tea is a very good idea."

*   *   *

SET FOR MURDER

It was a dark and stormy night. The shrilling of the telephone bell on the cabinet alongside his bed drew Detective Inspector Constable from a heavy slumber. He opened his eyes. Pitch black. He rolled over and lifted the receiver from its cradle.

"Hello. Yes?"

"Sorry to bother you at this hour, sir," came the voice of Detective Sergeant David Copper, "but I'm afraid we're wanted."

"What, now?"

"Yes, sir. Sorry, sir, but it was a special request. Something's happened at the film studios, and there are important people involved, so the Chief Constable says …"

"You can tell me all the details when you see me. Give me ten minutes to get dressed."

"Oh. Right." Copper sounded slightly disconcerted. "Sorry, sir, didn't realise you'd gone to bed. But there'll be a car on its way in just a sec. I'll explain everything then."

It was barely ten minutes later that the brisk rap sounded at the front door. Inspector Constable, already alerted by the sound of the approaching police car's bell, opened it to reveal a rather damp Sergeant Copper, trilby in hand, standing in the rain on the doorstep. At the kerb, engine still running, a uniformed P.C. at the wheel, stood the regulation black police Wolseley. Andy Constable picked up his hat and shrugged his way into his raincoat. "Shall we go?"

Seated in the back of the car alongside his colleague, Constable focussed his thoughts. "So, what's this all about?"

Copper still seemed troubled at having disturbed his senior officer. "I'm really sorry for waking you up, guv'nor," he said, "but I didn't think you'd be asleep at eleven o'clock."

"Stop apologising, sergeant," replied Constable. "I wouldn't be normally, but there was nothing worth listening to on the wireless, so I thought I'd look through the arrangements for the King's visit next month. Nothing like a mountain of instructions from on high to start your eyelids drooping."

"I'd forgotten about the royal visit, sir."

"It's all part of the celebrations for this year's Silver Jubilee. The King and Queen will be honouring His Worship the Mayor by taking tea at the Town Hall, so there are all sorts of special arrangements in place."

"Queen Mary's coming to the Town Hall for tea? Blimey, the mayor had better keep an eye on his silver teaspoons!"

"Sergeant Copper," said Constable severely, "that remark is not remotely amusing. I will not have my officers repeating idle tittle-tattle and taking in vain the name of the Queen, who is a very gracious lady. Is that clearly understood?"

"Yes, sir. I'm sorry, sir."

"So I should think." After a few moments of uncomfortable silence, Constable relented. "Anyway, shall we return to the matter in hand? Where are we going?"

"The Spanner Film Studios at Larchwood, sir," replied a chastened Copper. "I gather there was some sort of event going on in connection with a film they've been making, and someone's been killed."

"And why does this necessitate you hauling me out of bed in the middle of the night?"

"According to the word from the top brass, sir, it's a very sensitive matter. There are some big names involved – film stars and so on. The Chief Constable hasn't seen fit to allow me into all his counsels, sir ..." Copper chanced a sideways grin. " ... but apparently you were thought to be the man for the job. I don't really know any more than that."

"I dare say we shall find out more shortly," said Constable, as the car swept through the brightly-lit arch, boldly emblazoned 'Spanner Films'.

Spanner Film Studios had been founded some fifteen years before, in a disused aircraft factory left over in the aftermath of the Great War. For most of the 1920s they had churned out a constant stream of two-reel comedies, but with the advent of talkies some six years ago, they had branched out into full-length feature films, and had found their own particular niche in the market, producing a series of spine-chillers with a gothic theme under the general title of 'Spanner House of Horror'.

Constable registered surprise as the car drew up at the steps to the front door of a slightly unexpected Regency manor house. "This doesn't look much like a film studio to me," he remarked.

"I think all the film stuff is behind the house, sir," explained Copper. "Apparently the house was requisitioned from

150

the owner during the War, and after he lost his only son in action, he didn't want to live here any more when the government handed it back, and the film company bought it."

As the two detectives emerged from the car into the lashing rain, the man sheltering under an umbrella at the head of the steps descended to meet them. He looked to be in his fifties, portly, with thinning dark hair greased back. "Thank you for coming so quickly, gentlemen," he said. Constable was not expecting the American accent. "This is a terrible business. Are you the man in charge?"

"It would appear so, sir. I'm Detective Inspector Constable, and this is my colleague Detective Sergeant Copper. And you are ...?"

"I'm Omar Gould, inspector. I'm the producer of this movie, although after what's happened tonight, I don't know if it will ever get to the screen."

"Suppose you tell us exactly what has happened, sir," suggested Constable. "At present, we're rather short of details, other than that there has been a death."

"You'd better come and see for yourself." Omar led the way through the house to the rear door of the hall, which opened on to a covered walkway which turned to pass through a stable yard and onwards to a group of two or three hangar-like buildings beyond. "These are our sound stages," he explained. "It happened in here, on Stage 13." He held open a metal door and motioned the detectives to pass through.

A pair of large sofas flanked the entrance, lying in semi-darkness. All the lighting in the cavernous space was directed towards the film set, a construction of rough-hewn stone walls dotted with burning torches, a flag-stoned floor, tiny barred windows with an eerie green light filtering through them, and pointed Gothic arches. Three film cameras were positioned at intervals across the front, with a folding wood-and-canvas chair marked 'Director' between two of them, while a large table stood out of the way against the studio wall to the left, laden with various medieval-looking items. Near it on the studio wall, and half concealed by the scenery, a board held a row of large electrical switches. Chains and shackles were affixed at various points around the set walls, while alongside a smouldering brazier was a stand containing an assortment of iron devices,

151

evidently instruments of torture, whose precise uses Constable preferred not to think about. To the right of the set stood the rack, its wheels gleaming in the atmospheric pool of light around it, incongruously fitted up as a bar with glasses and a selection of bottles. And in pride of place, in the centre of the rear wall, stood a monstrous contraption in the form of a female figure, over seven feet high, reminiscent of the Egyptian sarcophagi which Constable had seen in the British Museum. This device, however, was not made of wood, but of cast iron. The door stood open, revealing a fearsome array of spikes on its inner side and at the back of the interior. And sprawled on the floor in front of it, blood-soaked from innumerable piercings, lay the body of a woman.

"What the hell ..." muttered Constable. "Copper, you'd better take a look, just to be sure." A grim nod followed swiftly from the kneeling sergeant. The inspector spoke briskly. "Right, Copper, get back in touch with the station. Tell them we want the usual team as soon as they can – photographers, fingerprints, the works. Mr. Gould, is there a telephone the sergeant can use?"

"There's one in the front hall of the house."

"Leave it to me, sir," said Copper, and headed back towards the entrance.

"Do you know who the dead woman is, sir?" asked Constable.

"Oh yes," said Omar Gould. "It's Myra Marks."

"Myra Marks? Who's she?"

"Have you not heard of her, inspector?" Omar sounded surprised. "She's quite famous in our business. She's a journalist - gossip columnist with one of the daily newspapers. They call her 'The Iron Maiden of Fleet Street'." He shuddered. "It's a bizarre coincidence, isn't it?"

"I don't know what you mean, sir."

"Iron Maiden, inspector. That's the name of that device. The Iron Maiden of Nuremberg. A medieval instrument of execution. It's the real thing, too – we tracked one down and had it imported for the film, to add more authenticity."

"A little too authentic for my taste, sir."

Sergeant Copper reappeared at that moment, puffing slightly. "It's all in hand, sir. Everybody is on the way."

"Well done, sergeant. We can make a start."

"What about everyone else, inspector?" enquired Omar Gould.

"How do you mean, everyone else? Do you mean to say that there are more people involved?"

"The rest of the guests."

"Guests? What guests?"

"For the party."

Constable suppressed a sigh of exasperation. "Why don't you start at the beginning, Mr. Gould," he said, "and tell me exactly how this came about."

"We've been making a movie, inspector ...

"That much I'd gathered, sir."

"And tonight we were celebrating the end of shooting."

"What, she's been shot as well?" ejaculated Copper, aghast.

"No, sergeant," continued Omar. "The shooting of the film. We did the final scenes today – we actually managed to finish on schedule, for once."

"And what is this film, sir?" Copper produced a notebook and prepared to take details.

"It's a comedy horror movie entitled 'Love Me To Death'."

"Not much to laugh about in this situation, is there, sir?" retorted the unimpressed sergeant grimly.

"So what with the coincidence of today being February 14th," Omar pressed on, "I decided to celebrate the occasion by having a little St. Valentine's Day cocktail party here in the Chamber of Horrors set."

"And ended up with your own St. Valentine's Day massacre, by the look of it."

"That will do, sergeant." Constable took the reins. "As you point out, not really the occasion for levity. Mr. Gould, do carry on."

"It seemed quite an amusing idea at the time, inspector," said Omar defensively. "Just a small gathering - the stars of the movie, some of the team involved with the production, and one or two guests. And Myra Marks was one of the guests."

"Which brings us to the all-important question of how your party guest ended up lying dead on the floor, with lord knows how many stab wounds."

"We started at about nine o'clock," explained Omar, "and

people seemed to be enjoying themselves, talking and having a few drinks and so on ..."

"I noticed the bar, sir," said Constable. "I thought it looked a little out of place in a medieval dungeon."

"Everything was fine until about ten o'clock, when suddenly, all the lights went out. I thought it must be a power cut – we get those sometimes when the studios are all working at once, because it overloads the power supply. It's all the strong lighting, you see. Anyway, everyone was taken by surprise, and there was a lot of shouting and jostling in the dark, and there was what sounded like a door slamming. A few seconds after that, the lights went back on – they could only have been off for a minute, if that – and we all stood looking at one another, wondering what had happened. Then someone noticed that there was blood seeping out from the bottom of the door of the Iron Maiden. And when we opened it up, Myra's body just sort of slumped out." Omar looked pale at the recollection.

"And then, sir?"

"As you can imagine, inspector, there was a great deal of shock and surprise. Some of the women were screaming, and nobody seemed to know what to do, so I took control. I sent everyone to the dressing rooms off-set, and then I went through to telephone for the police."

"Which is where we came in, Mr. Gould. Very smart thinking, if I may say so, but then, I suppose as the producer, you would be the man in control, I assume. Am I right?"

"Yes, ultimately, inspector. Some people get confused between the role of producer and director when you're making a movie. As producer, my job is to put the whole deal together and get the money in place."

"And Myra Marks would have fitted into this picture how, exactly?"

"She was great for helping you to make contacts. Being a journalist, there was nobody she didn't know in this business, and sometimes she knew one or two things which, shall we say, helped me to persuade a few reluctant backers to put their cash into a film. But where's the harm in that?"

"I see – a little gentle coercion to help you along the way, eh?"

"I don't know that I'd put it as strongly as that, inspector.

But I will certainly miss her influence, if that's what you mean."

"Of course, a critic can have influence which might harm your interests as well as benefit them, sir," observed Constable. "But I think we can leave speculation of that sort to one side for the moment. At present, I'm more concerned with these other people that you've mentioned. Who would they be?"

"Perhaps you'd better come and meet them for yourself," said Omar, sounding slightly relieved that the conversation had turned away from what might have been a sensitive topic. "They're through here in the dressing rooms." He led the way through an arch at the rear of the set.

*

Behind the scenery, the detectives received their first lesson about the illusory world of the cinema. What had appeared from the front to be solid ancient masonry was revealed to be nothing more than a flimsy construction of plywood and battens, held up with a ramshackle arrangement of timbers, braces, and weights. Electrical cables snaked across the floor. An odd jumble of ladders, spotlight bases, dusty tapestries, a throne, and what appeared to be the funnel of a Mississippi riverboat leaned against one wall. Omar turned left and opened a door in the rear wall of the building, concealed by the scenery, which gave on to a corridor with several doors off it. "I suppose you'd better meet our leading lady first." He tapped on the first door and, in response to a gracious 'Come in', held it back so that the detectives could enter.

"Please, Omar, no autograph hunters – I'm far too upset." The words came from a woman apparently in her middle years, wrapped in an oriental silk robe in crimson and gold and reclining upon an opulent brocade chaise longue, a cocktail glass in her hand. Strands of dark hair peeped from beneath a gold lamé turban – a chiffon scarf in a matching colour was draped about her neck. The complexion was a flawless pale cream, the eyes heavily kohl-lined, the lips scarlet. The effect could scarcely have been more theatrical.

"No, Gloria, it's nothing like that," Omar hastened to reassure the woman. "These gentlemen are from the police. They've come to find out what happened to Myra. This is Inspector Constable, and this is Sergeant Copper. Inspector, may I introduce you to ..."

155

"There's no need for an introduction, sir," interrupted Andy Constable. "I'm sure anyone who's ever been to the cinema would recognise Miss Gloria Mundy. And may I say that it's an honour to meet you, madam."

"Why, inspector, how very kind." Gloria extended a hand, its nails varnished to a deep purplish-red, its skin, the inspector noticed, not quite as youthful as the owner's face would have indicated. Constable was uncertain as to whether he was intended to shake the hand or kiss it – he compromised by taking it and executing an awkward sort of half bow. "It's always gratifying to meet an admirer. I suppose I shouldn't ask what was your favourite of all my films."

"Well, there have been so many, haven't there ...?" floundered Constable.

"I liked the one where you were the all-powerful ruler of that lost African kingdom," piped up Copper, coming to the rescue of his superior.

"Ah yes." Gloria sighed in reminiscence. "'*Her*' – that was certainly one of my triumphs. And then you must have seen me when I portrayed Victoria in '*What A Great Queen*'. Of course, those were in the days before sound came along. Acting was so much more of an art then. All in the eyes, you see, so that everyone could understand you, the world over. Not like this modern Tower of Babel where everyone is so obsessed by words."

"But you did win an academy award just recently, didn't you?" Constable recollected.

"Yes I did, inspector." Gloria bestowed a gratified smile on the detective. "How very sweet of you to mention it. Yes, it was as best supporting actress for playing The Queen of Spades in '*The Count at Monte Carlo*' – of course, only a minor rôle, but I believe I brought a certain grandeur to the character. A small thing, but mine own, as you might say."

"Sadly, Miss Mundy, we are here on rather more serious business. Much as I'm sure that Sergeant Copper and I would be delighted to hear about your career, it isn't really relevant to the death of Myra Marks."

"Ah, but that is just where you're wrong, inspector." Gloria became more animated as she sat up and directed her penetrating gaze towards her questioner. "Dear Myra has been following every step of my career. Of course, in her position, it is absolutely incumbent on her to keep up to date with everything that is going on in the film world and what all the major stars are involved with. Oh, not just the stars, of course – there is so much more to the film business, with all the various interests concerned. And that, I'm sure, is one of the main reasons she was here tonight – keeping abreast of events. Why, she was even taking an interest in this latest little film of mine." She smiled deprecatingly.

Constable became aware that Omar Gould was beginning to fidget in the background. "Mr. Gould, is there something worrying you?"

"I was just thinking, inspector," suggested Omar diffidently, "whether you might be wanting to speak to the other people who are waiting next door in the Green Room. They have been there for quite a while, and they'll surely be wondering what is happening. Only I wouldn't want you to miss out on anything they can tell you."

"That is a very good thought, Mr. Gould. The fresher the memories, the more reliable they usually are. Miss Mundy," Constable turned back to the actress, "I think we shall want to speak to you further, but for the moment, will you excuse us while we take some statements from your fellow guests."

"By all means, Mr. Constable." Gloria gestured grandly. "'*Go, go, seek some otherwhere*', as Queen Anne once put it." Her brow furrowed. "No, that's wrong. It was Queen Elizabeth, I'm sure. But you must carry on with your duty. I shall be here when you need me." The gracious inclination of her head was clearly a signal of dismissal, and her three visitors left the room as she reached for the conveniently-placed cocktail shaker at her elbow.

*

"My name is Lois Turner, and I play Georgia Mayle." The young woman seated on the sofa to the left of the door in the Green Room seemed eager to be the first to introduce herself.

Out in the corridor, Omar had consulted his watch nervously. "Do you suppose this will take long, inspector?" he had asked.

"Not really a question I can answer at this stage, Mr. Gould," Constable had replied. "It depends very much on how many people we have to talk to and what they can tell us."

157

"Well, you have the people in here, and of course there are our other stars. I don't want to keep them waiting longer than I must, because you must know how temperamental some of them can be."

"I can imagine, sir." Constable had thought for a moment. "Copper, I think it's best if we divide our forces. You find out who's in the Green Room and take some initial statements – then you can go and meet the investigation team from the station. I'll go with Mr. Gould and try to prevent any ruffled feathers. I will meet you back on the set shortly."

"Very good, sir." Copper had pushed open the Green Room door. Having introduced himself and laid out the situation to the group of people seated around the room, he opened his notebook.

"Yes, Miss Turner – do carry on. Is that a major rôle in the film?"

Lois giggled prettily as she shook her blonde head. "Oh goodness no, sergeant – I'm just a beginner. This is my first film, and it's such an honour for me to be appearing with a big star like Miss Mundy." She glanced adoringly at the young man seated alongside her. "And I never thought I'd have the chance to work under such a great director as Mr. Vail here. He's been so helpful and understanding. In fact, everyone on the film has been so nice to me. I can't think why movie people have such a reputation for back-biting."

"That's good to hear, Miss Turner," said Copper. "So you haven't had any difficulties with, say, adverse reviews in the press? From people like Myra Marks, for example?"

"Oh no, sergeant." Lois was wide-eyed. "Just the opposite. I hadn't met her before, and I was only introduced to her this evening, but she seemed to know who I was, and she'd promised to do an article about me in her column. We had quite a long talk – I suppose you might even call it an interview. And she was so interested in my past work when we spoke – isn't it awful that she's dead?"

"Indeed, miss." Copper moved on to the man alongside Lois. "So, can I come to you next, Mr. ... Vail, isn't it?"

"That's correct – Noah Vail. I'm sure the name's familiar to you, sergeant – after all, when it comes to directing movies, there aren't many names bigger than that."

"I'm sure I'll take your word for that, Mr. Vail." Copper did not sound wholly convinced.

"I know it may not sound very modest," continued Noah, "but in this business you have to push yourself all the time or you're finished. I'm sure everyone here knows that." He cast a look of appeal round the room.

"And your relationship with Myra Marks, sir? What can you tell me about that?"

"Oh, Myra's great." Noah sounded extremely enthusiastic, before recollection dawned that the woman under discussion was lying dead nearby. His face became serious. "Was, I mean. She always had a knack of finding the angle on a story which would make the best headlines." His enthusiasm reasserted itself. "And you know what helps to make a great movie? I'll tell you – great publicity. You know what they say, sergeant – there's no such thing as bad publicity."

"Hmmm. I think you may find, sir, that the sort of publicity you're likely to receive after tonight's incident will do you no good. But of course, that's not really our concern at the moment." Copper turned expectantly to the woman sitting in a chair next to Noah. "Madam?"

"Oh, pay no attention to Noah, sergeant," she commented. "He's forever letting his mouth run away with him. This is restrained – you should hear him on the studio floor. Anyway, you don't really want to hear what I think of Noah, do you? You'd rather know about me." She sat up a little straighter. Her dark hair, cut in a long finger-waved bob, swung across her face and she pushed it back with one hand. "Right. My name is Tamara Knight, I'm thirty-seven, single, and for my sins I'm the scriptwriter on this masterpiece."

Copper smiled at the cynicism evident in Tamara's words. "Not the finest work you've ever produced, then, miss?"

Tamara smiled in return. "Actually, I suppose I shouldn't complain. Work is work, and the pay isn't bad, and somehow or another, Omar has even managed to get some very good people in the cast. I expect that was why Myra was making a point of going around talking to everybody tonight."

"Yes, miss?"

"Oh, without a doubt, sergeant. The thing about Myra was, like her or loathe her, she was very good at her job. Even the

159

slightest sniff of a story, and she was like a dog with a bone. She would never let go. And she loved scandal."

"And how about you, miss? Did you like her or loathe her?"

"Me, sergeant? I didn't really care one way or the other," replied Tamara airily. "But I will say one thing – I'm glad she had nothing on me. I've seen her wreck so many careers."

"A woman with enemies, then?"

"I think we can all put two and two together," said Tamara. "Otherwise why would someone want to murder her?"

"Quite so, miss." Copper moved on to face the next man, a tall slim individual who looked to be in his forties, sitting subdued and unobtrusive in a corner of the room. "And you are?"

"Eustace – Eustace Potter," the man replied briefly.

"And your connection with the film, sir?"

"None at all, sergeant. I'm a private detective."

Copper raised his eyebrows in surprise. "So how come you're here tonight, sir? Is this something to do with security for the film company, or what?" he asked, slightly puzzled.

"No, I'm here as Myra's guest."

"You were a personal friend of Miss Marks, then, were you, sir? I didn't know. In which case, can I offer my condolences."

Eustace gave a small, almost silent laugh. "A very old friend, sergeant. In fact, I guess you could say I knew Myra better than anyone else. We first met about twenty-odd years ago. She was just starting out as a journalist, which in those days meant she had to be pretty determined in a business full of men, and I had a flair for finding out things about people which they'd rather keep hidden, so together we made a pretty good team."

"Professional colleagues, you're saying," Copper sought to clarify. "But I'm still not entirely clear as to what brought you here tonight."

"Myra insisted," replied Eustace. "I don't usually get to go to these showbiz parties, but Myra said there was something she needed help with tonight – something that was too good to miss – and she could be very persuasive, so I came along to give her what she wanted."

"Thank you, Mr. Potter. I think that will do for now, but I'll probably come back to you later to get more of a detailed idea of the events of the evening." Copper's eyes swept around the

160

room. "That goes for the rest of you ladies and gentlemen, of course. Which just leaves you, sir." His gaze fell on a small, somewhat rat-faced man whose age might be anywhere between forty and sixty, perched on a stool behind the door, whose clothing of plain white shirt and black trousers put him at odds with the smart cocktail dresses and suits of the others in the room. "And who might you be?"

"My name's Lyon, sergeant – I'm in charge of properties." The reply came in the distinctive accent of London's East End.

Copper did not at first grasp what was meant. "Sorry, sir – you mean you look after the studio buildings, or what?"

"No, not property – properties. Props. Set-dressing - all the bits and pieces that the actors handle when they're working. Books, candelabra, goblets, swords, torture instruments, all that sort of thing. There's a whole table-full out there on the set – you must have seen them."

Light dawned. "Indeed I did, sir. Thank you for the explanation, Mr. Lyon. Sorry, can I just make a note of your first name?"

"Ennio."

Copper blinked. "Come again?"

"Ennio, sergeant – E,N,N,I,O." Copper continued to look baffled. "It's an Italian name – my mother's grandfather was from Italy. Mother thought it was a good idea. It would make me stand out from the other kids." Ennio let out a bitter snort. "Well, it did that all right."

Making a note, Copper moved on. "And what were you doing here this evening, sir?"

"Working," came the brief response. "The great Omar wanted someone to act as a barman for his party, and I needed some extra money, so I said I'd do it."

"Which I assume led you into contact with Myra Marks?"

"That woman!" Ennio's sudden vehemence came as a surprise. "Yes, and not for the first time, either." There was obviously more to come. Copper waited patiently. "She'd been at the studios before when I've been working on other films. She'd stroll in like she owned the place, getting in everyone's way, holding things up. I remember once when we were in the middle of a session, she demanded an interview with one of the stars there and then because they were due to sail to America next day

161

on the *Berengaria* and she had a deadline to meet. And nobody ever said no because they were all too afraid of her. Not me! I saw her tonight, fiddling about with the things on my props table. She had hold of this really valuable dagger – it's a genuine antique, from Florence, you know - so I was straight over there and told her not to interfere. And she was so rude."

"Yes, sir?"

"She said to me, 'Don't be ridiculous. Interfering is what I do for a living.' Called me a silly little man. I tell you, if any of those bottles of poison of mine had been genuine, I might have been tempted to doctor her drinks." Ennio seemed to realise he was becoming carried away, and subsided. "Anyway, I didn't. Somebody beat me to it."

"As you say, Mr. Lyon." Copper closed his notebook with a snap. "And now, if you wouldn't mind staying put for the time being, ladies and gentlemen, I have to speak to my boss to see what he wants to do next." As he left the room, those remaining were exchanging looks, and as he closed the door he heard the voice of Tamara Knight saying "Well ..."

*

"'*Mr. Arthur Jefferson*'?" Constable paused to read the name beneath the silver star painted on the door in front of him. "Who's he? I've never heard of him."

"That's his real name," replied Omar, suppressing a smile. "He uses it when he's not actually appearing in public – it helps to keep away any unwanted attentions from fans. But I think you'll know him. Well, we'll see." He knocked on the door and, following a shouted 'Yes?', put his head round it.

"I've got the police here about Myra. Is it all right if we come in?"

"Sure," came the reply, and Omar gestured Constable to precede him into the room.

The man seated at the table in front of the mirror was unmistakeable. The hair sticking up in an uncontrollable tuft, the exaggeratedly-arched eyebrows, the long, slightly pasty face, seemingly born to wear a silly half-smile. A bowler hat sat on the table before him.

"Stan," said Omar, "this is Inspector Constable."

"Mr. Laurel! Good evening." Constable managed to contain his surprise, and even succeeded in advancing, hand

162

outstretched, with a passable display of nonchalance. "I'm sorry to disturb you, but I'm having to ask some questions about the death of Myra Marks."

"Of course, inspector. Go right ahead." The voice was familiar from a hundred comedy shorts. "Take a seat."

Constable gathered his slightly scattered wits. "I suppose the first thing I need to know, Mr. Laurel, is how you came to be at the scene of the crime?"

"It is a crime, then? Not some sort of horrible accident?"

"I'm afraid not, sir."

"I see. Well, it was all Ollie's fault."

"I beg your pardon, sir. You're blaming Mr. Hardy for Miss Marks' murder?"

"No, no, I mean that it's Ollie's fault that I'm here in the first place. You see, we were asked to do this film, and he said we should because there was no future in comedy and we should broaden our outlook. But then I said, if his outlook got any broader he wouldn't be able to get through a doorway, and he hit me. He does that a lot, you know, inspector."

"I thought that was all in fun, sir. You know, part of your comedy characters."

"That's because you don't know Ollie. Anyway, we agreed to do the movie, and here we are."

"I imagine a horror film would be something of a departure for you, sir. If I may ask, what sort of parts are you playing?"

"Ollie is Count Igor Blimey, who is the mysterious owner of the castle, and I play the hero, Willie Eckerslike. I'm supposed to be the main love interest, but I've only got a tiny part."

A thought struck Constable. "You keep mentioning Mr. Hardy, sir. Is he about, because obviously if he is, I'll be needing to talk to him as well."

"He isn't here, inspector," interrupted Omar. "He went back to his hotel before the business with Myra happened. He came over to me and said something about having a headache and that he was leaving. Personally, I think it was because he was afraid the bar might be starting to run dry, but he certainly couldn't have had anything to do with Myra's death."

"Thank you for that, Mr. Gould," said Constable. He reflected for a moment. "I've just had a thought, sir. You

163

mentioned 'other stars'. Would it be a good idea if you were to leave us alone here with Mr. Laurel and go and have a word with whoever-they-are, ask them if they wouldn't mind being patient for a little while longer, and tell them that I'll be in to see them shortly." The suggestion, although politely couched, was clearly more of an order.

"Oh. Yes, I'll go do that, inspector," responded the slightly disconcerted Omar. "Would you like me to wait in the Green Room once I've done that?"

"An excellent plan, sir." Constable smiled blandly and held the door open. Closing it behind Omar, he turned his attention back to Stan Laurel. "So then, Mr. Laurel, what can you tell me about Myra Marks' movements this evening?"

"I think she talked to just about everyone at some time or another," replied Stan readily. "I got talking to her because I thought she might be interested in doing a feature about my early career. I have some very funny stories about my act in the music halls in the north of England, especially the one about the chorus girl and the goat ..." He chuckled in recollection. "You see, what happened was, she was bending over ..."

Constable preferred not to be side-tracked by anecdotal reminiscences, however amusing. "If we can just stick to the events of this evening for the moment, sir. You were talking to Myra Marks ...?"

"And then, just in the middle of one of my best stories, she suddenly said she had to talk to someone else, and she rushed off."

"And who did she go and talk to?"

"That was Gloria Mundy. She was standing right behind me, and Myra grabbed a bottle of champagne from the props guy who happened to be passing – he was acting as the barman and waiter, you see – and Myra poured some into her own glass and then into Gloria's, and said something about 'needing a drink after tonight'."

"Did you happen to hear any more of their conversation, sir?"

Stan nodded emphatically. "I did, inspector. I wanted to know what was so much more important than me. Myra said to Gloria 'I've nearly finished that article, darling, and I bet you can't wait to read it'. And then Gloria said something about all her fans, and Myra said 'I've just got to add tonight's notes, and you're done. Your public will learn so much in next week's issue'. Then she got a notebook out of her bag and waved it in Gloria's face. And I thought, well, that's obviously why Myra's not interested in me tonight, because she's doing this thing on Gloria."

"And was that all?"

"Oh no, inspector," said Stan. "Myra hasn't been around this business for so long without learning how to deliver an exit line. She said to Gloria, 'At last everyone will appreciate the true value of your career. You'll never be forgotten, unlike some things'. And then she smiled and went off to talk to somebody else."

"Was that the last you saw of Miss Marks?"

Stan paused to consider. "No. I saw her talking to Noah Vail. He's our director," he explained in response to Constable's look of enquiry. "He was telling her about some new film he's going to direct for ParaMetro Studios later this year. He said he was meeting the studio bosses tomorrow, and she said 'Who isn't?'. I thought she sounded a bit triumphant about it, but I guess she would always have been on the lookout for important people to interview."

"Did she and this Mr. Vail seem friendly?"

Stan shrugged. "I don't know about that. Myra did say that she hoped Noah got on with ParaMetro better than he did with Omar for everyone's sake, and I heard her make some comment about 'a good deal at stake' and 'what percentage?'. I didn't really listen all that closely, because it was obviously about money, and I leave all that sort of thing to my agent. I remember Noah made some remark about what sounded like 'the cost of silents', and I can't think why, because nobody's made a silent movie for years."

"And was that the end of the conversation?" asked Constable.

"Almost," said Stan. "Myra said 'By the way, you'll never guess what I found in the pocket of your director's chair', and she patted her handbag, but then Ollie came over to say he was leaving, so I didn't hear any more."

"Was this the last you saw or heard of Myra Marks, sir?"

"I think so, inspector. I went out with Ollie to see him off the premises, and we were chatting for a while, and it was only a

165

few moments after I came back to the party that the lights went out ..."

"... and we know what happened at that point, sir," finished Constable. "So we'll leave it there for the time being."

"Will you want me any more, inspector?" enquired Stan. "I don't think there's anything else I can tell you, and Ollie and I have to leave early in the morning to catch the boat train to Southampton."

"Back to Hollywood, is it, sir? Ah, the glamour of the film star's life!" Constable smiled. "I think I'm happy to let you go, Mr. Laurel," he continued after a moment's thought. "We'll track you down if we need to." On this gnomic utterance he left the room, leaving Stan with a somewhat uncertain expression on his face.

*

As Constable emerged into the corridor he came face to face with Copper coming through the door from the studio.

"Everybody's just arrived, guv'nor," reported the sergeant. "The fingerprints people are going to start dusting everything once the photographer's finished, and the doctor's just about to take a look at the late lamented."

"Not lamented by everyone, evidently. I'm starting to get a few straws in the wind that the lady may not necessarily have been universally popular."

"Same here, sir. Just a few words here and there." Copper swiftly related the information he had gleaned from his interviews in the Green Room.

"So," said Constable, "with all that in mind, let's see if we can find out who took exception to Myra Marks. One thing I've discovered – she had a handbag."

"Which wasn't included in the bloody huddle on the floor, as far as I could see, sir."

"Yes, thank you for that picturesque description, Copper," replied Constable drily. "A little more respect for the dead, if you please. But let's see if we can track down her bag." He led the way back into the studio.

Amidst the hubbub of flashing bulbs and shouted instructions, a bespectacled middle-aged man was kneeling alongside the body of Myra Marks. "Ah, Inspector," he said, looking up as the two detectives approached. "In terms of picturesque corpses for me to study, you appear to have outdone

166

yourself on this occasion. I imagine you're not going to want my professional opinion as to cause of death?"

Constable allowed himself a small grim smile. "I'd be highly astonished if you were able to give us any surprises on that score, Doctor," he replied.

"Surprising as to the quantity of injuries, if not the nature – I've done an approximate count, and as far as I can see there are some fifty-two puncture wounds."

"That was quick work, Doc," said the admiring Copper.

"In my business we do not always have the luxury of leisure, sergeant," responded the doctor severely. He softened. "Not that, in this case, swift action would have been of much use to the victim. Death would have been immediate."

"And we know when it happened, down to the minute."

"In which case," sighed the doctor, rising to his feet and brushing off the knees of his trousers, "as you seem to have the how, the where and the when, I don't see that I can make much of a further contribution to your activities. If you would be good enough to have the lady sent down to my examination room, I will continue my work in the morning, and leave you to work out the who. If you will excuse me, I intend to resume my interrupted good night's sleep. Inspector – sergeant." With a brusque nod, he turned and strode towards the exit.

"Copper, we appear to have our orders," said Constable, watching the departing back. "If you would be good enough ..." He intoned, but then broke off with a chuckle. "Oh, dear lord! Look, organise the appropriate people to have the late Miss Marks taken away in the van, and if you can find a P.C. who can count that high, get them to verify the number of spikes on the inside of that Iron Maiden thing."

"Righty-ho, guv'nor," replied Copper. "Here, he's a bit of a card, that doc, isn't he?"

"And technically he outranks you, sergeant, so you'd better not let him hear you say it, true or not," said Constable. "And while you're doing that, I shall do what we started out to do, which is to find that missing handbag." He began to prowl around the studio.

Amidst the jumble of scenery behind the set, with its attendant miscellany of coils of rope, buckets, canvas bags of carpentry tools and discarded and broken light fittings, nothing

167

was to be found. An inspection of the table of props revealed a wide selection of weaponry, caskets of jewellery which Constable assumed to be imitation rather than the genuine article, pewter jugs and beakers alongside bottles containing dubious-looking fluids, and an ancient-looking leather-bound tome open at a page of incomprehensible arcane symbols. Heading towards the bar, the inspector noticed that the director's chair positioned between Cameras 2 and 3 had a saddlebag-like pouch over one arm holding various papers and a clipboard, but an examination revealed no sign of a handbag. Past Camera 1, the bar itself held only ranks of glasses and bottles, glinting innocently, while beneath it, amongst the chains and pulleys of the rack, lurked nothing more sinister than two cases of champagne and some empty bottles.

Copper returned to the inspector's side. "All sorted, sir," he reported cheerily. "Stretcher-bearers organised, spikes being counted as we speak. Any luck on the handbag front?"

"Nothing so far."

Copper looked around. "How about that one?" He gestured to a crocodile-skin handbag lying almost concealed by a cushion on one of the large sofas flanking the entry door from the covered walkway. The dark red leather merged almost perfectly with the maroon velvet of the upholstery. The sergeant smiled innocently.

Constable took a calming breath. "How very helpful of you to notice the one place I had not yet reached, Sergeant. What would I do without your assistance?"

"Glad to be of service, guv'nor. There's this new thing I read about in one of the papers called 'the power of positive thinking'. It's probably all mumbo-jumbo, but if it helps ..."

"Stop babbling, man. Open up the bag and see what's in it."

"Will do, sir." Copper took a seat on the sofa, opened the handbag, and began to examine its contents. "There's a letter, sir."

"So who's writing to Myra Marks?"

"Oh. That's interesting, sir. It isn't to her at all. It's addressed to Tamara Knight."

"What is she doing with a letter addressed to Tamara Knight?" Constable wondered. "Who is it from?"

"A firm Rees-Kay Publishers in Soho, sir. Ever heard of

them?"

"No. What do they say?"

"It says '*Dear Miss Knight, We are pleased to enclose our cheque in the sum of 100 guineas, made out to Cash as requested, being an advance payment in anticipation of sales of the recently-submitted manuscript of your latest book, 'The Lovely Lady's Chatter', to be published under your usual 'nom de plume'. A proof for your perusal and correction as required has been despatched under separate plain cover. We look forward to similar works of specialist fiction from your pen, and confidently expect substantial interest from our private clientèle of discerning gentlemen.*' And it's signed '*Yuri Pelling, Managing Editor*'."

"Now that, sergeant, is a very interesting piece of information."

"I'll say it is, sir. A hundred guineas! Do people really get paid that much for writing books?"

"I dare say some do, sergeant. It probably depends on whether the readers enjoy them. And what the critics say about them."

"So could that be what this is about, sir? Myra Marks was about to write some sort of review of Tamara's new book?" Copper took a second look at the letter. "Oh no, sir – it can't be. This letter's almost three years old. It's dated March 1932. So what's Myra doing with it?"

"We can't very well ask her, can we?" retorted Constable reasonably. "But perhaps Miss Knight will be able to throw some light on the matter. In the meantime, what else is in there?"

Copper burrowed. "Bits and pieces, sir – handkerchief, lipstick, and so on – purse with some money in it - and some keys." He held them up. "This bunch looks like house and car keys, sir."

"Which probably means there's a car somewhere outside. You can go and look for it in a minute. What about the other set?"

"Just one key on here, sir." The key was the simple type used in any ordinary internal door, on a large wooden fob reminiscent of those kept at a traditional hotel reception. It bore the legend 'Spanner Film Studios', with the letters G.M. hand-written on it. "Key to a dressing-room, do you suppose, sir?"

"A reasonable deduction, sergeant. Although why Myra Marks has someone's dressing room key is something of a

169

mystery. Anything else?"

The expression on Copper's face changed. "Only this, sir." He produced from the recesses of the bag, half-wrapped in a chiffon scarf, a small dagger. The blade gleamed dully, the hilt glinted with jewels. Although it was no larger than a toy, the blade appeared sharp and ended in a wicked point. "This is a bit of a turn-up, isn't it?"

"As you say. So what do we make of it?"

"Perhaps it's the actual murder weapon, sir." Copper began to sound excited as he held it out for Constable's inspection. "Maybe Myra Marks was actually stabbed with this, and the business with the Iron Maiden was some sort of ruse to put us off the scent."

"Hold your horses, sergeant," responded the inspector. "Let's not get carried away. For a start, as far as I can see, there's no blood on the blade or on that scarf, and as we know, there was quite a substantial amount of blood in evidence around the corpse. Secondly, don't you think somebody might have thought it a little suspicious if the murderer was seen lugging a dead body across the floor towards the Iron Maiden in the middle of a party?"

"Could have been done in the dark, sir," Copper defended his theory.

"I somehow think that using the Iron Maiden to conceal a simple stabbing is rather over-egging the omelette. What interests me more is what this knife is doing there in the first place."

"The props man said she was fiddling about with one, sir. Maybe Myra Marks got wind that she was in danger and wanted to protect herself. Or ..." Copper warmed to his theme. "Maybe she went to stab somebody else and got shoved into the Iron Maiden as a sort of pre-emptive strike."

Constable shook his head. "Sometimes your flights of fancy astonish me, sergeant. Wouldn't you think that using the Iron Maiden against an attacker would be a fairly spectacular form of self-defence? I'm sure there's a simpler explanation. But we'll let our forensic colleagues have a look at it anyway." Constable gestured to the bag. "That's the lot, is it?"

Copper looked carefully inside. "Seems to be, sir."

"What about that?" Constable pointed to a small scrap of

170

paper, partly tucked underneath the cushion, which had been hidden by the bag.

Copper retrieved the item. "It's a newspaper cutting, sir." He perused it. "Looks as if it's been torn out of Myra Marks' column. But there's only part of it here."

"Let me see." Constable held out his hand for the cutting. "Hmmm. Torn out, but not torn up, by the look of it. So there's obviously something about the contents that means something to somebody."

"So what does it say exactly, sir?"

"It seems to be the tail-end of the column, where Myra Marks was retailing snippets of gossip she'd picked up. There's something about '*two stage-hands and an electrician on the floor of the wardrobe department*'," he read. "I shudder to think what that was all about – and then it goes on to say '*Shhh! Which busty starlet is about to marry her childhood cowboy sweetheart, after being paid a fortune at Nineteenth Century Cox for a VERY unimpressive acting career – plus some other more private performances?*'."

Copper frowned. "Doesn't say who, though, does it, sir?"

"No," countered the inspector, "but I dare say anyone in the know would be able to pick up the hints."

"Tends to hit on the head that remark by Noah Vail about bad publicity, doesn't it," remarked the sergeant. "But there's more in that clipping, isn't there, sir?"

"Just a trailer – isn't that what they call them in the film business – about what was going to be in her next column. It says '*IN OUR NEXT ISSUE – New York ... Hollywood ... London ... Skid Row??? Where next for one of the biggest names in movies? Don't miss Myra Marks' latest shock revelations in next week's issue!*'. She didn't appear to hold back on the sensationalism, did she? Or the self-regard. Called herself '*Myra Marks – the star reporter the stars watch!*'."

"Strikes me she should have been watching out for herself a bit more," commented Copper.

"And you aren't wrong there, sergeant," agreed Constable. He thought briefly. "I'm just wondering what our next move ought to be."

The decision was taken out of his hands by a commotion coming from the direction of the door to the dressing rooms corridor. Through it burst a man in a tailcoat and striped trousers, his crinkled hair parted in the centre, with round spectacles gleaming above a large square and obviously false-looking moustache, and a cigar clamped firmly between his teeth. He was followed by an anxiously-trotting Omar Gould.

"Where's the man in charge?" barked the newcomer. "I demand to see the man in charge!" He confronted Constable. "Is that you? Are you the police captain around here?"

"This is Detective Inspector Constable," squirmed Omar. "Inspector, this is Mr. Groucho Marx."

"Don't be a fool, Omar – he knows who I am," grated Groucho. "Now, go away and produce something while I talk to the inspector so that I can get out of here." At a nod from Constable, Omar faded towards the dressing rooms with a look of relief. "Now, Mr. Constable, I'd like to know why I'm being held here."

"Not held, Mr. Marx," said Constable. "But I do need to ask everyone some questions about tonight's events."

"I don't see why," replied Groucho. "A child of five could solve this case." He looked about him at the surrounding ring of slightly stunned police officers. "Somebody fetch me a child of five!"

"I'm assuming, sir," said Constable, attempting to keep hold of the conversation, "that you're here because you have a part in this film."

"Of course. I play Serge B. Samovar, the lawyer. I suggested the name 'Serge' myself. What I was really hoping for was a new blue suit."

"This would be a comedy character, sir?"

"Certainly he's a comedy character – what did you expect? I always say, laugh and the world laughs with you. Cry, and you're probably watching this movie."

"Well, Mr. Marx, I'd be very grateful if you can help me out."

"By all means, inspector. Which way did you come in?" The eyes gleamed wickedly behind the glasses.

"And I'm sure posterity will thank you."

"Why should I do anything for posterity? What has posterity ever done for me?"

Constable gritted his teeth in the face of the increasingly

172

surreal nature of the conversation. "So tell me, Mr. Marx, were you by any chance related to the dead woman?"

"Myra Marks? No. The only relatives I have are my brothers Harpo, Chico, and Zeppo. And of course, the funniest one of all, my distant cousin Karl."

The inspector, conscious of the tightening circle of spectators around him and the rising volume of chuckles of mirth, glared at the attendant officers, who swiftly turned their attention back to their varying tasks in hand. He lowered his voice and drew Groucho to one side, attempting to inject a serious tone. "Did you see Miss Marks at the party this evening?"

"I certainly did. I saw her talking to that producer fellow, Omar Gould. Now there's a man with his finger on the pulse. At least, I think it was her pulse he was taking." Groucho's eyebrows rose and fell rapidly.

Constable pressed on grimly. "And did you hear anything of what was said?"

"I think they must have been talking about turning some novel into a movie, because Myra said something about 'things being taken from books', and Omar said this film will be worth a fortune. And they must have arranged for Omar to do an interview, because Myra said she was really looking forward to her piece."

"I see." Constable nodded thoughtfully. "Tell me, did you hear her speak to anyone else?"

"In a way, inspector, yes I did. You see, I was talking to Lois Turner." Groucho sighed. "Now there's a lovely girl. She reminds me of you." Constable looked startled. Beside him, Copper was unable to suppress a snort of amusement. "In fact, she reminds me more of you than you do."

"So what happened then?" enquired the inspector in a somewhat strained voice.

Groucho launched enthusiastically into his narrative. "Lois was telling me – by the way, have you noticed those great big baby blue eyes of hers – she was saying how she got this part, and how life is never easy for an *ingénue*, and how she was up against several much more experienced girls, and she had to do several auditions for the director, but in the end she was cast purely on merit and acting ability. Just then, Myra came up, and she'd obviously overheard Lois's words, because she said 'Of course you were, darling. I know that'. And then she leaned over and whispered something in Lois's ear."

"Did you manage to catch what it was, sir?"

"All I heard were the words 'Noah' and 'sack'. And then Myra said how she must get around to scheduling that article about Lois. Something like 'After that, nobody will be able to touch you', and then she said 'We'll talk later. Don't forget, darling, I hold the key to your future' and then she held up her purse."

"Was there anything else said?"

"No, not then, because Myra headed over to the bar to get another drink. I think she'd had quite a few already. Who'd have thought it – a journalist on the sauce! And I didn't see her after that."

Constable turned to his junior colleague. "I hope you've managed to make some useful notes from Mr. Marx' statement, sergeant," he said, one eyebrow raised quizzically.

"Oh yes, sir," replied Copper. He sounded dubious. "I think I've got everything that's relevant. That's as long as Mr. Marx is absolutely sure of what he's told us."

"Of course I'm sure," retorted Groucho. "Who are you going to believe – me, or your lying eyes? I've told you everything I know." He assumed an air of mock outrage. "Enough of this – I'm leaving!"

"Please, Mr. Marx," intervened Constable, "there's no need to leave in a huff."

"Alright." Groucho grinned and waggled his eyebrows again. "I'll leave in a minute and a huff! Now will someone please call me a cab?"

Copper couldn't stop himself. "Alright sir – you're a cab!" The ensuing silence was deafening.

"Sergeant Copper," said Constable in restrained tones which promised later retribution, "would you please escort Mr. Marx to the door and telephone for a taxi for him? Thank you for your help, sir – I'm very grateful. And while you are about it, sergeant, take these keys, see if you can find Myra Marks' car outside, and check whether there's anything of interest in it."

"Very good, sir," muttered Copper. He avoided meeting the inspector's eyes. "I'll be as quick as I can. If you'd like to come with me, Mr. Marx." He escorted Groucho to the door to the

174

exterior, which closed behind the two with a thud.

*

Constable took a seat on the sofa as the investigation proceeded around him. The body of Myra Marks was placed on a stretcher and borne away. The photographer, innumerable flashbulbs expended in taking shots of the Iron Maiden and the position of the body, loaded his equipment into its bulky case and left with a brief nod of acknowledgement to the seated inspector. The fingerprints team, records made to their seeming satisfaction, departed leaving traces of powder on various items and a faint haze hanging in the air. For a few moments, Constable was left alone to muse in the cavernous hush of the studio.

The silence was broken by the sudden reappearance of Sergeant Copper, who had evidently been running. "I've found some stuff, sir," he panted, sounding eager to please. "The car was parked just outside, and there were a couple of things in it that I'm sure are useful, plus there was something in the hall."

"Slow down, sergeant. Take it gently. What was in the car?"

"There's this, sir – another letter." He held it up.

"Miss Marks certainly seems to have been cavalier with her correspondence. Or is it someone else's again?"

"That's just it, sir – this one isn't to her either. Or from her, for that matter. It's from some company called MM Estates Management."

"And do we have another mysterious document from the past?"

"No, sir – this one's only two days old, dated the 12th of February. And it's addressed to Eustace Potter at what looks like his business address, somewhere in the Balls Pond Road."

"Highly salubrious," commented Constable. "Well, don't keep me in suspense. If you've got your breath back, tell me what it says."

"Looks as if he's in trouble," remarked Copper. "Listen to this. '*Dear Mr. Potter, We are informed that the rental for the above office premises has not been paid for the past three months, in contravention of the terms of your lease. You are therefore advised that, unless the outstanding sum, plus a payment on account for the forthcoming quarter, is settled within seven days of this letter, we shall have no choice but to place the matter in the*

175

hands of our solicitors ... blah, blah ... *legal proceedings* ... blah blah ... *recovery of debt and repossession. We regret the necessity for this action, but you will understand that our principal feels that she has no choice'*."

"Hmmm, interesting," mused Constable. "And who's this letter from?"

"Signed by some woman called Marie A. Mann, '*pp MM Estates Management*'. Obviously the owner of the business."

"Not quite so obviously, sergeant. So, financial trouble in the world of private detection, by the look of it."

"That's not the only financial thing, sir. Miss Marks had this in her car as well." Copper passed across a buff bound folder entitled '*SPANNER FILM STUDIOS Financial Report 1935*', boldly emblazoned '*PRIVATE AND CONFIDENTIAL – Not to be published before 6/4/1935*'. "I don't know a thing about finances, but it strikes me that if this thing is supposed to be secret until the 6th of April this year, what's she doing with it? That's more than six weeks away."

"The lady was a journalist," Constable reminded him. "And we know they have all manner of nefarious ways of laying hold of information that others don't want them to have. Perhaps there's something in here which would have made tasty copy for the lady's column."

"It's certainly not going to come out now, is it, sir?"

"My point precisely, sergeant. So, what else?"

"I found this business card lying next to the phone when I called for the taxi for Mr. Marx. Can't think why I didn't see it before." He handed the card to his superior.

"Perhaps it wasn't there to see," suggested the inspector. "'*Meyer Goldman, President, ParaMetro Film Corporation, California*'," he read. "That rings a bell. His name came up in the conversations that Stan Laurel overheard. Well, at least there's one person we can rule out as a suspect, since he wasn't at the party."

"No, but he may know something, sir. And look, we know where he's staying." Copper drew the inspector's attention to a hand-written jotting on the back of the card – '*Savoy, 11.00a, 2.15*'. "Must be the Savoy Hotel – nothing but the best for these American movie moguls. And that must be an appointment – or two."

176

"As you say, American, so that tells us something, doesn't it?" Constable was rewarded with a blank look. "Keep thinking, sergeant – you'll get there. In the meantime, I think we should go and have another little word with our friends in the Green Room. With a bit of luck, they will be simmering nicely, and we may get some extra useful information out of them."

In the Green Room, a group of weary faces turned to greet the two detectives as they entered.

"Sorry to have kept you all waiting for what must seem like a very long time, ladies and gentlemen," said Constable breezily, not sounding in the least contrite. "As I'm sure you must realise, investigations of this nature take a time. But now that we've spoken to everyone ..."

"Excuse me, inspector," interrupted Omar Gould. "Not quite everyone. What about the lady in Dressing Room A?"

"What?" exploded Constable. "Mr. Gould, it really would have been extremely helpful if you had given me a full list of people on the premises before we began. No matter!" He cut short Omar's attempts to protest. "We shall go and speak to her now. Come along, Copper – it doesn't do to keep a lady waiting, whoever she is. Along here, is it, Mr. Gould? Right. Thank you. Everyone, please wait here. I shall be back shortly." He turned abruptly and, with Sergeant Copper trotting behind, headed briskly up the corridor.

*

The woman who responded to the knock posed strikingly in the doorway. Her full-length gown, fashioned in some sort of silvery-blue lace which gave tantalising hints of transparency, clung to sensuous hips and a formidable bust, on which was displayed an extravagant sparkling waterfall necklace. A white fur stole was casually draped around her shoulders. The lips were red and inviting, the eyes dark and smouldering, and the platinum-blonde hair was dressed in an elaborate confection of waves and curls which closely followed the shape of the head and framed the face perfectly. Not tall, she would always effortlessly dominate any room she occupied.

"Well, boys," said Mae West, "I knew you'd eventually come up and see me some time."

Constable was dumbfounded at the vision before him. "We're sorry to disturb you, madam," he spluttered.

177

"Why so formal?" she replied. "The name's Mae. When people start calling me madam, I start to worry that I'm going to be charged with keeping a disorderly house." She smiled. "You'd better come in." She stood back and beckoned the detectives inside. "Omar told me the police would be along to see me."

"Yes, madam … Miss West … Mae." Constable was still attempting to gather his wits. "Let me introduce myself. My name is Detective Inspector Constable, and as I'm sure you realise, I am investigating the sudden death of Myra Marks. This is my colleague, Detective Sergeant Copper."

"How do you do, sergeant," said Mae, looking the young man up and down. She extended a hand. "I'm very pleased to meet you."

Copper blushed to the roots of his hair as he took the proffered hand and shook it nervously. "How do you do, Miss West. How are you?"

Mae lowered her eyelashes seductively as she kept hold of the officer's hand. "Well, I have to say, sergeant, I feel like a million tonight. But please, one at a time. Now, is there anything I can do for you, or do you want to ask me about the murder?"

"We do have some questions, Miss West," said Constable, seeking to rescue his colleague. "I apologise that it's such a late hour – I know most people are usually in bed by this time."

"I know what you mean, inspector," responded Mae. "Usually, if I'm not in bed by this time, I go home." She sank into a graceful posture on a couch, waving the inspector to take a seat alongside her. Clearing his throat uneasily, Constable took an upright chair across the room, while Copper indicated his preference to remain standing within easy reach of the door.

"Just for our records, Miss West," said Constable, gesturing to his colleague to begin taking notes, "can you tell us how you came to be involved with this film?"

"Every horror movie needs a beautiful young virgin," answered Mae. The eyes of both detectives widened with incredulity. "Well," she continued, laughing, "that certainly ain't me! Maybe I used to be Snow White, but I drifted."

"I suppose it's no secret that you've got something of a past." Constable put it as delicately as he could.

Mae chuckled knowingly. "Honey, I've got *all* of a past! But as I'm sure I don't need to tell you boys, a woman with a past interests men. They hope history will repeat itself. And in answer to your question, I play the glamorous countess with a mysterious secret."

"And how well did you know Myra Marks?"

"Well, if it hadn't been for me, she would probably have had nothing to write about most of the time. It sure ain't no mysterious secret about me and men – well, Myra provided the column, and I told her all about the inches."

"But surely that made for a lot of scandal?" enquired Constable.

Mae seemed totally at ease with the suggestion. "You know what they say, honey – when women go wrong, men go right after them."

"Tell me, Miss West," said Constable, determined to eke out some actual information amongst all the highly-charged banter, "when did you see Myra Marks tonight?"

"I was talking to that private dick, Eustace Potter," replied Mae. "I've been involved in quite a few court cases, one way or the other – chiefly the other – and you never know when you're going to need the services of a good dick. You wouldn't believe the amount of trouble husbands can cause."

"Have you had many husbands, Miss West?"

"Do you mean my own, or other people's?" asked Mae archly. "Oh, don't get me wrong, inspector – I'm a great believer in marriage as an institution. It's just that I ain't ready to live in no institution."

"And what happened during this conversation of yours with Mr. Potter?" said Constable, desperately attempting to stick to the point.

At last Mae seemed prepared to co-operate. "Myra came up to us, and she heard us talking about divorce, and she said to Eustace 'Well, darling, if there's one thing you and I both know about, it's divorce, isn't it?'. And then she said something about reporting results to her, and she made some remark about people just doing as they're told if they don't want to end up on the outside. Then she turned on her heel and was gone."

"Just one second, Miss West," intervened Copper, urgently scribbling as he tried to keep up with Mae's rapid speech. "Right, got that. And do you know of anyone else she spoke to?"

179

"The scriptwriter, Tamara Knight. Of course, you may not know, sergeant, but I'm a writer too. I've written a book, and a play."

"Oh, really? What's the title?"

"'*Sex*'." Mae smiled enticingly at Copper, who gulped. "I based it on personal experience," she continued, "and I wrote the story all myself. No ghost-writer involved. It's all about a girl who lost her reputation and never missed it."

"But what about the censorship laws?" ventured the sergeant.

"Let me tell you, honey, I'm a firm believer in censorship," said Mae. "I've made a fortune out of it."

Once again Inspector Constable intervened in order to rescue his junior colleague. "So, this conversation with Tamara ...?"

"Myra came up, and she said 'You two ladies have so much in common. Tamara used to do a lot of writing before she began working in films'. I was surprised – I told her I hadn't known that. And Myra said nobody did, and that Tamara's work had a lot of readers, but that she'd never gotten the recognition she deserved. And that she had the proof. Myra promised that she'd make sure she used her column to put that right. She had that notebook of hers in her hand, like always. 'It's all in here' she said."

"So it sounds," said Constable slowly, "as if Myra Marks was planning on doing Tamara Knight a favour?"

Mae shrugged. "Seems so. And that's the first time I've heard of something like that happening! But then I thought, why am I standing here talking to two women when there are men in the room? So I left them to it. I had other interests. After all, you only live once, but if you do it right, once is enough!"

"Is there anything else we should know that you can think of?" asked the inspector.

"Not offhand," said Mae. And as the two detectives prepared to leave the room, she put a restraining hand on David Copper's shoulder. "But I'll be sure to get in touch if I think of anything. And you can take my number." She slipped a small card into Copper's top pocket. "Then you can send this nice young sergeant to come up and investigate me - anytime."

*

180

"Is there any chance I could get danger money for this job, sir?" enquired a still-rattled Sergeant Copper as he leaned against the corridor wall.

"Didn't you tell me once that you joined the police force to get a wider experience of life?" countered Inspector Constable. "So don't complain when it happens."

"I think that lady's got rather more experience to offer than I can cope with at my age," grinned Copper. "Give me a nice bank robber with an iron bar any day. Anyway, what next, sir?"

"Back to the Green Room, I think, and carry on with what we were about to do. All this eaves-dropping on overheard conversations is all very well, but we still don't have a sense of who was where at the crucial moment when the lights went out. That's what I want to find out." Constable turned the handle of the Green Room door and entered, to find an atmosphere of mixed unease and weariness.

"Inspector, can you give us some idea of what's happening?" Omar Gould rose from his place at the end of the sofa to confront the detective. "And what else you want from us? All this waiting around is getting to be very inconvenient."

"Nowhere near as inconvenient as it is for Myra Marks, sir." Constable gave a wintery smile. "So if everyone would like to extend their co-operation just a little further, perhaps we shall be able to conclude matters sooner rather than later. Now, Sergeant Copper here has the advantage over me, since he knows who each of you is. I don't. Perhaps you'd like to remedy that, Mr. Gould." Somewhat grudgingly, Omar performed the introductions. "Thank you, sir. I'd like to make a start by trying to establish where everyone was when the blackout occurred. Was any one of you actually speaking to Miss Marks when the lights went out?"

Those assembled looked at one another for a moment, uncertain, and then Noah Vail spoke up from his seat on the sofa alongside Lois.

"I suppose I might have been nearest to Myra," he said. "I'd just been with her a few moments before the power cut out and it all went dark, but nobody was far away. Anyone could have pushed her into that Iron Maiden thing. And believe me, inspector, I've directed a few movies in my time, but I don't reckon you could ever beat this for melodrama. As far as I'm concerned, the whole scene was just like something from a cheap

181

novel – in fact, that's what it ought to be. You could get Tamara to write it and Lois to pose for the cover picture."

"An interesting suggestion, Mr. Vail," said Constable, "but I don't think it advances us very far. But that reminds me – you mention your directing career. We've been told about a meeting you're due to have with another company about directing a new film, which Myra Marks seems to have known about. Sounds as if 'Love Me To Death' may be your last venture with Spanner films – maybe there are some strained relations involved. Any comment?"

"Huh!" snorted Noah. "What, maybe you're hinting at some sort of disloyalty on my part? Don't talk to me about loyalty. You should try talking to Omar about that. If ever a man needed to worry about his future, it's him, and Myra knew it all."

Somewhat taken aback by Noah's vehemence, Constable turned to Omar to follow up the suggestion, but he was forestalled by Lois Turner, who took Noah's hand. "Noah, you shouldn't get upset over things that aren't anything to do with you," she said. Her eyes flashed a warning. "We all know what a fine director you are, and nothing is going to stand in the way of that." She turned to face Constable. "Noah's right, inspector – I saw him with Myra, and I was just on my way over to him when the lights went off, so of course I couldn't find him."

"So where had you been before that, Miss Turner?" asked Constable.

"Oh … um … I'd just been speaking to Eustace Potter." Lois displayed an odd degree of embarrassment. "But I'd made an excuse because I wanted to get away from him - he was trying to stir up trouble and talking about some old pictures. Silly really, because as I told you, this is my first film – everyone knows that."

"Indeed yes, Miss Turner. In fact, I think you were heard to have a conversation with Myra Marks on that very subject – casting, and so on."

"Exactly." Lois nodded eagerly. "So naturally, inspector, I wouldn't have had any reason to do Myra any harm, because I needed her help for my career." She batted her eyelids innocently, but then her eyes lit up with a sudden gleam of spite. "But if you want someone who did have a motive, you should just ask Eustace about his past instead of worrying about other people's." She sank back alongside Noah, her hand still in his, a small smile of self-satisfaction on her lips.

"Mr. Potter," said Constable, facing the private eye as he sat quietly in his place in the corner, "why don't I do as Miss Turner proposes and come to you next? Because there are some very interesting items which we've found in Miss Marks' possession, including a recent letter whose contents on the subject of your finances I'm sure I don't need to remind you about, plus some other confidential information which you may have had a hand in obtaining. Anything to say about that?"

"Yes, well, detective to detective, you seem to be pretty good at your job," admitted Eustace grimly. "All right, so maybe times have been hard, and it's not as if I've been so busy lately. Those one or two little jobs I'd done for Myra were just bread-and-butter research, and she always had ways to persuade a man to do things that perhaps were just slightly beyond the rules. But what the hell – you can't hold a grudge forever, and we were a good team once."

"It's as much the present as the past that I'm concerned, Mr. Potter," said Constable. "And these 'little jobs' that you mention don't quite account for the fact that you were here at the party as a guest. So I think you were still working."

"It's true," agreed Eustace. "Myra asked me to try to get some dirt on Lois's background to keep up her sleeve for the future, and that's the main reason I was with her at the time you're talking about. But Lois said she wouldn't talk to me without a drink, so I was just going to the bar when everything went black."

"So did he or didn't he reach you at the bar, Mr. Lyon?" Constable continued his progress around the group. "Were you actually in position at the time, or were you out and about amongst the others, as we've been told? Were you perhaps in contact with Myra Marks at that particular moment? Giving her more champagne, as you had before?"

"I wouldn't have given her the time of day," replied Ennio. "Anyway, you didn't need to give Myra Marks anything. I've seen her around on enough occasions to know that she'd never wait to be given anything – she'd just go and grab it."

"Ah, now that reminds me," said Constable. "We happened to find in the lady's handbag a certain small jewelled dagger which looked to be rather valuable. Would you know anything about that?"

"So she did take it!" cried Ennio. "I knew it! I could tell she was up to something. Typical!" He realised his attitude might lead to damaging conclusions. "But hang on, inspector, if you think there's some sort of connection between Myra snaffling one of my props and her getting murdered, you're barking up the wrong tree. She ended up with more holes in her than a colander, didn't she? So if you think my little dagger had anything to do with that, all I can say is ..."

Constable halted the flow with some difficulty. "Rest assured, Mr. Lyon, we're not considering the dagger as a murder weapon. Not unless my scientific colleagues tell me otherwise, that is. It just so happens that it was one of a number of items of interest in Myra Marks' handbag."

"Well, if you want to know about her handbag, inspector, I can tell you something," volunteered Tamara Knight.

"Indeed, Miss Knight?" Constable's interest was awakened. "And what might that be?"

"I wasn't particularly close to them," explained Tamara, "but I happened to look across, and I saw Noah bump into Myra, and that was what made her drop her bag so that her things went all over the floor. And it looked to me as if he did it deliberately."

"What? That's not true!" protested Noah.

Constable silenced him with a gesture. "Go on, Miss Knight."

"Then Noah tried to help her pick her things up, but Myra wouldn't let him. But I know Gloria got down and helped, but then she went off towards the dressing rooms. I'm surprised she could remember the way on her own, because usually she's got a flock of people fussing around her bowing and scraping, and she never has to do anything for herself, and in fact she left Myra to finish picking things up on her own. And just a couple of minutes after that, the lights went out, and I heard a scream and then the slam."

"Can you confirm that, Miss Mundy?" Constable looked enquiringly towards Gloria who was lounging almost buried in a gigantic deeply-upholstered armchair, a cocktail glass still in her hand. She smiled brightly at him.

"Of course I can confirm it, sergeant," she replied. "I remember it very distinctly. The last time I saw Myra, she was standing right in front of the Iron Maiden. Yes, I did pick some things up that had fallen from her bag, but I can't tell you what happened after that because I had to go out for a moment." Constable thought he could interpret the faint blush which came to her cheek. "And I was just coming back from my dressing room when the whole studio was plunged into darkness." An expressive gesture emphasised the drama of Gloria's narrative. "I, of course, could see nothing at all, but there was a great deal of shouting, and I'm sure I heard Mr. ... er ... the detective gentleman ..." She waved her hand.

"Eustace Potter?"

"Yes. I'm sure I heard him say 'I'll do it' as he passed me. Of course, it is possible that it wasn't him at all. Everybody was milling about, and I ended up with Omar next to Camera 3 – that's the one to the right as you look out from the set, isn't it, Noah dear?" The director gave a nod in reply. "And then ..." A dramatic pause. Gloria lifted her head and shot a piercing look towards the inspector. "The lights came on! And oh, the horror!"

Constable, slightly disconcerted by Gloria's theatricality, cleared his throat. "Thank you, Miss Mundy – you paint a very vivid picture." Gloria inclined her head graciously at the compliment. "So now, Mr. Gould," continued the inspector, "finally we come back to you. You were with Miss Mundy as the lighting was restored – is that so?"

"Yes, I suppose so." Omar Gould seemed pre-occupied with something. "Now look, inspector, there's something that's bugging me. I wouldn't want you to get the wrong idea from what Noah said about me. If he thinks I wasn't on to what he was up to, he's a fool. He may think I don't know he's meeting Meyer Goldman from ParaMetro over lunch tomorrow, but what he doesn't know is that I'm having dinner with Meyer tomorrow night. He and I go way back, and we don't have a lot of secrets from one another. Don't believe everything you read in the papers about studio wars – it's just friendly rivalry."

"So if Mr. Vail didn't know about this meeting, who did?"

Omar thought for a moment. "Gloria did, and I think she'd told Tamara, because she'd just asked me if they could tag along. I told Gloria to forget it, which shouldn't be a problem."

"This is taking us away from the point a little, Mr. Gould. What I need you to tell me is where you were when the lights failed."

"Well, like Gloria said, I must have been somewhere near Camera 3, but I wasn't actually speaking to anyone at that moment. Then the power went out, and there was all that yelling and pushing, and the sound of the slam. And once the lighting came back on, there was Gloria next to me, and everyone looked at one another for a moment, but then someone noticed the blood and screamed."

"And that's it?"

"That's it, inspector," returned Omar simply. "Now you know as much as we do."

Constable smiled. "Ah, if only that were true, Mr. Gould." He thought for a moment. "Right, everyone, I'd like you to stay here for a little while longer if you would. Sergeant Copper, would you please remain with everyone, just in case someone remembers something of interest for you to record." The instruction was accompanied by a look carrying an unspoken message that any conferring between the suspects was to be discouraged. Copper caught on and nodded. "In the meantime, if you'd like to come with me please, Mr. Lyon?"

"Me?" Ennio jumped to his feet. "What do you want me for?"

Constable declined to explain. "Just a few moments of your time, Mr. Lyon." He led the way from the room, Ennio following with a troubled look.

"What's this all about, inspector?" asked Ennio as the two emerged on to the film set.

"Nothing to trouble yourself about unduly, Mr. Lyon," Constable reassured him. "I just wanted to make sure that the dagger which Miss Marks had in her possession was the only similar object to hand. Just in case, you understand, that the stabbing theory which has been advanced is not quite so far-fetched as it appears. So if you'd be good enough to look over the items on your table, that would be much appreciated."

"Oh. Right." Ennio seemed relieved. He went over to his table and began to inspect the items on it, while Constable stood by, idly surveying the surroundings.

"It's all here, inspector," reported Ennio after a brief check. "Just the dagger missing."

"Helpful to know," said Constable absently, his attention

186

elsewhere. "I'm just looking at these burning torches around the walls. They've been going ever since we got here. Wouldn't they be some sort of fire danger, or is this whole construction fireproof?"

Ennio chuckled. "They're not real, inspector. They're electric. It's a new idea of mine I'm trying out. Those aren't actual flames – they're small pieces of coloured silk, and there's a light bulb inside, and a fan to blow the fabric so it looks like flames."

"Very ingenious," said Constable admiringly. "Obviously another instance of the illusory nature of the film business." A truth dawned on the inspector. "Which would explain, of course, why they weren't giving out any light during the blackout."

"That's right. In fact, the only real fire around is this brazier, but we need that to be real because there are some scenes where it has incense thrown on it to create a cloud of smoke. But when we're shooting, someone's normally standing by with a fire extinguisher in case it gets out of control." Ennio's eye was suddenly caught by something unexpected. "Just a second, inspector – there's something in there. Hold on – I'll see if I can get it ..." He picked up a pair of long tongs from the stand alongside and succeeded in retrieving the item which fell to the floor. "What's that doing there?"

The object was charred almost to destruction. As Constable knelt to examine it, he could see a thin wire spiral with what appeared to be some remnants of burnt sheets of paper adhering to it. He suddenly realised what it was. "And that," he declared, "is what remains of a reporter's notebook." He picked up the now cooled item.

"You're right!" declared Ennio. "That was Myra's."

Constable stood. "And how, I wonder, would you know that, Mr. Lyon?"

Ennio looked sheepish. "Oh, I just recognised it from when ... when she ..."

"Yes, sir?" Constable waited.

"Oh, all right." Ennio capitulated. "She tore a page out and gave it to me, and I recognised it from that."

"And she did this because ...?"

The little man sighed. "Because she was going to give me a back-hander, if you must know, inspector. She said if I slipped some of the bottles of champagne out to her car on the sly, there would be something in it for me."

"I thought you didn't like the lady," remarked Constable. "You 'wouldn't give her the time of day', I thought you said."

"Nor would I usually," said Ennio. "But when you're skint, a few quid make all the difference, don't they? And Omar's not going to miss it, is he? And with what he's paying me, can you blame a chap? So she wrote down her car registration on a page from her book and gave it to me, and said I could nip the stuff out to her car later when nobody was paying attention." He fished in his pocket and produced a crumpled sheet. "Here, look, if you don't believe me." He handed the paper to Constable, who flattened it out and held the torn edge against the spiral spine. It matched.

A slow smile lit the inspector's face. "Mr. Lyon, I think this could be one of the most useful pieces of evidence we have. Thank you for your help in finding it."

"That's all right," replied Ennio. He preened slightly. "Glad to help. Shame you can't read whatever it is she'd written in the book."

"That," said Constable, "may be the most important fact of all."

*

"That chap Lyon said you wanted to see me, sir."

Inspector Constable had despatched Ennio back to the Green Room with instructions to send Sergeant Copper through to him. In the intervening minutes, Constable had paced back and forth, his eyes focussed on nothing in particular, considering, weighing up facts, discarding some while pairing up others, until a clear pattern of events composed itself in his mind. His gaze returned to his junior colleague.

"Yes, sergeant. I think we're about ready."

"What, you mean you reckon you know what happened, sir? Already?" enquired the slightly surprised sergeant.

"Not only what, but who and why, young David," replied Constable in unusually expansive tones.

"So what did the trick for you, sir? I mean, I've got all sorts of notes, and I'm nowhere near sorting it all out."

"Oh, various things," said Constable. "I wondered about that dressing room key we found in Myra Marks' handbag; there was of course the matter of why and how she had obtained the

188

various documents in her possession; and then there's that business card. That tells us something. And after we've looked at whose movements can and cannot be accounted for at the time of Myra Marks' death, we come down to the most crucial consideration of all."

"Which is ...?"

"What revelation was so threatening that it had to be prevented by murder?"

"And now you know, sir." It was a statement rather than a question.

"I do. So if you would please ask everyone to come through here to the set, we will put an end to the matter."

Copper knew better by now than to ask his superior for a straight answer as to the identity of the culprit. 'Let the guv'nor have his moment of theatre' he thought. With a brisk "Will do, sir", he turned and headed for the dressing rooms corridor.

A few moments later, the remaining individuals stood before the inspector in a somewhat uneasy group.

"Miss West has already left, sir," reported Copper. "She seems to have gone while we were in the Green Room talking to the others."

"No matter," said Constable airily. "I'm sure she told us everything we needed to know. And of course, you can always contact her if you feel the need." A glint of humour in his eye was rewarded by another faint blush from his colleague. The inspector reverted to a more serious demeanour. "However, since everyone else is here, perhaps you'd like to make yourselves as comfortable as you can while I share certain facts with you." He waved towards the sofas, and the group seated themselves, Noah taking proprietorial possession of his director's chair. Several of the company, Copper noted, were having difficulty tearing their gaze away from the traces of congealed blood in the spot where the body of Myra Marks had lain.

Constable took a deep breath and confronted the company. "From what we have heard here tonight," he began, "Myra Marks seems to have been one of the most dangerous women in the business, particularly the movie business." The reaction was a general murmur of puzzlement. "But being dangerous to others meant that she was in danger herself. As tonight's events have clearly taught us.

189

"What do we know about her relationships with others? I think that her nickname, the Iron Maiden of Fleet Street, probably tells us a great deal. I'm sure she never courted popularity. It doesn't sound to me as if she would have allowed personal feelings to get in the way of her career or a good story. But evidently, ruthlessness has its perils.

"So let's examine some of the facts we've learnt. I'll begin with Eustace Potter – a slightly unusual member of this gathering, since he is not connected with the film business as the rest of you are. He was here tonight at the personal instigation of Myra Marks – he was her guest. Now, he told us that he knew Myra better than most, and had done for over twenty years. Of course, there was one thing that he didn't exactly spell out for us, but in all honesty, Sergeant Copper and I would not be very good at our job as detectives if we were unable to work out that, when Myra said that she and Eustace knew all about divorce, it was from a personal standpoint. Am I right, Mr. Potter?"

"It's true," said Eustace, "but it's no secret. Myra and I had been married. I don't know how many people here were aware of it, and frankly, I don't care. It was nobody's business but ours."

"And yet I can't help being intrigued by the nature of the relationship," said Constable. "You were evidently both on sufficiently good terms to be working in co-operation, and yet you could hardly be said to be described as exhibiting all the emotions of a bereaved husband, sir. Ex-husband, I should say. And as your career stayed in the back streets, your ex-wife's moved onwards and upwards, bringing her power and the wealth that went with it. Enough wealth to extend to the ownership of a string of business properties, perhaps? Rented out in some instances to small firms whose finances were not always secure. Everyone has given the impression that Myra Marks was a tough lady – was she a tough landlady as well?

"What about the rest of you? The other suspects, people from the artificial world of the movies, where illusion reigns and appearance is everything? It seems Myra had a talent for finding out the truth behind the façades – truth which, in many cases, could bring careers crashing to the ground. So on the subject of careers, let's begin with the young lady whose career in films is just beginning."

"Me?" said Lois Turner, regarding the inspector like a

startled fawn. "But why would you think that I ...?"

Constable overrode her protests. "Bear with me, Miss Turner. Let's not be too hasty with the performance as the innocent young girl in danger. True, we know that you're just starting out in films – but the question has been raised as to where you came from. What sort of work got you started? And did Noah Vail let slip an awkward fact when he made that remark about you posing for a picture on a book cover? Are there, perhaps, other pictures? I also have to bear in mind your own relationship with Mr. Vail. We've seen a certain personal closeness, and one wonders how and when that began. I don't mean to throw up any concerns about your personal morality, but I would merely remark that the casting couch is an old tradition, and great fodder for newspaper stories."

Noah jumped to his feet. "That is an intolerable suggestion, inspector," he said hotly. "I am a professional director, and I would never ..."

"Quietly, Mr. Vail, if you please." Once again, Constable quelled the interruption. "I shall be coming to you soon enough. But just to wrap up – I think that's the correct film terminology, is it not? - to wrap up the matter of Miss Turner, when Myra Marks was overheard to mention 'the sack', did she mean that Lois had been in it with Noah, or that she was about to be given it by him? Good copy either way. And perhaps she had some concrete evidence. There was a dressing room key in her handbag, which I think she had discovered in Noah's possession, in the side pouch of that very director's chair he's occupying. The label said 'G.M.' - did that refer to the most obvious likely owner, Gloria Mundy, or to Lois's character, Georgia Mayle? Perhaps that key allowed, if I may use the expression, easy access to Miss Turner."

"This is all speculation, inspector." Noah seemed to have recovered his equilibrium. "I'm sure you can't prove any of this."

Constable declined to comment on the assertion. "Then, since we're talking about speculation, Mr. Vail, let's turn to you. Aside from any questions over your dealings with members of your cast, you're a famous director, or so you told us, and nobody has contradicted you, at least, not publicly. But Myra was overheard to make a very interesting remark about you not getting on with Omar Gould, which leads me to wonder if you might have been about to jump to ParaMetro Films before you

191

were pushed. We know you were due to meet the president of ParaMetro tomorrow for lunch – but who might have got there before you? My colleague Sergeant Copper found one of the business cards belonging to Meyer Goldman, the ParaMetro boss, and that, combined with another remark of Mr. Gould's, gives us the answer to that. Which brings me to Mr. Gould himself."

"Now look, inspector," said Omar, "whatever shenanigans there may have been going on, those are nothing to do with me. I told you, Meyer Goldman and I are just old friends, and as for what happens on the studio floor, that's not my province.

"Yes, I remember you told us that, Mr. Gould," replied Constable. "You're just the money man, in control of the finances. Or maybe not. Because you were heard to have a conversation with Myra Marks in which the subject of books was raised, and she made some comment about 'looking forward to her piece'. That was assumed to have something to do with the possible adaptation of a novel for a film, and Myra writing a story on the subject. But I have doubts on that score, largely because a copy of the Spanner Films accounts for the last year was found in Myra Marks' car. Perhaps those were the 'books' she meant. Had she found out that you, Mr. Gould, had not been taking plots from other sources, but something altogether more financially rewarding from the studio's revenues? And was Myra's 'piece' not an article, but her 'piece of the action', as I believe they say in gangster films – her share of the ill-gotten gains, a gentle little venture into blackmail? Oh, I know, I know," said Constable, forestalling Omar's evident intention of protesting. "All pure speculation once again, but perhaps that speculation will become a little less speculative once those accounts are more closely examined.

"That just leaves us with you two ladies." The inspector turned to Gloria Mundy and Tamara Knight, seated alongside one another on one of the sofas. "We have to consider what hold Myra Marks might have had over you. Miss Mundy, your very long and glittering career speaks for itself. You have legions of fans."

"People have been so kind," murmured Gloria.

"And those fans," continued Constable, "would eagerly read any article about their favourite star. But had Myra Marks stumbled on an uncomfortable truth. Is that star fading? And could that be the reason why the president of ParaMetro would have avoided meeting her? One or two snippets have been let fall which might support that suggestion. But why should Meyer Goldman also not be interested in Miss Knight's scriptwriting skills? Why shouldn't Tamara also be welcome at the proposed meeting?"

Tamara Knight raised a sardonic eyebrow. "Do you know, inspector, I have the strangest feeling that you are about to tell us."

"Then I shall try not to disappoint you, Miss Knight," replied Constable in similar tones. "I remember when we first spoke, that you told us how glad you were that Myra Marks had nothing on you. 'I've seen her wreck so many careers', I think you said. And I've got an inkling that you weren't quite as truthful with us as you might have been. Don't they use the term 'creative copy-writing' in the advertising business when they want to avoid a downright lie? And writing is what we're talking about, because in Myra Marks' handbag was a letter from some three years ago which mentioned another kind of writing. Books from Rees-Kay Publishers. Perhaps not the sort I'd find on the station bookstall next time I'm looking for something to read on the train? And could Myra have been about to spill the beans on your personal literary history, thus putting your future at risk?"

Tamara looked the inspector straight in the eye. "Inspector, I admire you. You seem to have discovered a great deal in a very short time. Not that I'm admitting anything, of course," she added quickly. "But if there is one thing I have learnt during my career as a writer, it's that a work of fiction which comes to no satisfactory conclusion will never be popular. And you seem to be singularly lacking a conclusion."

"Setting the scene, Miss Knight," returned Constable. "Isn't that what it's called in literature? And what I've said so far is merely to point out that everyone had a motive to stop Myra Marks' activities. Eustace Potter faced being thrown out of his offices by his ruthless ex-wife - except that in my opinion, this was just an empty threat to keep him under Myra's thumb. He was far too useful to her – all the documents we've seen here must have been obtained by him for her by fair means or foul. Then there's Lois Turner. I'm sure there's nothing unique about her. Like it or not, plenty of girls must have done things in their past to get a few steps up the ladder. Some scandal in the newspapers might have shocked a few people, but would it honestly put directors off casting her in future? For some of the less scrupulous, surely not – especially when they knew how friendly she could be in order to get a part. So I do not see that Myra's knowledge presented a danger to Lois's career.

"Likewise Tamara Knight. I say this purely as an individual rather than a police officer, so please do not quote me – if she wrote a few dirty books, so what? The state will not totter. My colleagues on the vice squad have no doubt raided enough dubious shops in the back streets to know that there will always be – how did the publisher's letter put it? - a '*clientèle of discerning gentlemen*' wanting more. As Mae West pointed out, she made a fortune out of censorship. As long as you keep at arm's length, Miss Knight, I for one am content to turn a blind eye.

"Fraud and blackmail, on the other hand, deserve a rather closer look. In the case of Noah Vail and Omar Gould, I wonder if what Myra quaintly called her 'percentage', otherwise referred to as 'the cost of silence', would have kept her quiet at her meeting with Meyer Goldman tomorrow. A meeting which was scheduled to take place before Noah's lunch and Omar's dinner – a meeting which had been arranged, according to the jottings on Mr. Goldman's business card, at eleven o'clock tomorrow morning, the fifteenth of February, or as an American would write it, 11.00a, 2.15. But I ask myself if it would have been in Myra's interests to throw away a potentially good source of income, both from Noah and Omar, by letting the cat out of the bag, when there were plenty more stories out there for her to exploit. And my answer is, surely not."

Constable drew a deep breath. "Which brings me to the one remaining person. That, Miss Mundy, is you. And I assure you that it gives me no pleasure to say these things, but I'm afraid they must be said." He looked away from the actress, unwilling to address her directly. "Gloria Mundy is a different matter. She has spent years building a fabulous career as a star of the silver screen. She is universally recognised – a legend. Which leads one to wonder what she was doing appearing in this, no offence intended, rather second-rate horror film. Have her abilities begun to wane? Should we draw unfortunate conclusions from the various remarks about forgetfulness that have been made by a number of people – even a momentary confusion over my own identity. And we have the evidence of a cutting from Myra Marks' column from her last issue, promising shocking revelations about the decline and fall of a prominent figure from the film world. True, the person was not identified, but to someone who might have been the subject, the comments could have hit home.

"Once again, I am moving into the realms of speculation, but it's surely not a coincidence that the cutting was present at the scene. I have no way of knowing whether Myra herself showed Gloria the cutting – unlikely, in my opinion - or whether Gloria herself had seen it in the press, or indeed whether some very helpful third party made the contents known to Gloria. But I believe that Gloria had an inkling that the curtain was about to fall, and when Myra's bag fell open, scattering her belongings, this presented Gloria with the perfect opportunity. While assisting Myra to retrieve the items which had fallen to the floor, Gloria managed to pick up Myra's notebook and conceal it among the flowing draperies of her robe as she made her way to the privacy of her dressing room. A brief glance at the contents of the notebook was enough to confirm her worst fears. Her reputation, so carefully nurtured over the years, was doomed. But how could Myra be stopped?

"Gloria returned to the studio floor, where she saw Myra standing in front of the Iron Maiden. In a flash, she knew what she had to do. She moved behind the scenery to the power switch and turned everything off, and then, drawing on her long and intimate experience of film studios, swiftly found her way to where Myra was standing in the darkness. With one hard shove, Gloria pushed her into the waiting Iron Maiden, slammed the door shut, threw the offending notebook into the brazier to be consumed by fire, and battled her way through the confusion, to be found standing next to Omar Gould when the lights came back on."

A long and stunned silence followed the inspector's words. Expressions ranging from horror to sympathy to downright incredulity were etched upon the faces of those present. At last, Omar Gould broke the mood.

"Mr. Constable, are you seriously suggesting that Gloria is a murderess? But that is absurd. Do you realise you're talking about one of the greatest movie stars of all time? How could you think such a thing?"

A smile of surprising sweetness spread across Gloria's

face. "Omar dear, please don't make this any harder than it already is. The inspector is quite right, you know. I killed Myra, and for the reasons he gave you. My career is over." She held up a hand to stifle the murmurs of protest around her. "Please, everyone, don't try to be kind. I know all too well that there is a time for everything to come to an end, and however much I may have tried to conceal it from you all, I couldn't carry on concealing it from myself. When one's abilities are no longer there, it is time to leave the stage. And yet I couldn't bring myself to let go. Films have been my life. I have no other existence. And if I could have chosen my own time and my own way, then this would all have been easier. But Myra Marks had other ideas. Her predatory nature couldn't see – forgive the immodesty – a towering colossus without wishing to pull it down. And so, before she could destroy me, I chose to destroy her." Gloria sighed. "And all in vain, of course. The newspapers will soon be full of the story of the star who fell. But better that a star should burn up in a blaze of glory than flicker out feebly like a spent candle. As they say, '*sic transit* ...'."

Gloria stood and faced Constable with the dignity of Marie Antoinette on her way to the scaffold. "I'm quite ready to go with you now, inspector. I'm sure that when we arrive at the police station, your photographer will be wanting to take some extremely unflattering stills of me." A last spark of mischief, mingled with sorrow, gleamed in her eye. "You may tell him that I shall be quite ready for my close-up." She turned to Noah Vail. "I hope you won't object, Noah dear, if I usurp your right to have the final word in this film. But as you would say, 'Cut and Print!'."

*

The warbling of a ringtone on the cabinet alongside his bed dragged Detective Inspector Andy Constable from a heavy slumber. He opened his eyes. Light was filtering through his bedroom curtains. He rolled over and picked up his mobile.

"Hello. Yes?"

"Morning, guv," came the voice of Detective Sergeant Dave Copper. "I hope you don't mind me calling you at this hour, but you did say you wanted to make an early start on ..."

"Yes, yes," interrupted Constable. "Give me ten minutes for a quick shower and a cup of tea to wake myself up, and I'll be with you."

"Oh, sorry, guv." Copper's apology did not sound remotely genuine. "Were you still asleep?"

"As a matter of fact, sergeant, I was," replied Constable, "and you won't believe it, but I've been having the weirdest dream. I'll tell you all about it in the car." Without waiting for a reply, he pressed the off-button and headed for the bathroom.

*   *   *   *   *

THE INSPECTOR CONSTABLE MURDER MYSTERIES

MURDERER'S FETE
(First published in paperback as Feted To Die)
Constable and Copper investigate the death of a celebrity clairvoyant at the annual garden fete at Dammett Hall

MURDER UNEARTHED
(First published in paperback as Juan Foot In The Grave)
A lucky win takes Constable and Copper on holiday to Spain, but murder soon rears its head among the British community on the Costa

DEATH SAILS IN THE SUNSET
Our detectives find themselves aboard a brand new cruise liner, but swiftly discover that some guilty secrets refuse to be buried at sea

www.rogerkeevil.co.uk

Printed in Great Britain
by Amazon